RARER
THAN RUBIES

EM LYNLEY

Dreamspinner Press

Published by
Dreamspinner Press
4760 Preston Road
Suite 244-149
Frisco, TX 75034
http://www.dreamspinnerpress.com/

Rarer Than Rubies
Copyright © 2011 by EM Lynley

Cover Art by Anne Cain   annecain.art@gmail.com
Cover Design by Mara McKennen

ISBN: 978-1-61581-930-0

Printed in the United States of America
Second Edition
July 2011

EBook First Edition released January 2011 by Ravenous Romance as *Thief of Hearts: Tempted in Thailand*.

For Dana and Emilie, who have encouraged and supported me more than I ever expected. I owe you more than I can possibly express or repay. Thank you.

PROLOGUE

"WE'LL be landing in Bangkok in approximately thirty minutes."

The voice over the loudspeaker broke into Trent Copeland's consciousness and he pushed it away, thinking it was simply part of his dream. He attempted to return to the comfort of his slumber.

"Sir, your immigration card." Someone shook his shoulder and pushed an official-looking form at him, and he realized he wasn't dreaming at all. It was real. And about to get even more real.

He blinked and sat up, bringing his reclining seat to a sitting position. He heard, as well as felt, a shift, as the jet literally changed gears and began its descent.

For a moment he stared at the paper, trying to trace the steps that had brought him here. Had it been only two weeks earlier that he'd been jolted out of the security of his routine by an unexpected and unwelcome phone call from his literary agent?

What had he been thinking, letting Beth and Cassandra plan this trip for him?

He better get plenty of inspiration for his next novel, or plenty of sex—or both—or someone was going to be in big trouble when he got back. *If* he got back. He took a deep breath and pressed his face to the tiny window, wondering what lay in store for him once he landed.

1

Two weeks earlier
Los Angeles, California

THIS wasn't really happening. It had never happened to him before. Okay, once. But never twice—in a row. His friends told him it was natural and sooner or later it happened to everyone. Now it was happening to *Trent*.

"Rejected? What're you talking about, rejected?"

"Trent, honey, I'm sorry. The publisher isn't interested this time around." Cassandra's slightly British-accented voice came through the phone clear as crystal, but still Trent didn't think he'd heard her correctly.

"Why not? I'm one of their top-selling authors!" If there were a *New York Times* best-seller list for gay erotic romance, every one of his books would have been on it. "Aren't I?" As soon as the words were out of his mouth, he knew he sounded like a child.

Trent got up from the couch, tipping his Siamese cat Godiva off his lap and causing her to loudly meow her displeasure as she landed on all fours. Trent paced around the living room, cordless phone pressed tightly to his ear. He wished he had a phone with a cord so he could twist it around his editor's neck. No, *Cass's* neck. What the hell kind of agent *was* she, if she couldn't sell either of his last two books?

"Yes, Trent, you are one of the top sellers, but your editor told me she'd read this one already. Twice."

"What the fuck? I just finished it! How could she have read it twice? Is she a psychic as well as an editor?" He stopped in the middle of the living room and Godiva, who had been tagging along at his heels, crashed into him with a less-than-ladylike snarl. She hopped back onto the vacant couch, out of his way.

"Well, honey, it *is* an awful lot like the last one you wrote, you know?" Cassandra's voice rose ever so slightly at the end of the sentence, as if he actually were a child she wanted to appease. It didn't work.

"Grrr," was all he could manage in reply. He started pacing again, trying to burn off anger and nervous energy while he crafted a suitable response. "What kind of agent are you, anyway? You're supposed to get them to want it."

"Trent, honey, I'm a pretty good agent, but I'm not a miracle worker. You always have the option of coming up with a new pen name and I can shop this to someone else."

"No!" Trent practically shouted. He remembered how hard it had been choosing a pen name in the first place. He and his two best friends since college days, Beth and Mick, had sat around in his crummy old apartment tossing around ideas; he'd had to endure asinine suggestions such as I.M. Hung from Mick. Finally, with Cassandra's input, he'd settled on J.T. Dallas, though he came from a little town in Oklahoma and hated when people thought he was Texan. But Cassandra said Texas sounded sexy to readers and *Dallas* brought back images of the rich and ruthless, which always helped sell romance. She'd been right, as usual, and it had proved a good decision. Since then, she'd been much more than an agent. She'd not only helped shape his heretofore successful career, but had become one of his closest and most-trusted friends.

He realized Cassandra had been talking while he'd been strolling down memory lane and he struggled to catch up to what she was saying.

"… but I think you just need a little change of pace, a vacation or something. Get a new perspective," Cassandra went on. "Shake things up a bit and spark your creativity…."

"I don't know how they can say this is like the last one!" He wasn't giving up. "This one is about a cowboy and a NASA scientist, while the last one was about a university professor and a… cowboy…." His voice trailed off at the end. "Okay, maybe there are some similarities. Slight similarities." He couldn't even convince himself. No wonder the editor had thrown it back.

"You've finished two books already this year. Take some well-earned time off and spend some of those fat royalty checks you're piling up."

"I don't need a vacation."

"Yes, you do. You can't just sit around all day watching Turner Classic Movies and Lifetime."

Trent grabbed the TV remote and quickly hit the mute button. *Damn*, she knew him entirely too well.

"Give me a call in a couple of days and we'll go for lunch with Beth and you can tell me where you decide to go for your vacation, okay? Gotta run, sweetie. Love you!"

Cassandra disconnected and Trent tossed the phone onto the couch, narrowly missing Godiva, who meowed imperiously before racing for safety behind the television.

"Sorry, baby." Trent plopped himself down on the couch and pouted while he figured out what to do next.

Maybe Cass was right and a vacation wasn't such a bad idea. He had gotten into a rut. He glanced down at the carpet and wouldn't have been surprised to find he'd worn a trail into the floor following the same path over and over and over. He should visit the travel agent around the corner and pick up some brochures. Better yet, he'd call Beth and she could help him choose a destination.

He'd get right on that, after he finished watching *Now, Voyager*, one of his favorite films. He adored the classic scene where Paul Henreid lights two cigarettes at once, before handing one to Bette Davis. It made him want to take up smoking, the way the *Thin Man* films left him craving dry martinis. Trent clicked on the volume, grabbed a box of tissues, and settled back onto the couch.

2

Saturday, two weeks later

"I DON'T know what possessed me when I asked you to plan my trip and surprise me. How could you have let me?" Trent was nearly wringing his hands as he opened the door to Beth. "This has to be the dumbest thing I've ever done."

"Trent, I've known you for what, almost ten years. Would you like me to give you examples of really dumb stuff you've done?"

They'd met as wide-eyed freshmen moving into the dorm at the University of Michigan, so she had quite a list of them; of that Trent was confident. "No, thanks. But I'm sure it's in the top ten."

"It's a pretty long list."

"Gee, thanks." He turned, and Beth followed him into the bedroom.

"Are you ready to *finally* let me know where I'm going? All you told me was it was going to be hot and I needed booster vaccines for the same diseases as when I went to Mexico. How can I possibly be prepared?" He was leaving in two days and he still had no idea about his destination. Beth had promised to tell him tonight.

"It is going to be hot. And I've got your tickets with me now, along with a couple of guidebooks and some other stuff I printed out to help you plan the specifics." She patted the messenger bag slung over one shoulder, before dropping it onto the floor next to the bed.

Trent lunged toward it, but Beth pushed him away.

"Later, at dinner. Now, let's see what you've packed...." Her voice trailed off as she hunched over the suitcase splayed open on the bed.

Godiva had planted herself on top of the contents, chin resting on paws and eyeing both Trent and Beth with exquisite boredom.

Gently disengaging the cat, Beth began to dig through Trent's carefully folded and packed—though now lightly cat-fur-coated—clothing. He felt exposed and vulnerable as she poked through his belongings.

"Hey! Do you know how long it took to get everything in there?"

She pulled a shirt out of the suitcase and waved it in the air. "You do not need this where you're going."

It was Trent's favorite: a dark blue long-sleeved shirt even he admitted was somewhat threadbare. He snatched it away and clutched it against his chest, feeling his blood pressure rising. From atop one of the pillows, Godiva let out a particularly disapproving meow, and Trent realized he was alone on this one.

Beth grabbed the shirt back and tossed it onto a chair in the corner of the room as Trent suppressed frustration. He enjoyed reading mysteries and watching thrillers, but in real life, Trent detested mystery and suspense. He did whatever he could to avoid them, while Beth seemed to thrive on spontaneity and surprise. The degree to which she enjoyed keeping him on pins and needles about his "hot" vacation bordered on sadistic.

"You have got to be kidding me." This time she held up his toiletries bag. "Trent, even I don't have this many things in my travel kit. This is bigger than half of my purses!" She upended the bag and dumped the contents out onto the bed. Shampoos, conditioners, gels, and mousses in fancy bottles tumbled out.

"I want to look good, don't I?"

"Do you seriously use all this stuff?"

"Not usually, but if I'm supposed to be meeting the man of my dreams, I ought to use all the ammo I can, right?"

"If you need all this crap to get someone to notice you, they aren't worth having."

Trent considered this for a moment. "Okay, maybe you're right." He took the hair gels out of the pile. "I do use all the rest of this stuff."

"Three kinds of body wash?"

"Yes. One is for relaxation, one for revitaliza—"

Beth harrumphed and shook her head. "*No one* needs three kinds of body wash. Pick one shampoo, one conditioner, and *one* body wash."

She looked him square in the eye. Her demeanor had grown serious.

"Trent, you know you don't need half the stuff you've packed." She picked up another example: Trent's "lucky writing T-shirt," which he'd been wearing when he got the news about his first book contract.

"I want to have my favorite things with me." What business was it of Beth's what he packed? He slammed the suitcase shut and pulled it closer to him. "I don't need your help packing. If I have the wrong clothes, then fine; I'll buy new ones when I get there." His heart was pounding, but he went on. "You know, I changed my mind. I'm not going anywhere."

"Trent." Beth's tone softened. She sat down next to him on the bed and stroked his knee reassuringly. "We both know this isn't about body wash or T-shirts."

"Then why are you unpacking everything?"

"This is about you letting go. You know you have to. It's been two years and we've all been patient while you've been trying to get over losing Marc. But you have to stop living in the past and surrounding yourself with security blankets."

"I don't have a blanket."

"You know, since Marc, you've been hiding behind your favorite, familiar safe things, and," she offered a concerned smile, "entirely too many aromatherapy products."

Trent didn't want to meet her eyes, because he knew she was right. Not about the body wash, but about retreating into a safety zone. That didn't mean he wanted or needed to do anything about it.

"You watch the same movies over and over. You order the same dishes at the same restaurants unless someone else orders for you. Last week at Splash, I thought you were going to have a panic attack because they'd run out of that halibut you like."

Trent opened his mouth to defend himself, but stopped when he realized he *had* gone a bit postal over something as trivial as an entrée.

Beth went on, "It's a major drama getting you to come with us to a new club or even a coffee bar. You've been avoiding anything new and it's not healthy for you. Your writing reflects this too. Cass has mentioned it time and time again."

She paused and reached for his hand. "It's time to make some changes."

Trent stared at her small hand covering his much larger one and let her words penetrate his brain. Sure, he had *habits*; lots of people did. But he hadn't realized the extent to which he'd relied on them until Beth spelled it out for him. His friends teased him about ordering his favorite dishes over and over, but he had always shrugged it off. Now he saw his behavior from a different perspective.

He hadn't just been following habits. He'd been actively avoiding change. No wonder he felt like his heart was pounding loud enough for Beth to hear at the prospect of this trip.

"You're right. I know I'm missing out on a lot of things in my life, but... I guess I think I'm happier this way."

"Are you happy?"

"I'm not *un*happy." Trent frowned. It wasn't completely true. He'd been more and more restless lately, but he hadn't figured out why. He had never been so thankful for Beth as a friend. "I've just been too afraid of breaking out of the safety bubble."

"Maybe this trip is too much to start with. I'm sorry I pushed you into it. I can cancel the reservations." A sly smile crept across her face. "Or I can go with you...."

"I can do this. *Alone*. I don't need a babysitter!" Now he was annoyed she didn't have any faith in him.

"Of course you can." Beth gave a smug grin and he knew she'd played him. He glared as menacingly as he could muster up and she just laughed. "One thing I do know about you, Trent..."

"What's that?"

"Once you put your mind to something, you have never failed to accomplish it." Beth punched his arm playfully before wrapping her arms around him and practically squeezing him to death. In playful retaliation, he pulled her close, face against his chest, until she mumbled something into his left pec.

"I was getting a little low on air, there." Her words came between gasps.

"Sorry," he said, completely unrepentantly. "Your hugs are lethal weapons, so I was just protecting myself."

She punched him again on the arm. Twice. "Hope you bruise easily. Now, back to this suitcase!"

"Can I take the hair dryer?" Trent tried to keep a pleading tone out of his voice.

"No!"

Trent looked at her, mouth falling open, and chose three items from the pile of his favorite bath products. Beth gathered the rest up and carried them into his bathroom, where she dumped them on the counter.

"Now, we'll work on the wardrobe."

Godiva gracefully settled into the now-empty suitcase and offered her own advice with an aristocratic meow.

NINETY minutes later Trent and Beth entered one of his favorite restaurants, a Thai place around the corner from his apartment. No driving or parking necessary. Cassandra and Mick, Trent's other good friend since grad school, were already there waiting, two half-finished beers in front of them.

"Get your ass in here, Trent. I'm just as curious as you are about this big trip Beth's got planned for you. Cass wouldn't tell me a thing." Mick clapped Trent on the shoulder as he sat down, and motioned toward one of the beers on the table after catching the server's eye. "All I know is it's apparently to someplace very gay and even you should be able to get laid there."

"Mick, that is not what I said!" Beth glared.

"Close enough."

Beth raised a hand as if to smack Mick, who cringed in mock terror. Trent ignored their scene-playing. He'd seen it dozens of times over the years. Mick invariably offended one or both of them, but Beth never let it slide.

"I'm all packed, though I think I'd enjoy a root canal more." Trent looked pointedly at Beth, who grinned innocently and poured beer into her glass from Cass's bottle.

Cass frowned at Beth and turned to Trent. "It couldn't have been that bad." She pinched Trent's arm. "Hey, you've been spending more time at the gym, haven't you?" She stroked his bicep and let out a girlish sigh.

"Yes, I have. I don't spend *all* my time watching TCM." Trent glared purposefully at Cass.

"Did Beth let on what we've got planned for your vacation yet?" Cass sounded businesslike again.

"It feels more like a forced exile, but no, she hasn't given me a single clue except it's going to be hot. I was hoping for Paris; it's really nice this time of year."

"You've been to Paris before, at least twice. Once with me and Mick," Beth said, thankfully leaving unsaid Trent's other visit had been with Marc.

"So, what's wrong with that?"

"Don't you want to go somewhere you've never been?" Cass ordered more beer by catching the waiter's attention with a wave of her hand.

"It doesn't matter where you go, Trent, what you need is to have lots of sex to get in the mood."

Sex was Mick's answer to everything. Not surprising, since he worked in the porn industry. He'd come to grad school at USC to study film writing, like Beth, but after finding well-paying part-time work on a porn shoot, he'd never had much ambition to move into mainstream film. Mick had found his calling writing and directing porn of all flavors.

"I can't believe I'm agreeing with Mick, but he's right. This trip is going to be an opportunity to go somewhere you've never been and really have an adventure. And that means sex, Trent. Face it, you can't write erotic romance if you're living like a fucking monk!"

"Is there such a thing?" Mick asked wistfully. "I love the paradox."

"This trip is to get your creativity going and inspire something different for your next book." Cass deftly brought the conversation back to reality, and her agenda.

"I don't really like trying new things, Cass."

"That's the point, Trent."

"Don't you trust me?" Beth asked with a smile on her face that didn't make Trent feel particularly trusting. Damn, he should have planned his own trip. *What had he been thinking?*

Mali, the owner of the restaurant, brought menus with their beers and greeted Trent and his friends. Trent was a regular here and had gotten to know Mali and her staff fairly well.

"Beth can order tonight." Trent glanced at Beth and started to hand his menu back to Mali.

Beth shook her head. "Open the menu, Trent."

Trent shrugged and opened his menu. Inside was a long white envelope. "What the hell?" He looked up to see Cass and Beth staring at him like he'd grown a second nose. Apparently they'd planned this all out and gotten Mali into the act as well.

"Open it!" Cass tilted her head expectantly.

Trent knew what was inside. He took a deep breath before opening the envelope. He pulled out an old-style paper plane ticket and grinned.

"I knew you like old-fashioned things, and an e-ticket would be so anti-climactic," Beth said. She definitely knew him very well. He felt a stir of anticipation—or perhaps dread—as he opened it.

LOS ANGELES / LAX

BANGKOK / BKK

"Bangkok?" Trent let it sink in for a moment. He wasn't sure how he felt about a trip to Thailand. At least he knew he'd like the food, but other than that, he knew nothing about the country.

"Happy travels, Trent!" Mali said and gave him a graceful *wai*, the hands-together greeting of Thailand, before rushing back toward the kitchen.

"So, what do you think?" Beth grabbed at Trent's arm.

"Wow. It's really not at all what I expected. I guess I'm excited. I don't know what I'd do there."

"There are zillions of things to do," Beth said. "In Bangkok alone there are hundreds of temples, a royal palace, a river, and lots of restaurants and bars. Gay bars even."

"Even Trent should be able to get laid in Bangkok," Mick chimed in. Sex was his favorite subject and he never held back with his opinion or unwanted details of his own experiences.

"Fuck you." Trent was a fan of the classics, after all.

"Bangkok is one of the most gay-friendly cities in the world. You'll find plenty of places to hang out, meet people, and, well, you know…." Beth's words trailed off.

"Get laid," Mick offered.

"Mick, must you always be so crude?" Cass asked. She could be pretty crude herself so the comment brought general laughter around the table.

"If I was going to be crude I'd've said 'fuck.' But with Trent, someone has to get to the point." Mick drained his glass and motioned for another. "For a guy who writes about sex, Trent, you are one of the most uptight people I know."

"I'm not uptight."

"Yes, you are," Beth and Cass said almost simultaneously.

"Trent's sex scenes are very… tasteful," Cass added.

"Just like my food. Tasteful," Mali said, appearing behind Trent. "Ready to order now?"

AFTER stuffing themselves silly with Trent's favorite dishes and a few special items Mali made to celebrate Trent's trip, they vacated their table for another group and settled across the room at Mali's beautiful mirror-backed full bar.

"Glenfiddich for me," Mick told the bartender as he slid onto a stool. "Cabernet," he motioned toward Beth, "Bourbon, neat," Cass, "and a girly cocktail for Trent. Something pink with an umbrella."

"No. Give me a Gibson." Trent had no idea what was in a Gibson, but he wasn't going to drink something pink just because Mick was a dick.

"Trent, you've never ordered a Gibson before!" Beth said.

"I'm trying new things," Trent replied, though it came out a bit more petulantly than he'd intended. "You're all over me because I'm in a rut, and then when I do something different, y'all freak out. I can't win."

"You're right. I'm sorry." Beth rubbed a soothing hand on top of his, on the bar.

The bartender served them quickly and while the others sipped theirs, Cassandra knocked her bourbon back in a couple of large gulps. Even Mick seemed taken aback, but for once he didn't say anything.

"Off to the Ladies," Cass said and hopped off her stool.

"I'll go with you," Beth said.

"Don't get into any trouble while we're gone." Cassandra waited for Beth to grab her purse.

"We'll be just fine," Trent replied, laughing.

"I wasn't talking to you." Cassandra glared at Mick, who sneered in response. "Trent, I want you to get into some trouble, please. Anything to liven up your life a little. Mick's life is already a bit too lively for anyone's good!"

"So, Bangkok," Mick said. "Bang. Cock. I just love saying the name: Bang. *Cock*. I wish I were going with you!" Mick sidled up closer to Trent and lowered his voice. "Anyway, I hear they have these bars there, with these girls, right? Only they aren't all girl, if you know what I mean." Mick leered knowingly and jabbed Trent in the ribs with a bony elbow.

"I don't know what you mean, Mick, and quite honestly, I don't want to." Trent scooted his stool a few inches farther from Mick. He let his gaze wander the room as he took a few sips from his drink. He couldn't face Mick when Mick talked like this.

"So, just in case you're not a hundred-percent sure you want a guy, right, you can sort of have it both ways at once with these guys—girls—fuck, I don't know what you call 'em, but they have fantastic tits, and they still have their junk and—"

"Mick, just shut up." Trent stared open-mouthed at the extent of his friend's sexual imagination. Trent might write what some might say bordered on porn for a living, but at least his characters weren't sick fucks like his supposed best friend.

"Can I have your autograph?" A young blonde woman walked toward them, a thankful distraction from the conversation. She was pretty and wore fashionable clothing. Her shy smile belied the effect of a skirt that flirted with the line between short and totally inappropriate, exactly the direction Mick's eyes zeroed in on.

"Sure, baby, anything you want." Mick grinned and visibly pulled his gaze from the woman's thighs to her face, with a short pause on her ample and well-displayed cleavage.

Trent hoped he hid the sneer that sprang momentarily to his face at the comment and Mick's inability to comprehend the concept of subtle. Poor woman was just Mick's type, too, all innocent face and curvy young body.

"No, not yours." She turned to face Trent. "*Yours.*" Her coy smile widened and Trent thought for sure she'd blushed. Mick was the one sneering now.

"Do you know me?" Trent asked. He did occasional signings and his photo was on the cover of his books, but he didn't think anyone would actually *recognize* him in public. Some of his readers were female but he assumed they knew he was gay and not interested.

"I don't care who you are; I just want your autograph. Here's mine." Her voice turned husky and inviting as she passed Trent a cocktail napkin with her name and phone number on it.

Hell, now Trent was blushing.

"I—uh—sorry. I'm—"

"Gay," Mick interjected triumphantly, again looking at the woman like she was on the menu and he'd been on a crash diet. Like he might actually have a chance with her.

"Ah. Oh." She completely ignored Mick and continued to face Trent. "I figured it was worth a shot." She turned on her heel and walked back to the table where her friends sat. Trent watched her sit down and wave at him with a good-natured smile. Meanwhile Mick glowered next to him at the bar.

"So, lemme have her number? It's not like you're gonna use it."

"No way!" Trent ripped up the napkin and dumped the shreds into Mick's half-full tumbler of single malt. The look on Mick's face was worth the price of the drink Trent was certain he'd be buying to replace it. "I'm not letting you get your hands on her. If she was interested in you, she wouldn't have come on to me right in front of you."

"Who came on to you?" Beth asked as she and Cassandra returned and perched themselves once more on their seats.

"A girl. Gave me her number and everything." Trent grinned sideways at Mick. "Well, she *offered* everything."

"Maybe you should call her. I think anyone would do at the moment," Cassandra said.

"Anyone would do what?" Trent didn't like her tone.

"Trent, honey, for once, Mick's right. You just need to get yourself laid. A mindless fuck to reboot your system. Even with a girl." Cassandra picked up her glass and knocked back the contents in one gulp and put it back down on the bar with a crack. "Get everything working again properly."

"Everything works." Trent snuck a glance in the direction of his crotch.

"Then share the love with someone, boy!" Cassandra clapped Trent on the back. Sometimes she was more like a guy than… well, than Trent was.

Mick sat there nodding with a smug look on his face and even Beth's initial wide-eyed astonishment quickly faded to agreement.

"Well, someone had to say it, sweetie. Besides Mick." Cassandra nodded to the bartender for a refill then turned back to Trent and put a hand on his shoulder. "Since Marc you're just not the same. Not the same writer, not the same man. You need something big to shake your life up again and get past it."

"I hardly thinking fucking a girl is going to help me."

"Well, you remember what I told you about those Bang. Cock girls…" Mick leered.

"This trip is really going to be good for you, Trent." Beth squeezed in between Trent and Mick and wrapped an arm around Trent's waist. "Who knows? Maybe it will completely change your life."

Trent was suspicious of the look that passed between Cassandra and Beth. What had they planned for him in Thailand?

"We'll see," Trent agreed tentatively. But he knew they both had his best interests at heart, and he trusted them. Didn't he?

3

Tuesday morning, Bangkok

THE sun shone brightly as the plane flew low over the densely packed city bisected by the wide, winding Chao Phraya River. He'd spent the final ten minutes of the journey face pressed against the tiny airplane window. As the green-gray squares of an enormous agricultural quilt gave way to tightly packed urban sprawl, Trent found himself in awe of the sheer size of the city below. A mixture of anticipation and nerves fought in Trent's gut as the plane touched down in a nearly perfect landing.

He stretched and a smiling, purple-silk-clad stewardess handed him his daypack from the overhead bin in the first-class cabin. He thanked her and waited for the doors to open so he could get off this damn flying tin can. Even the relatively comfortable seating in Thai Airways "Silk Class" wasn't roomy enough, and his legs and back ached from the long flight. They really ought to have a section just for people over six feet tall. "Tall Class"? Probably not much of a demand for it on Thai Airways, he mused, as he towered over the other passengers lined up in the aisle.

He knew he'd crossed the International Date Line but he couldn't remember whether it was yesterday or tomorrow in Thailand. He dug in his pocket for the itinerary to see if he could figure it out while he waited to disembark.

On the other hand, he wasn't exactly sure what he was going to do once he got off the plane. He'd collect his checked bag, and there was supposed to be a driver waiting for him to take him to his hotel. He had guidebooks and maps, and plenty of information Beth had gathered for him, and wondered for about the hundredth time whether he should have let her and Cass plan his trip for him after all. He'd spent a good part of Sunday with Mali at the restaurant, and she'd gotten him good and excited about the trip, but now he was here, doubts and fears multiplied.

As he psyched himself back up for the adventure, the airplane door opened and the line began to move.

WELCOME TO BANGKOK, read the banner, as he blindly followed the couple in front of him. They seemed to know their way around; hopefully they were heading in the direction of Baggage Claim. Signs in the curly Thai script Trent had recently become slightly more familiar with were everywhere, but there were enough signs in English for him to figure out where he needed to go.

At Baggage Claim he quickly found his suitcase and headed for Immigration and Customs. While one man searched his suitcase and backpack, another asked him half a dozen seemingly innocuous questions about his trip, and without much of a delay he was released and headed for the exit, where he expected to be met by his prearranged limo. He looked forward to traveling in style.

REED ACTON'S target had a hell of a nice ass on him.

Reed watched the tall, shaggy-haired Westerner in the dark pink shirt collect his bags and head for the exit. He'd seen the transfer, one of the customs officials tucking a folded piece of paper into the tall man's daypack. So far so good. Now to follow the guy and catch him before he left the airport.

It was Tuesday and there were plenty of pink shirts floating around the airport. Thai tradition—or superstition—dictated pink an auspicious color for Tuesdays and even modern Thais followed the custom. But not many of them were as tall as Reed's target, making him easy to spot even from a distance.

"Need a ride anywhere, friend?" Reed asked as he caught up to Fuchsia Shirt and uttered the prearranged phrase. Damn, he was even better-looking up close. And taller.

The guy slowed his brisk pace only slightly as Reed tried to keep up with him. "No thanks. I have a limo waiting for me." He barely even glanced out of the corner of his eye as he replied. There was a hint of an accent in his voice, but Reed couldn't place it. Something from the Southern U.S.

"What?" Reed assessed the situation. That wasn't the scripted response. *Oh, fucking fuck.* The customs agent had given the map to the wrong person. This airport transfer was unnecessarily complicated, and Reed cursed his superior, who had planned it. There were better places to transfer the documents than a crowded airport, and he still didn't see the need to have the paper go through this many hands.

"I don't need a ride." Fuchsia Shirt's tone was decidedly less friendly as he turned toward Reed and slowed enough to give him a once-over. "Hey, are you American?" the guy added in a surprised tone and stopped suddenly, causing two people following closely to crash into him, cursing in Thai. "Oh, I am so sorry!" The man's tone was so remorseful Reed would have thought he'd run over their kid or something.

He stared up at Fuchsia Shirt, who continued to apologize even as his victims scurried away into the crowd of people leaving the terminal. Reed took in the bright hazel eyes and the wide, slightly crooked grin with its large white teeth. And tall! Reed was over six foot, but this guy had several inches on him. Judging by the way his shirt clung to his upper body, he must have spent hours in the gym, and it all paid off. Reed realized he hadn't answered the question Tall, Hot and Handsome had asked him.

All Reed knew was he had to get the map out of the backpack before this tourist noticed it or he might just throw it away. If that happened, the game was up and it would be a disaster for Reed.

"Yeah, I'm American, but I work here in Bangkok. Sure you don't want me to give you a lift? Keep you from worrying about anyone trying to cheat you on taxi fare or send you to a crappy hotel," Reed suggested. He had to think fast about how to get into the guy's bag short of stealing it.

"Mr. Dallas?" A middle-aged Thai man wearing tan cotton pants and a short-sleeved pale pink shirt came up, and the tall American nodded.

"Yeah, that's close enough." He smiled and laughed softly, with a hint of embarrassment.

"I'm Phaibun, your driver. I take you to hotel now." Phaibun glared at Reed as he took Dallas's arm and steered him toward the exit. "Don't let hustlers hurt you. Watch out! Don't trust."

Phaibun had meant Reed when he'd said "hustlers," though it couldn't be farther from the truth. Reed raced to the motorbike he'd left outside near the taxi stand, hoping he could catch up to Phaibun and Dallas, follow them to the hotel and retrieve the map. The task would be much harder now, especially if Dallas thought he was trying to scam him or something. But Reed could be charming when he needed to, and it wouldn't be particularly difficult—would actually be more than pleasant—to spend time with Dallas and get the damned map. Otherwise Reed could kiss this deal, and possibly his life, goodbye.

There was also a chance this Dallas guy could get hurt, too, and Reed certainly didn't want that on his conscience. He ran for his motorcycle, dodging slow-moving travelers and receiving more than a few angry remarks, but he couldn't afford to lose Dallas and the map.

As SOON as Trent stepped outside of the airport building he hit a wall of heat and humidity so thick it nearly stopped him in his tracks. Each step forward was a battle against an invisible force that immediately sapped his energy. He'd grown up in Oklahoma, where the mercury regularly hit the nineties during the summer, and you could fry an egg on the hood of your car, but he'd never experienced heat like this before. He slowed his steps as he followed Phaibun, who wheeled Trent's larger suitcase behind him and seemed to move easily through the oppressive heat.

Outside the airport stood a row of shiny black luxury cars, mostly BMWs and Mercedes, and Trent's mood brightened at the thought of putting the AC on full blast once he got inside. But Phaibun led Trent past all of them to the end of the row to a dusty, ramshackle vehicle that looked like a cross between a motorcycle and the surrey with the fringe on top. It was mainly open, with just a covering over the driver and passenger seats, but no windows except for the windshield. The vehicle in question was painted bright yellow and blue and sported a TAXI sign on top, but Trent had never seen anything like it before. He silently thanked God for that and began to walk away, but Phaibun grabbed at his elbow until Trent stopped and turned around.

"Dallas, it's okay, it's okay!" Phaibun intoned. "You never ride in tuk-tuk before, I think?"

"Tuk-tuk?" Trent shook his head as he stared warily at the vehicle. He glanced longingly at the beautiful, shiny black Mercedes parked next

to it and felt his good mood ebbing away and his blood pressure rising. A
rivulet of sweat trickled down the middle of his back and Trent squirmed
slightly, fighting to keep his calm, if not his cool.

"Very popular in Thailand. See?" Phaibun motioned his arm
toward the dozens of similar vehicles lined up outside the airport. People
stood on line for them and no one else looked fearful for their life.
Maybe it would be okay, Trent hoped, as he opened the door, which
squealed on its hinges, and settled into the tiny backseat with his
backpack still clutched tightly to his chest. The vehicle was cramped and
he had to sit at an angle to make enough room for his legs. Phaibun
stowed Trent's suitcase in the back and hopped into the driver's seat. He
started the engine and joined the line of tuk-tuks exiting the airport.

"You know how to get to my hotel?" Trent asked almost as an
afterthought, shouting to be heard over the put-putting of the tiny
vehicle's engine. He hoped the guy knew, since Trent wasn't even sure
what hotel he was booked into; Beth had left that little tidbit of
information off his travel itinerary.

"Yes, sir, Dallas. I know where to take you. No problem, sir!"

"Please don't call me 'Dallas.' It's 'Trent,' really."

Phaibun turned to reply, "Okay, Mr. Trent, sir."

"Or 'sir.' No 'sir.'"

"Okay, Mr. Trent."

Trent cringed as his driver seemed to focus more attention on him
than on the road. He didn't want to be "mister" either, but he'd won a
small battle if not the war, and he wasn't going to distract the driver
again. He glanced around at his surroundings once he became
accustomed to the stomach-jolting erratic movements of the small
vehicle.

Two garlands of flowers and several amulets on thick orange string
hung from the rearview mirror and swung wildly as the tuk-tuk
navigated turns or wove in and out of traffic. Trent wondered how the
driver could see clearly enough to drive. To distract himself he checked
for the name of the hotel on the piece of paper he still had wadded up in
his hand and realized it wasn't there; just the address. Great. More of
Beth's mystery adventure. He just hoped whatever Beth and Cassandra
had arranged would meet his approval.

He wouldn't say he was fussy, but he had come to enjoy and expect
certain amenities when he traveled, and he'd heard terrific things about

the hotels in Bangkok. Superb food, wonderful service. His stomach growled, reminding him it was time to eat, no matter what time the clock displayed. He'd order something decadent and eat by the pool. He couldn't imagine wanting to do any running around or sightseeing in this heat and instead daydreamed of his air-conditioned room. He'd be there soon and he could cool off, relax, and eat, not necessarily in that order.

If the heat and the tuk-tuk had taken Trent by surprise, it was nothing compared to the traffic. It was so thick, and the constant stopping and starting combined with the pervasive odor of auto fumes soon made Trent lose his appetite. He couldn't wait to shower off the grime from the exhaust, now mingled with sweat to form a disgusting layer of dirt. It was going to use up a good portion of the bottle of his scrumptious body wash. The thought he might run out of it during this trip worried him, and he wondered whether he'd be able to find a suitable replacement in the hotel shop.

Finally, the traffic broke up and the tuk-tuk accelerated, creating a warm breeze; it was a welcome relief from the heat and smell of the traffic jam. Trent began to enjoy the ride as they passed car after car plodding along, less agile than the smaller tuk-tuks. Along the road, Trent could see all manner of carts full of street food. Occasionally he caught a whiff of something absolutely heavenly. His stomach growled, reminding him he hadn't eaten for hours. The food on the plane hadn't exactly been what he'd call a full meal, and he'd charmed the flight attendant into giving him a second meal. At least international flights still offered meal service. Then again, he'd flown first class, so he'd more than paid for it.

They passed numerous temples on the journey. Though surrounded by high fences, the unique colors and traditional architecture soon became familiar and Trent had no idea just how many temples there were in Bangkok alone. He saw a line of saffron-robed monks lined up outside some of the temples, holding out bowls while men walked past scooping some sort of food into each man's bowl. Trent was surprised to discover the monks varied in age from children to elderly men.

Maybe he should have read that damn guidebook Beth had given him *before* his trip.

REED'S motorcycle wove in and out of traffic and he easily kept the blue-and-yellow tuk-tuk in sight. Almost too easily. He needed to make sure he wasn't spotted or he'd risk arousing Dallas's suspicions. Reed would have to retrieve the map while the guy left his backpack unattended in his room. He'd fucked everything up in the airport and now Dallas knew what he looked like, and worse, thought he was a hustler. It would be next to impossible to gain his trust now and find a better way of retrieving the map besides breaking into his room. Reed could always get a room at the same hotel and casually run into Dallas, but there was always a chance he'd discover the map and throw it away before Reed was able to make friends with him.

The tuk-tuk didn't head in the direction of the five-star international hotels, which caught Reed by surprise. Dallas looked like the type to stay in the upscale area of town. If not one of the big international chains, at least one of the more expensive locally owned inns. When Dallas's tuk-tuk headed for Silom, everything clicked. It was the center of gay Bangkok.

Reed hadn't been certain, though enough about Dallas hinted at it. Maybe it was the slight swing of his hips rather than his shoulders. Or his clothing and the brand-new backpack. His jeans were too perfectly tailored. He probably had the shirt custom made, judging by the way it clung to every curve and angle of his arms and chest. Or the way he'd checked out Reed's body before his face until that damned Thai driver showed up. Reed tried not to recall too much detail about Dallas's body as he followed the tuk-tuk and stopped about twenty feet behind as it parked in front of its apparent final destination, the Pink Tiger Hotel.

Yup. That clinched it. Gay. Reed smiled. This would be *much* more pleasant than he'd expected.

"Wait a minute, dude. This has got to be the wrong place!" Dallas hopped out of the tuk-tuk after the driver, who was pulling the rolling suitcase from the baggage compartment behind the passenger area. He shouted loudly enough Reed could hear and even the jumble of college-age kids walking on the opposite side of the street turned to look at the commotion.

"Yes, sir. No, sir." the driver handed a piece of paper to Dallas, who snatched it from the much shorter Thai man's hand. Dallas glared, mouth opening in what could have been protest, though no words came out.

"No, no, no, this is a mistake! I'm supposed to stay in a fancy new place. Not this old run-down hotel." He practically spat out the final word as if his mouth couldn't quite manage to call this establishment a hotel.

"Miss Beth e-mail says you stay this place. I leave you and baggages here now, Dallas, sir." The driver pulled the bag out of the back of his vehicle and placed it on the sidewalk and got back behind the wheel. Dallas was grumbling loudly about "Miss Beth" though Reed couldn't make out the rest of the words. Finally Dallas turned toward the Thai.

"How much do I owe you for the ride?"

At least the guy was honest, even if he was angry. Reed tried not to laugh at Dallas's obvious predicament though it certainly was pretty fucking hilarious. If Reed hadn't already come to the conclusion Dallas was as queer as a three-baht note, he might have suspected "Miss Beth" was an angry ex playing a horrible joke, but obviously that wasn't the case. Reed had to admit he was intrigued now. How had Dallas ended up here, and why?

"No owe me. Miss Beth paid my services already for one week. I can take you on sightseeing or taxi service, but I leave you here now." The driver pointed toward the hotel.

This is definitely getting interesting. Reed smiled to himself, and for a few minutes he forgot about the map he still had to get out of Dallas's backpack.

"Can you take me to another hotel? One of those fancy international places? I'll pay you extra. Lots extra." Dallas wasn't giving up, but Phaibun shook his head. He rummaged in the breast pocket of his shirt and handed Dallas another small piece of paper.

"You want taxi sightseeing, call me." Phaibun pointed to the tuk-tuk. "Cell number, okay?" He drove off, leaving Dallas openmouthed on the sidewalk, squinting at the card in his hand.

Reed could probably win over Dallas by offering to get him to the Four Seasons Bangkok, the Peninsula, or even the Dusit Thani, the top Thai-run luxury hotel. He started to cross the street, as Dallas grabbed his suitcase and headed at top speed into the Pink Tiger Hotel. By the time Reed got inside, Dallas was already filling out a form at the check-in counter. The clerk handed Dallas a key and an eager Thai bellboy of about ten ran to the counter to grab the suitcase. There was a slight struggle over the bag until Dallas released it, though he watched warily as the boy began to wheel it toward the stairway on the other side of the lobby.

"I can help you find a better place, if you're interested," Reed said as Dallas stepped in his direction, but before he could get a reply, the hotel clerk came out from behind his desk and began yelling at Reed in a mix of Thai and English.

"Watch out for hustlers!" the clerk warned Dallas, who watched as Reed was shoved roughly in the direction of the front door. The boy grabbed Dallas's arm and yanked him toward the stairs.

Fuuuuuuuck, Reed nearly growled as he ended up on the sidewalk outside the hotel. Twice now he'd been kept from talking to Dallas. Hot and interesting or not, this guy was fucking up Reed's plans and he had to do something about it fast.

TRENT had been beyond furious when the tuk-tuk taxi thing pulled up outside this dinky old hotel—maybe "hotel" was a bit elegant for what it really was. Beth had booked him a room here rather than the luxurious international hotel he'd expected, apparently in pursuit of adventure. He'd deal with her when he got home. He'd just pay someone at the Pink Tiger Hotel to book him a room at another hotel—he'd choose the best one in that guidebook *and* make Beth pay for it—but once he'd walked inside he'd been surprised by the high ceilings and the bright airiness of the lobby. Multiple ceiling fans provided an unexpected coolness and the lobby was nicely, if simply, furnished with heavy wicker chairs and couches covered with clean bright cotton cushions. The few guests he saw in the lobby—all male—were Westerners who looked clean and happy. They gave him appraising glances, but he was too preoccupied to care about potential dates now.

Chakri, the desk clerk, commanded all of Trent's attention. He giggled flirtatiously and batted long fake eyelashes while he checked Trent in. Despite the makeup, Chakri wore men's clothing and made no attempt to disguise he was male. No fake tits here. Trent grinned at Chakri's easy mix of male and female.

"You want fun, let Chakri know! Fun follows Chakri everywhere!"

Trent laughed at the diva-like way Chakri used third person. He'd been cute and friendly and it now it seemed downright rude to ask him to find Trent a better hotel. Trent's momma had raised him right. As much as he liked his AC and pedicures, he wasn't about to insult someone right in their own lobby. He'd figure it out on his own. He'd grab a shower and a nap—wait: food, then nap!—and deal with the change of hotel later.

He was supposed to be here for an adventure and so far, nothing had been what he'd expected. Wasn't that the definition of "adventure"? He wasn't exactly having fun yet, but so far the trip had successfully jolted him out of his routine and definitely out of his comfort zone.

After checking in, the good-looking guy who had talked to him in the airport had turned up in the lobby. *What was he doing here? Is he following me?* Trent chided himself for such a far-fetched idea. This wasn't one of his books, after all. But so far the taxi guy and even the kid who took his suitcase had warned Trent away from him, calling him a pretty-boy hustler. Trent now knew all about the "girls" who were really boys—Thailand was famous for them, as Mick had filled him in with more detail than Trent needed or wanted—but he hadn't expected another American would try to scam him. Or was he just some gay hustler? Whatever the guy was after, Trent would have to be on his guard if he saw him again.

Once upstairs, Trent looked around his room. Just like downstairs, the room was bright and clean, its white walls freshly painted. No AC. That was the worst of it, but the fan whirring overhead and a couple of windows with sturdy screens might do the trick. A quick examination showed no holes in either one, and Trent let out a sigh of relief. He could just imagine the enormous man-eating insects that would come in through an open window around here. The desk clerk had mentioned they were close to the river, which meant even more unwanted insect life. But overall the room was clean, even with its battered furniture and pale polished-wood floor, dented and scraped from a parade of previous guests. On a small desk, a glass bowl containing various buds and petals floating on water perfumed the room, adding an unexpected touch of Thai elegance.

A white envelope lay on top of the pillows. Intrigued, Trent sat on the bed and opened it. It was from Beth, probably faxed or e-mailed.

Congratulations, Trent! If you made it this far you've already taken the first step in your Thai adventure. Sorry about the hotel, but all the expensive gay hotels were booked up for months and this was the best I could do on short notice. You won't spend much time here anyway. If you do, hopefully you won't be alone!

If you have any problems, call Phaibun. He's Mali's cousin and you can trust him completely.

Now go and explore!

XOXOXOXOX – Beth

Trent laughed. Beth knew him pretty well and had suspected he might have tried to change hotels.

Really, his main gripe now was the room didn't have a private bathroom and he would have to use shared facilities at the end of the hall. Chakri made it sound like a feature rather than a drawback—"naked hot guys!"—but Trent couldn't remember the last time he'd had to use a communal shower, and he shivered at the thought. He'd get revenge on Beth for this later, but at the moment he was absolutely dying to clean up. He took an experimental sniff at one armpit and recoiled at his own unpleasant smell. The body wash should fix him right up. He smiled and let out a little anticipatory sigh.

Trent slipped out of his jeans and damp shirt and tossed them on the bed. He unzipped his suitcase and dug out his toiletries bag, then grabbed the towel hanging from a bar next to the sink in one corner of the room. Wrapping the towel around his waist, he was about to leave the room when he decided against leaving his backpack there. It might get stolen and he'd have to deal with replacing money, passport, plane tickets, and his precious little notebooks. He slung the backpack over one shoulder, locked the door behind him, and shuffled down the hall to wash off the Bangkok grime.

The shower area at the end of the hall had three stalls, each with its own small changing area, a remarkably clean bamboo-patterned shower curtain, and a couple of large plastic hooks. He hung up his towel and his backpack before turning on the water—lukewarm—and slipped under the relatively refreshing spray. He slid the curtain closed behind him and was frustrated to discover it wasn't quite wide enough to span the width of the stall. Well, at least this way he could make sure no one swiped his backpack while he was in there.

After the oppressive heat, the cool water was incredibly refreshing. He grabbed his favorite body wash and started soaping himself, letting the power of aromatherapy relax him after the long flight and frustration of discovering Beth and Cassandra had set him up in this hotel. He'd stay here one night—more than enough to show them he had broken out of his rut—and then he'd move over to a four- or five-star place with a Jacuzzi in the room and turn the AC up so high he'd need mittens and a parka.

As he washed, he recalled the American hustler who seemed to have followed him from the airport. *Too bad the guy's trouble. He was pretty hot.* He certainly could have been part of the adventure, but Trent probably wouldn't run into him again. He thought about the guy's almost-too-short dark-brown hair and the way his blue-gray eyes practically twinkled when he'd spoken to Trent. It didn't take long before Trent's body started thinking about what it was missing and he felt the blood flowing into his cock, a warm glow growing heavy and insistent between his legs.

REED hovered on the staircase down the hall from Dallas's room, after slipping in through a side entrance without any of the hotel staff noticing him. He hoped Dallas would head to the shower as soon as he settled in. He was right, he thought, as Dallas, wearing only a towel around his waist, soon emerged from his room. Reed was so caught up in the view, especially since the towel was rather small and ended mid-thigh, he didn't immediately realize Dallas still had the backpack with him. No chance of sneaking into his room to get the map now. But Reed wouldn't let the backpack out of his sight. So what if that meant he had to head in the direction of the shower, noticing the way Dallas's muscles glided beneath the smooth skin of his back and shoulders, and the bunched knot of muscles in his well-developed calves. Damn, this guy must spend half the day in the gym. Maybe he was one of those underwear models.

Reed tried to stay out of Dallas's line of vision as he watched the man enter the shower area, disrobe, and slip under the water. He didn't even attempt to keep his eyes off the man's body, most of which was visible due to the narrow curtain.

What a gorgeous ass. Reed wondered what it would feel like to stroke its firm perfect shape or squeeze it, feeling the hard muscles beneath the skin. Dallas had brought some body wash in a fancy-looking blue-and-gold bottle, and was slathering himself in it. Reed almost chuckled at the idea of this powerfully built hunk of a man using such a girly soap. He preferred plain old soap. In his line of work, sometimes showers were few and far between, and he focused on getting clean when he was lucky enough to have one.

Any criticism Reed had of Dallas faded into oblivion when the man turned and Reed got a view of the guy's cock. Jesus, Mary, and Joseph, it was beautiful. Thick and long, and getting longer as Dallas slid his soapy hand up and down the length. Reed grinned to himself at how his day was turning out. Sure, he'd had a couple of setbacks, but he hadn't lost sight of the map, and now here he was getting a free show from the hottest guy he'd ever seen. *Just gotta make sure he doesn't see me!* Reed reminded himself and pressed his back against the wall again.

Dallas's cock was fully hard now, dark and swollen, and Reed watched as he continued to stroke himself, long smooth pulls along the shaft and some thumb work around the head. Thankfully, Dallas's eyes were shut tight, but the way he scraped his teeth across his lip now and then had Reed's own cock responding, and he shifted himself to ease the tightness in his crotch. With the other hand, Dallas at first pinched at his nipples, then let his hand fall lower to cup his sac or roll his balls in his hand. Reed lost track of time completely while he watched as—too soon—Dallas grunted softly and came against the wall. Hell, after watching that performance, *Reed* really needed a cold shower. He looked at the obvious bulge at his crotch and tried to rearrange himself so it wouldn't be so obtrusive.

4

DAMP towel around his waist and hair dripping wet after his refreshing and satisfying shower, Trent flopped onto the bed when he got back into his room. He was still thinking about the enigmatic American guy. He didn't have his laptop, so he grabbed the little notebook he liked to scribble in when random ideas came to him, or to record things or people he noticed. At the moment he wanted to write down a few things about that dangerously sexy guy he'd fantasized about in the shower. It might make a good scene in one of his future books.

As he pulled the little notebook out, a folded-up piece of thick, glossy paper—a map—fell out of his pack. Odd. This one was in Thai. He didn't remember seeing that in the stack of maps Beth had given him. He already knew Mick had deposited a few surprises, and this could be another: maybe some Thai sex map. Or had Mali left it for him? Whatever it was, Trent knew he didn't need any of his maps right now so he just tossed it onto the small table next to the bed and grabbed a pen and started making notes. After a couple of minutes, he closed his eyes and again conjured up the image of how the guy had looked: dark wavy hair, slightly longer in front. And those eyes. Steel blue. If he were writing he'd say they were the color of a summer thundercloud. And those dimples. Gorgeous! And that was just his face. The body was something else too. Well-defined muscles, nipples that stood out enough to be obvious through the fabric of his shirt. Trent admitted he was a nipple man.

He imagined even more, just as he had in the shower, and it didn't take long for the same reaction to come over him. He felt himself hardening again, cock still damp from the shower, now pressing against the towel wrapped around his waist. He pulled the towel off and stared at

himself for a moment until his stomach started growling. He couldn't
remember the last time he'd eaten, which meant it was entirely too long
ago. He needed food more than another orgasm right now. He finished
his notes, threw on some clean clothes—this time light chinos and a
short-sleeve teal polo shirt—and grabbed the backpack. He made sure
the room was locked behind him and went in search of food.

The wall of heat hit him again as soon as he walked out of the
hotel, but he was starting to become accustomed to it. As he wandered
down the street from his hotel he realized he was definitely starving now.
So hungry in fact, he'd probably eat anything—even at one of those
street stalls or tiny little restaurants they'd passed on the way to the hotel.
He turned the corner onto a busier street and was delighted to see the
hustle and bustle, so different from home, but also somewhat reassuring.
The sidewalks were crowded and a variety of sights, sounds, and scents
jolted him fully awake and aware. Jet lag was a distant memory.

A variety of people came up to him, all of them friendly and all
trying to sell him something—or someone. A couple of skinny Thais
offered in turn pretty girls or pretty boys. Another offered a "very very
young boy—you like?—first-time boy." Trent shuddered at the thought.
A tall guy with stringy blond hair, red-rimmed eyes, and a German
accent offered him opium. *These* were the people Phaibun had warned
him about. Compared to this motley bunch, the man who'd approached
Trent in the airport was Bill Gates. Well, not literally—Airport Guy had
been *hot*—but he was certainly clean, well-dressed, and looked safe and
harmless compared to these people. Maybe he used that to sucker the
unsuspecting: by pretending to be the clean, safe alternative to the less-
trustworthy-looking scammers who had come up to him so far.

This was the first time in a long time he'd been on his own in a
new place. He hadn't realized how insular he'd become, how much he'd
relied on routine and familiarity—and TCM—so much in his daily life.
The only place his imagination soared was in his books, and from his
publisher's latest feedback, he hadn't really been soaring very high
lately. Another loud grumble from his stomach told him to stop musing
and start hunting for lunch.

Delicious aromas of a variety of foods teased his senses, and his
mouth began to water. He spied a cart across the street, tended by an
elderly man. Half a dozen lacquer-shiny ducks hung from a bar slung
across two upright poles attached to the cart and there was a line of

people—four Thais and one Westerner—waiting to be served. Trent crossed the street and watched as the man chopped up delicious-smelling duck meat into thick chunks with a heavy cleaver, mixed it with rice and heaped it onto plates, then drizzled a thick dark sauce onto the dish. Smiling customers forked over a couple of bills, grabbed their plates, and hurried to a table set up next to the cart.

Unable to resist what seemed like a popular dish, Trent joined the line. When it was his turn, he put up two fingers and the man nodded, chopped up a double portion of duck, the cleaver thudding loudly on the cutting surface, and prepared Trent's meal. The way the man handled the cleaver made Trent check to see if he had all of his fingers. Yup, all ten appeared to be there. After chopping the meat, he served it in a bowl with rice and an aromatic sauce drizzled over the top.

Trent was mesmerized by the process and the man's speed. It had taken less than a minute! He handed over the equivalent of about five dollars in baht and was surprised to receive more than half of it back as the man gave him a wide, broken-toothed smile. Trent beamed, took the dish, and headed for the table. He grabbed a fork with bent tines from a plastic container on the table and dug in.

He thought he'd died and gone to heaven! Even at Mali's supposedly authentic restaurant, he hadn't tasted anything this, well, heavenly. Anise, ginger, garlic, and lemongrass blended with other flavors Trent couldn't recognize. The result was sublime. Spicy, salty, sweet, and tart all at once, his taste buds seemed alive in a whole new way. And all made on the side of the street by a guy who looked like a reject from a community-theater production of *The King and I*. And for about two bucks. The best meal he'd eaten in LA paled in comparison, though it cost fifty times as much as this simple dish.

It was so tasty, he got in line for more, and the vendor heaped extra duck on this time and grinned, shouting to his fellow vendors along the street. Apparently they had spotted a sure thing with Trent, but he laughed along with the Thais and settled down to enjoy a second bowl.

This time he noticed the others sitting at the table with him. One man spooned something from one of the condiment jars: sliced chilies. Trent recalled seeing these at Mali's but never used them. When in Thailand.... He reached toward another jar, filled with what looked like red chili powder, and felt a hand on his arm.

"That's very, very hot." The man sitting next to him pointed. "Take only a tiny amount." The man was middle-aged and Thai, but he spoke English well.

"Thanks." Trent pointed to the other bowls. "What are all these?"

"Thai food has four main tastes: hot, sour, sweet, and salty. Each of these allows you to vary the mix to your personal taste." He indicated which flavor each enhanced and proceeded to sprinkle something from each jar onto his plate.

Following the man's example, Trent took a tiny amount from sweet and hot, and then tasted his food again. It *was* better! *Delicious.* He'd experiment with proportions while he was here. Then he could show off to everyone next time they were at Mali's.

Before he'd finished eating, a woman from another cart came over and offered him a plate of what appeared to be rice with sliced mango. She put it down on the table in front of him and said something in Thai. The last thing he needed was everyone trying to sell him food. Trent tried to give the plate back to her but she wouldn't take it. He fished a few bills from his pocket but before he could hand them to her he felt a hand on his arm.

"She said it's a gift for you since you like Thai food so much," Trent's dining partner explained. "It's good luck for her to make a gift."

"Really?"

"Yes. This is a Thai specialty. Sticky rice with fresh mango."

"*Khob khun kaa.*" Trent ventured. He'd heard Mali say it a million times and hoped he remembered correctly.

The woman burst out laughing, then covered her mouth and glanced at the man next to Trent, who had also begun chuckling.

"Isn't that 'thank you' in Thai?"

"Yes, but…" The man lowered his voice. "That's how women say thank you. Men say "*khob khun* krub.' Last word *krub*, not *kaa.*"

Trent's cheeks flamed.

"*Khob khun krub,*" he said, then repeated it as he looked up at the woman.

She gave a kindly smile and made impatient eating motions with her hands, so he took a forkful of rice and stabbed a piece of the bright orange fruit. *Delicious*. He'd eaten this a dozen times at Mali's, but here, with all fresh ingredients and the atmosphere, it tasted better than ever. He made appropriate sounds of enjoyment and, now satisfied, the woman beamed again and headed back to her cart.

I think I'm going to like it here, Trent thought, as he polished off the dessert.

REED had followed Dallas down the stairs when he left the hotel—at a safe enough distance not to be seen, either by his mark or by the eagle-eyed guest house staff.

"Bye, Mr. Trent!" the desk clerk shouted, waving as Dallas walked across the lobby.

Trent Dallas. Or Dallas Trent? Either way it was a ridiculous name, but it explained that soft accent—Texan, or thereabouts. Reed made a mental note. Just in case he needed to resort to something besides following the guy around Bangkok. Not that Reed minded much. Except for the heat, he was almost enjoying watching Dallas. Maybe he'd even get another shower show later.

He followed Trent a few blocks until he stopped at a street stall for duck. *Good choice*. Reed's own stomach reminded him he hadn't eaten a thing since before Trent's plane had landed this morning. He put food out of his mind for the moment as he planned how to get the backpack away from Trent without exposing himself again—so to speak. While Trent ate his lunch, obviously enjoying it since he got a second bowl, Reed found a kid of about ten years old who was dirty and scrawny and looked like he could use a good meal.

"What you want me doing?" the boy asked Reed in passable but heavily accented English.

In fluent Thai, Reed explained what he needed, and the boy nodded, but his eyes were wide and darted over in Trent's direction as Reed spoke. He took hold of the boy's shoulder firmly, turning him away so his furtive glances wouldn't alert Trent to Reed's presence or his plan.

As soon as Trent got up from the table and started walking down the street again, the boy began to follow him, and Reed followed behind the boy. Gradually the boy closed the gap, glancing now and then over his shoulder at Reed, who refused to acknowledge the boy's wide, searching eyes, but nodded slightly in encouragement. Finally, Reed got fed up with the boy's delay of the inevitable and said "Now!" in Thai.

The boy rushed up behind Trent, grabbed the backpack, and darted into an alley where he was supposed to toss the backpack behind a Dumpster. Reed watched from across the street as Trent spun and looked frantically around, shouting in the general direction the boy had run. The sidewalk was crowded and he bumped into several people before giving up the chase. Once Reed was certain Trent hadn't seen the boy go into the alley, he moved to recover the backpack.

Finally I've got the fucking map! Reed hadn't expected it to take more than an hour this morning to retrieve the thing, and he still couldn't quite comprehend how he'd failed not once but twice to make contact with Trent. Well, in two minutes this would all be over. He slipped behind the Dumpster to snatch up the pack, which by now had taken on proportions of the Holy Grail. Not so far off, he reminded himself. That map would be almost priceless in the right hands, which was why he had to get it today. He still had a few days before he was supposed to hand the map over to Supachai, but he needed time to get his ducks in a row for the next stage of the plan.

Heart beating with barely suppressed excitement, Reed unzipped the eggplant-colored backpack and rummaged around in the smaller pocket where he'd seen the customs officer slip the map that morning in the airport. The first thing he noticed was a new box of large-sized condoms and tubes of three different flavors of lube. Well, if Dallas wasn't a kinky bastard, Reed chuckled. Piña-fucking-colada-flavored lube? He scratched his head and kept digging around in the pack.

It's not here! What the fuck? This couldn't be happening! Reed nearly shouted but checked himself just in time. He still ran the risk of Trent wandering into the alley and discovering him looking through the pack. Reed quickly but thoroughly examined the rest of the pockets and pouches and threw the bag onto the ground with a soft grunt when he realized the map wasn't there.

Dallas couldn't be onto him, could he? He looked innocent and harmless enough, but he couldn't possibly be part of the Thai group trying to acquire the Ruby Buddha, could he? Reed wouldn't put it past Supachai to hire someone else if he didn't trust Reed completely. Or worse, could Dallas be working for the Yakuza or Hong Kong Triad trying to cut Supachai—and Reed—out of the deal completely?

Reed had to find out more about this guy, and fast. If there was another set of players in the market for the artifact, that would really fuck things up for him.

Thinking fast, Reed picked up the backpack and slung it over his shoulder. He jogged out of the alley to discover a crowd of people gathered around Trent on the sidewalk. Several Westerners and a handful of Thais were all shouting and competing to explain what they'd seen to a uniformed police officer.

"I found your backpack in the alley." Reed walked up to the cluster and handed the pack to Trent, who blinked in surprise to see his property returned so quickly. He gave Reed a long glance under furrowed brows. "I saw the kid pull it off your shoulder and I just ran after him. When he saw me he dropped it, but kept running. Sorry I couldn't catch him."

Reed repeated his story in Thai for the police officer, who smiled and nodded in delight over not having to write up yet another report of a stupid *farang* who let his bag get stolen right off his shoulder. The quick resolution to the problem dispersed the tiny crowd, who now had no reason to hang around, and Reed found himself alone on the street with Trent.

"Thanks," Trent said, but the expression on his face told Reed he was far from happy.

"Happens all the time around here. Stolen backpacks, picked pockets. It's worse at night."

"I'll bet." Trent practically glared at Reed and his tone was disbelieving, almost condescending. He unzipped the backpack and sifted quickly through the contents, obviously checking to see if all of his belongings were still there.

Fuck. He suspects I had something to do with this. That was no wonder, considering so far everyone had done their best to let Trent think Reed was a hustler. Truth be told, he really was out to get just one thing from Trent, but it wasn't his money. If they'd met under different circumstances it wouldn't be the map to the Ruby Buddha either, Reed mused. Why'd he have to meet such a hot guy in the middle of a deal like this? It just wasn't fucking fair.

"Are you following me around?" Trent put his backpack on again, this time putting both arms through the straps. Obviously he wasn't taking any more chances. Reed knew he wouldn't get another chance to get into the pack, but where could the map be? Had Trent found it in his pack and, knowing it wasn't his, already thrown it away? Or was he working for a competitor and had already passed it off? Reed hadn't let him out of his sight for very long, but there might have been someone waiting in his room at the Pink Tiger.

But this guy appeared too clueless to be part of any underworld organization. No one was that good an actor. The only explanation was Trent somehow realized the map was valuable and had hidden it, hoping to sell it to someone who would pay big money for the information.

"No, man. Bangkok's really kind of a small place for *farangs*, you know? I run into the same people all the time. I'm Reed Acton, by the way." He started to put a hand out but Trent didn't look to be in a trusting, hand-shaking mood yet. He also didn't volunteer an introduction.

"*Farangs*?" Trent rolled the word around on his tongue and squinted in puzzlement.

"Foreigners…Westerners. It's kind of an insult, but if you spend enough time here you get used to it."

"But you speak Thai. You said you live here?"

"Yeah, for work." Fuck. This conversation was getting into dangerous territory for Reed. But he didn't want to just walk off on his own, and suddenly it had nothing to do with the map. He wanted to get closer to Trent Dallas and breathe in the beautiful scent of him— probably courtesy of that fancy body wash Reed had watched him apply earlier—and lick along the curve of his jaw, and then maybe rip off that shirt Trent was wearing and trace every muscle on his chest and abs. Reed had seen what was under there and this time he wanted more than to look. He wanted to touch, and taste, and….

"Well, thanks for getting my bag back. Do you want a reward or something?" Trent's voice jolted Reed back to reality, and with difficulty he pulled his mind out of Trent's pants. Which was too bad, because he was just starting to plan out what he wanted to do with that ass.

"No, no." Reed shook his head. "I don't want money. If that's what you're thinking, that I'm trying to scam you or something, you're dead wrong."

"Well...." Trent looked at Reed out of the corner of his eye and Reed knew he wasn't convinced Reed was harmless.

"Look, let's sit down for a few minutes and grab something to drink. The heat is getting to me." Reed wiped the back of his hand across his sweaty brow and smiled up at Trent, getting another suspicious look in return. But Trent looked hot and sweaty too—though it just made him look even sexier—and let Reed lead him to a table set up under a canvas canopy near half a dozen street vendors.

Reed ordered cool coconut drinks for them. Trent eyed the drink warily at first, but when he saw Reed slurp down half the glass in one long pull, he cautiously sipped and smiled in delighted surprise. The coconut drinks were one of Reed's favorites, though some vendors made them too sweet. He loved the soft fresh coconut flesh that floated in the glass and he'd usually save a few pieces to suck on and savor after he'd drained the liquid contents. From the look on Trent's face, he seemed to be relaxing, and Reed decided to take a time-out here and put him at ease.

"I admit I saw you in the airport and thought it might be fun to hang out. I know a lot of places to go in the city, if this is your first time here..." Reed smiled, hoping Trent would trust him, no matter how suspicious Reed's behavior might have been up until now. He wished he could forget about the map and enjoy a few fun-filled days with Trent Dallas—preferably in a bed in Reed's air-conditioned apartment where they ordered in food and didn't get dressed the entire time. It would be nice to spend time with a normal guy, have some uncomplicated mind-blowing sex and not have to be thinking three steps ahead all the time. *Maybe in another life.*

"How do I know I can trust you? I mean, what were you doing in the airport anyway?" Trent repeatedly poked his straw at the pieces of coconut at the bottom of his glass.

"I had to pick up a package for my boss." Thankfully Reed could tell the truth. "It got misdirected so I have to get it from a different location later today." He paused for a moment. "You can eat that. It's coconut flesh." Reed took a bite from a piece he pulled from his own glass, to demonstrate it was safe.

"Really? I've never seen it so soft."

"It's from young coconuts. I guess they don't leave them on the trees long enough to get really hard. They're much easier to open when they're young too."

Trent fished a piece out and took a tiny bite. He quickly ate the rest of it. "Mmm."

"See? You can trust me." Reed laughed. He enjoyed watching Trent consume the rest of the coconut pieces, picking each up and licking it to catch the last drops of the drink before sucking it into his mouth with a tiny slurp.

"Eating coconut and going somewhere with you are two entirely different things." Trent tilted his head slightly then licked his lips, and Reed had to keep from jumping across the table and kissing him. Did Trent know how he was torturing Reed as he imagined what else those lips and tongue could be doing? The smile on Trent's face led Reed to believe that maybe he did. Damn tease! But Reed was enjoying the game. He couldn't remember the last time he'd felt a spark like this for anyone.

"Fair enough."

They chatted casually for another ten minutes. Reed kept the conversation mainly about Thai food—deftly avoiding personal topics—until Trent seemed to have relaxed and become less suspicious. Reed noticed Trent's appraising glances and grinned, hoping his dimples might be extra convincing. God, he hated doing it this way but he was on a short timetable and he didn't have the luxury of being smooth about it.

"Have you decided you can lower the threat level on me to blue or green?"

Trent laughed and Reed's spirits picked up. He liked the sound of Trent's laugh.

"Well, I might go as low as yellow, with an option for blue."

"That's progress." Reed grinned and finished off his drink. "Any chance of meeting up later on?"

"Look, Reed, I want to hang out on my own the rest of the afternoon and explore, but maybe tonight? I'm not feeling like I want to be on my own at night until I get the feel of the place. I'm sure something a lot worse than losing my backpack could happen to me."

"Bangkok's not as dangerous as it seems despite your unfortunate brush with the criminal element." Reed threw a reassuring smile toward Trent, adding just a tiny bit of heat. "But tonight sounds great. Let's meet at a restaurant for dinner and then hit some of the nightlife?"

"And you'll make sure nothing happens to me, right?" Trent laughed again and Reed didn't think he'd ever heard anything so wonderful. He did know he wanted to make Trent Dallas laugh again. There were plenty more sounds he wanted to bring out of Trent, but all that could wait for later.

"Why don't you meet me at one of my favorite restaurants tonight? Eight o'clock?" Reed dug around in his pocket for paper but came up short. "Got some paper? I can write down the address."

"Yeah, sure." Trent pulled a small cobalt-blue spiral-bound notebook out of his pack and started to hand it to Reed. Suddenly he pulled it back and Reed thought the guy might be blushing. Trent tore out a piece of paper and handed it to Reed along with a pen.

He scribbled the address in both English and Thai, but now he was curious about what was in the tiny notebook. He wished he'd had time to look in it when he had the pack in the alley, but if he played his cards right, he'd have a chance later on. While Trent slept in post-coital bliss, Reed could peruse the notebook and see what in there was so embarrassing. Again, here he was getting ahead of himself. *Slow down. I haven't even made it through dinner and I've already got the guy in my bed.*

"Okay. See you there tonight."

"By the way, I'm Trent." Trent put out his hand to shake and Reed took it, feeling awkward. He'd seen the guy jerk off already, so introductions seemed out of place. They'd moved well past handshakes, though of course Trent didn't know that.

"Nice to meet you." He smiled again as he let go, his hand still slightly smarting from Trent's powerful grip. "See you at eight!"

Trent grinned and walked off, his step light and bouncy, and Reed watched his cute little ass.

I've got a date. He was thrilled with the way things were going. It took about two minutes for the joy to wear off when he realized he still didn't have the map—and didn't fucking know where it was—and he hated the fact he was probably going to end up hurting Trent somehow when it came time to figure out where it was.

5

TRENT spent the better part of the afternoon wandering around the Chatuchak Market, a course of action decided upon after skimming through the guidebook. When he'd stepped into the lobby after lunch, Chakri was about to go off duty and had offered to take Trent there on his motorbike. If Trent had thought his first tuk-tuk ride was unnerving, he certainly wasn't prepared for the way Chakri darted around cars, buses, trucks, and other motorcycles. Trent had to hang on tightly to avoid being spun off the back of the bike, though maybe that had been Chakri's intention all along. Even the sparkly pink helmet Chakri had insisted Trent wear didn't make him feel safe. He'd definitely call Phaibun to take him back to the Pink Tiger.

Once there, he found the market was worth the mortal peril he'd endured on the journey.

Housed in several large open tentlike structures, Chatuchak Market was unlike anything he'd ever experienced. It was a combination trade show and farmers market on steroids. Hundreds of stalls competed for his attention—and wallet. His mind and body were soon reeling from the cacophony of sounds and explosion of scents, some delicious like those emanating from the now ubiquitous food carts or the barks and squeals and chirps of the various animals for sale. One could find anything, from enormous and almost certainly illegal reptiles to pastel-dyed chicks.

One stall exclusively sold charms depicting the king. Similar in size and shape to a cameo, literally thousands of images of the king decorated the stall, each with a different-colored background. The vendor explained: yellow gave one success in business, green protected against ghosts and wild animals (hopefully neither was prevalent in Bangkok) and black promised its wearer complete invincibility. Trent chuckled and half considered buying a black one, not sure what kind of protection he'd need during his trip.

Among his favorite stalls were the ones selling Buddhist beads and medallions. He sifted through bins of random items, puzzling over the identity of the different deities depicted on flat, coinlike medallions, much like the Catholic saints, dangling from cords like the ones he recalled on the rearview mirror of Phaibun's tuk-tuk. Some shops even had monks' bright saffron robes for sale. Trent debated buying one but feared possibly angering the shopkeeper.

"Many people buy the robes to donate to a temple." The shopkeeper's voice startled Trent and he dropped the plastic-wrapped robe he had been holding. "A lot of the items here are intended as donations. Especially by women. They can't be monks, so it's their way of making merit."

"Making merit?" Trent hadn't heard the phrase before and listened in fascination as the man told him how people gave donations to temples or food to monks as a way of ensuring good luck, health, or happiness for the donor, depending on the item and the recipient. This explained what he'd seen earlier: the line of monks receiving food.

He settled for purchasing a prayer-bead bracelet for himself, made of heavy saffron-colored ceramic beads on a thick silk cord. As soon as he'd paid and left the shopkeeper's stall, he slipped it onto his left wrist, thrilled with his first purchase. It wasn't the hand-tailored suit of Thai silk he'd envisioned or the designer shoes he'd planned to acquire, but this small token of Thailand, and the shopkeeper who had explained something of Thai culture to him, meant so much more. Throughout the rest of the afternoon he found himself unconsciously fingering the beads, and it made him incredibly happy. He'd come back to this market to find gifts for his friends if he didn't come across anything more appropriate during his visit.

From the market he decided his next stop should be a temple. He chose Wat Pho, home of the most iconic image in Thailand: the reclining Buddha. As he wandered around the grounds, he glanced at his tour book and read details about the temple and Buddhist ritual, which made his visit all the more meaningful. While the beauty of the Buddha statue itself was breathtaking and unique, Trent wanted to discover the larger meaning and importance of the statue. He could have spent hours just staring at the Buddha, taking in the tiniest detail, but one glance at his watch reminded him he needed to get ready for his date. He headed back to the hotel.

TRENT dressed carefully, choosing clothes that accentuated all his positives. He was still slightly suspicious of Reed and the circumstances under which they'd met, especially the "coincidence" of Reed finding and returning the stolen backpack, but Trent was happy to let his cock make the decisions for him tonight. He liked the idea that Reed was mysterious and maybe a little bit dangerous. Meeting him felt like Trent had walked into one of his own stories. Mysterious, hunky guy with a dark past who wanted to get into Trent's pants. It couldn't have been more perfect if he'd written it himself. All he had to do was let Reed have what he seemed to want and everyone would be happy.

Trent took another shower but this time he refrained from any jerking off, which he now regretted. He'd been in a constant state of half-arousal since then, and his balls were aching. Every time he thought about Reed—especially his mouth with its full pink lips—he could feel himself getting harder, and he willed his erection away with the reminder that later on he'd give in to all those urges and take a chance on hooking up with a total stranger. *Adventure, yes, siree.* Beth would be proud of him. Even Mick would approve.

If Trent imagined his dream guy, Reed looked pretty damn close. A few extra inches—in height—might be a nice plus, but Trent had pretty much given in to the idea he was going to be the taller in just about any relationship. Reed was in great shape—muscular shoulders, arms, and chest—but Trent liked the way his waist tapered in and his ass and hips were slim. Not feminine at all, but not beefy or burly. There didn't seem to be an ounce of extra weight on him, either. He was solid.

Trent had arranged for Phaibun to drive him to the restaurant and he was waiting downstairs when the tuk-tuk sputtered to a stop in front of the guest house.

"Oh, big date tonight!" Phaibun eyed Trent's clothing, grinning like a fool. Trent just nodded. He wasn't about to mention it was with Reed, since Phaibun had already tried to warn Trent away from him in the airport, and he didn't want to deal with the older man's scorn.

"Yeah, we'll see about that." Trent settled himself into the passenger seat and enjoyed the ride to the restaurant, getting a chance to see many parts of town he hadn't seen before. Signs and shop-fronts were lit up with garish neon and a mixture of exotic Thai script, Chinese characters and English.

"Hey, Phaibun?" Phaibun turned to glance back at Trent, and he cringed and frantically waved his hand in a circle, indicating Phaibun should watch the road.

"Yeah, Trent?"

"What're all those things hanging from your mirror?" Trent still couldn't figure out how the man could see clearly enough to drive.

"For safety and good luck!" Phaibun announced, strumming the fingers of one hand through the flower garlands and amulets hanging there, causing them to swing even more violently than the simple motion of the vehicle. Ironic, considering they obscured the driver's view and seemed more likely to *contribute* to than prevent an accident. But who was he to argue with Thai logic? And even after only a day here, he'd come to realize the Thais had their own customs and traditions, rooted as often in superstition as Buddhism. There was no room for Western logic in this equation. Trent smiled to himself. So far he definitely had been relaxing and enjoying his vacation; and now there was the anticipation of meeting Reed for dinner—and whatever else the night would bring.

The streets seemed even more crowded and bustling at night than they did during daylight hours. Rows of stalls lined the way, piled high with all manner of goods: knockoff designer purses, scarves, and watches attracted the obvious tourists, while Thais flocked to booths selling CDs and DVDs with impenetrable Thai script. Other vendors offered electronics, belt buckles, T-shirts, just about anything imaginable. Trent's head spun at the sheer variety of offerings. Of course there were the ubiquitous food stalls, with aromatic smoke billowing from grills and pastel-colored sweets brightly displayed. He did a double take at a cart of what seemed to be large insects on sticks. Not surprisingly, tourists gawped at the offerings while only Thais seemed to be buying.

"Very good restaurant," Phaibun shouted over his shoulder as he slowed the tuk-tuk when they neared the destination, though the thought of chowing down on giant grasshoppers had reduced Trent's craving for food. "Local people like very much. *Farangs* don't go. No one speaking

English." Phaibun double-parked the tuk-tuk on a relatively quiet side street, devoid of the ubiquitous neon signs and noisy touts.

"My date speaks Thai." Trent felt a tiny rush of pride, but it quickly vanished when he saw a hint of suspicion in Phaibun's expression.

"Okay, you know what you doing." Phaibun shrugged. "If you need ride later, you call me. But probably you don't call me, right?" Phaibun winked in a way that would have been annoying if it had been Mick, but for some reason Trent found it amusing and simply laughed. He was in far too good a mood to care what a Thai taxi driver thought of him.

The restaurant was dark and filled almost exclusively with Thais. A sarong-clad hostess with long, red fingernails and sleek hair hanging down past her waist greeted him. She spoke only a smattering of English but she recognized Reed's name, nodding vigorously, then led Trent to a table, which apparently Reed had reserved. Trent ordered a beer and waited for Reed, trying not to glance at his watch every two minutes. He busied himself with stirring a spoon through a dangerously thick red chili sauce on the condiment tray.

Forty-five minutes after their appointed meeting time, Reed was a no-show and Trent had had two beers. He picked at the label of the beer, green and gold with two elephants on it. Chang Beer, apparently a popular local brand. He'd nursed the first bottle for nearly half an hour, but the second one didn't last quite so long. When Trent ordered a third the waitress came back instead with a tumbler of golden liquid. He stared up at her in confusion.

"Mekong... Thai whiskey," she said, with a smile.

He cocked his head and wondered whether he should drink it. An unopened beer seemed safe enough but this he wasn't so sure about. He'd heard plenty of warnings about avoiding food or drink which might turn out to be drugged. Hell, he really needed a drink right now. Throwing caution to the wind, he shrugged and downed the glassful.

Fucking fuck! He nearly roared as the harsh liquid burned his throat and windpipe on the way down. Whatever noise he did make attracted the attention of the people seated nearest to him, and they laughed in that way locals apparently reserved for *farangs* and their ridiculous antics. But the Thais were generally so kind they didn't seem condescending, simply amused.

"Oh, so sorry, sir!" The waitress rushed back to his table with another beer but Trent waved it away. Instead he pointed at the empty glass and held up two fingers. He needed more of the stuff to dull the ache of disappointment over Reed's failure to appear.

Am I that much of a loser? Trent wondered as he waited for the waitress to return with the whiskeys.

Now he was a bit tipsy and very hungry. He managed to order dinner, though he wasn't quite sure what he'd end up with. In the end he found each dish tasty, though he didn't have much of an appetite as he contemplated why he'd been stood up.

Reed had run into him three times that morning and Trent thought for sure the guy was genuinely interested in him—or at the very least his money if not his body. He'd tried to shrug off the stolen backpack but the more he considered it, the less of a coincidence it seemed. If only Reed hadn't been so charming and sexy when they'd sat and chatted over coconut drinks earlier in the day. But what purpose could Reed have for making a date and not showing up?

Even worse, Trent was still incredibly horny, and the idea of another shower-time hand job didn't appeal to him. Hell, he was in Bangkok, where you could find someone to do anything you wanted provided you paid enough, if Mick was to be believed. It was supposedly the sex capital of the world! There was no reason Trent had to be alone. He remembered the Web sites Mick had printed off for him: "escorts" of all sizes, shapes, and ages were available, and all at incredibly reasonable prices. Trent could find companionship, even if he did have to pay for it. He ate a few more bites of his dinner, wishing he'd been able to enjoy the delicious food more, paid his bill—leaving a very generous tip for the waitress—and left.

He called Phaibun and browsed the street stalls while he waited for the Thai to retrieve him. Touts at bars and clubs of all kinds beckoned him in, half with their doors wide open so he could see the topless girls dancing on stage.

"Not interested." He found himself repeating this over and over. One bar tout mentioned boys, and Trent was about ready to follow him inside when he heard Phaibun shouting his name and honking.

"Trent date not so good?"

"No, Phaibun. Bad date. Very bad date." Trent climbed into the back of the tuk-tuk.

"Still looking for some fun? Phaibun know where to find fun. Safe fun with clean boys."

Trent stared at the man in open-mouthed shock before he remembered he was staying at the Pink Tiger, so even a blind man would know he was gay. He thanked Mali and Beth for Phaibun, forgetting they'd booked him into a cheap hotel with no AC. But at the moment, his cock was in charge, and that was all that mattered.

"Take me someplace with clean boys." Trent let out a heavy sigh and Phaibun sped off.

The first club wasn't to Trent's taste. It was dim and smoky and full of Western men sipping expensive whiskey and groping smiling Thai boys, not really a turn-on for Trent. Plus, a lot of them really *were* boys and far too young—or at least they looked too young to him. The whole thing turned his stomach. Trent wondered about how prevalent this was: boys selling themselves. Worse than that where the men who thought it was acceptable to pay for their services. Most of the patrons looked like middle-aged family men, based on the predominance of wedding rings in plain sight. What would their wives and kids think if they saw what was going on right now? This was not at all what Trent wanted or needed.

"Okay, we go another place." Phaibun tugged at Trent's arm and pulled him back into the street and the relatively fresh air. Despite the still-intense heat of the night, Trent gulped in air.

"What kind of boy you want? Phaibun knows other places."

"No boys."

Phaibun frowned slightly and furrowed his brows. "You want *girl* instead? Or ladyboy?"

"No." Trent sighed. "No tits. No young boys. Older ones. Adults. You understand?"

"You want old man?" Phaibun looked even more disgusted than Trent had felt inside the club.

"No. Twenties, thirties, like that age."

Phaibun nodded. "What kind look like?"

"Not so… girly-looking. Maybe with some muscles and…."

If he might once have wanted a slim, smooth-skinned boy with almond eyes, after meeting Reed, the typical Thai wasn't going to do the trick. Trent wanted a man. Someone with hard muscles rippling beneath his skin, and broad shoulders, and some stubble on his chin. Trent admitted he wanted a particular man, but he did his best to forget Reed and his manly attributes. Apparently Trent wasn't *Reed's* type, after all.

Trent gave Phaibun what he thought was a general description of the body type he liked, but realized with a tug at his heart he'd pretty much described Reed to a T.

"You want Tawan. Muscle-boy club." Phaibun nodded with a knowing smile, raised one hand into a fist, and flexed his bicep. Trent had to admit Beth couldn't have found a better driver. The guy was a veritable font of useful information and he certainly seemed to be honest.

The Tawan Club was famous for its muscle-men shows. Mick had included an article about it in the "Bangkok Sex Resources" packet he'd collected for Trent. Half a dozen men—professional Thai bodybuilders, according the Website—paraded around the stage and through the audience, and Phaibun frowned in disappointment.

"Fake-fake muscle."

"What?" Trent knew the ladyboys had fake tits—that was pretty obvious—but what were fake muscles?

"Pills. Drug muscles."

"You mean steroids?"

"Yes! Forgot English word." Phaibun nodded and sipped fruit juice. He'd refused to drink any alcohol at all, for which Trent was grateful. "You like these?" Phaibun's brows shot up hopefully but the look of disappointment returned when Trent shook his head.

Fake-muscle men getting blow jobs from guys with huge racks. None of the guys really appealed to Trent, even less when he realized it was all just for show. Even if Phaibun knew the places the gay locals went, they wouldn't necessarily trust Trent enough to let him in, and an interpreter would really ruin the mood. He could just go back to the Pink Tiger and find some tourist who could scratch his itch.

Phaibun wasn't about to admit defeat. He was going to get Trent laid. They split another hour between two more bars. None of the young men were going to be right, so Trent did his best to get shit-faced drunk, but Phaibun wouldn't let him. In fact, the kind older man went into both places with Trent and made sure he didn't get into any trouble.

"Trent, you should go out of Bangkok. Many dangerous things and people here." Phaibun muttered something in Thai to a pretty boy who had sidled up and wrapped his arms around Trent's neck, letting one hand snake down in the direction of his crotch. The boy hissed back at Phaibun, turned on his heel, and left in search of another target, one without a chaperone. "My hometown much slower pace and kindly peoples. Beautiful old history places. Many Buddhas."

"Where're you from?"

"Khorat. Countryside with very beautiful places and slow life. Old temples. Was Khmer city before Bangkok was capital."

"Khmer?" Trent recalled reading Thailand had been under Khmer, or Cambodian, rule some thousand years earlier. It sounded perfect. "Yeah, I want to get out of Bangkok. Good idea. Can you drive me?"

"No. Too far for tuk-tuk. You take bus." Phaibun smiled broadly and nodded.

Trent blinked a few times. He might even have seen two Phaibuns, which was definitely a very bad thing.

"Time you going guesthouse, Trent. Miss Beth and Mali kill me through e-mail if I let you getting in trouble!"

Once again, Trent had Beth to thank for looking out for him, even from five thousand miles away. Admittedly, he still had quite a few reasons to be pissed off at her, but she'd been thoughtful enough to hire Phaibun, and he'd been a lifesaver. Too bad Trent hadn't heeded his original call about Reed and avoided all contact with him. Otherwise, Trent might be happy in bed right now with one of those pretty Thai boys, instead of drunk off his ass feeling sorry for himself because some ruggedly handsome hustler had stood him up.

Phaibun helped Trent to his feet and down the street to the tuk-tuk. The air wasn't exactly cool but it helped clear his mind on the drive back to the guesthouse. Before Phaibun left he made a plan to collect Trent from the hotel early the next morning and take him to the bus station so he could visit Khorat. Again, Phaibun refused Trent's offer of money, *wai*-ing him instead. Then he zipped off down the street while Trent tottered up the pathway to the guesthouse entrance.

The male desk clerk waved cheerfully as Trent entered the lobby, reluctantly pulling his attention from what appeared to be an episode of *Miami Vice* dubbed in Thai. Trent scratched his head at Don Johnson speaking in a low-pitched Thai voice. Suddenly, gunshots from the television echoed through the empty lobby, bouncing back from the high ceilings, and Trent instinctively ducked at the sound.

Alak, the night clerk, giggled girlishly at the reaction. Trent tried to process the incongruity of a guy wearing heavy eyeliner and pearly pink lipstick and the fascination with American crime drama. Like Chakri, Alak dressed as a man, but the plastic pink butterfly hairclip was a cute touch.

When he got to his room, the door swung open as soon as he touched the key to the lock. It was immediately clear his room had been ransacked.

Fucking hell! Now he knew exactly why Reed had arranged their so-called date. To get Trent out of the room in order to look for whatever he hadn't found in the backpack earlier in the day. Reed had to have had something to do with it getting stolen, after all. Again, Trent cursed his stupidity and gullibility at letting himself fall for Reed the way he had.

Trent scratched his head as he assessed the damage. Nothing appeared to be missing. As he cleaned up the mess of scattered clothes and belongings, he was even more determined to get out of Bangkok and away from evil influences and danger—like the drugged-out kids in the streets and one handsome but treacherous Reed Acton.

REED had just parked his bike around the corner from the restaurant when they grabbed him. He sensed a presence behind him a beat too late, and someone pinned his arms behind his back before he managed to react.

He knew exactly who it was and why they were doing this. He also knew his attention had been focused on Trent, or he would have been on his guard. He heard a metallic click as handcuffs were fastened around his wrists and he knew he couldn't get away at this point. *Fuck! They couldn't have had worse timing.* Dark fabric covered his head, nearly suffocating him, and he was shoved roughly into a vehicle, pushed up from behind into what must be the backseat. Unable to break his fall, he sprawled face down on the seat, instinctively turning his head so he wouldn't get a bloody nose. At least he wasn't being shut into the trunk. God, he hated when *that* happened.

No one spoke to him during the short ride, but the radio blared Thai pop as the vehicle bounced over potholed streets and veered around sharp turns, leaving Reed constantly unbalanced. It was safest to just lie down on the seat and wait it out, concentrating on the sounds and order of the turns, trying to memorize the route so he could retrace it later on.

Twenty minutes later he was dragged unceremoniously out of the vehicle and marched into what turned out to be a very comfortable house when the blindfold was finally removed. He was immediately pushed down onto a chair, his hands pinned painfully between his body and the high back of the chair. One of his two guards proceeded to cuff his ankles. *Overkill.* Reed wasn't going anywhere.

"How about taking the cuffs off?" he asked politely in Thai. He received a backhanded smack across his mouth from one of the beefy Thais and assessed the damage by the amount of blood pooling in his mouth. He wasn't sure how long he waited before the man who'd commanded his presence finally entered the room, accompanied by Boontung, his second in command, who came over to inspect Reed's restraints, making certain to inflict some pain during the procedure. The older man settled on a plump, luxurious sofa, while Reed remained seated in the uncomfortable wooden chair, hands still pinned behind his body.

"Where's the map?"

"That's what I love about you, Supachai. Always straight to business without any annoying social chatter." Reed stared at the man, putting on his best cocky, you-can't-scare-me expression.

"Since you're handcuffed to a chair, I see no need to pretend we're socializing, but I can if you like." Supachai stared at Reed with slitted eyes. He knew he held all the cards and he liked it that way. "Where's the map, Reed, my friend?" He used particularly polite Thai, and the incongruity amused Reed, distracting him from his painful predicament.

"I was on the way to meet the mark when your goons," Reed glared pointedly in the direction of said goons, "picked me up off the street. Maybe I should say knocked me down onto the street. Otherwise I'd probably have it right now."

"You were meeting the mark? You look more like you're going on a date." Supachai's cruel eyes raked over Reed's body, and he looked down at his clothing. He *did* look like he was going on a date: tightly fitted dark pants and a forest-green hand-tailored Thai silk shirt. The tailor's wife suggested the fabric, saying it brought out the color of his eyes. This was the first time he'd worn it. He'd been saving it for a special occasion, and Trent Dallas fit that description perfectly.

"So, I like to mix business with pleasure." He laughed with a confidence he didn't quite feel, but it annoyed Supachai, making it worth another smack across the mouth, this time from the lieutenant, Boontung. He hadn't expected the blow, and the force of it knocked his head back painfully.

"How's that for pleasure?" Boontung leered and gently smoothed two fingers along Reed's cheek and jawline, then down his throat. A caress combined with a threat.

Reed decided to avoid finding out where Boontung drew the line between pain and pleasure; he wanted neither from the man, whose earlier physical invitations Reed had rebuffed. Knowing Reed was hot for Trent clearly upset Boontung, and he would enjoy the payback.

Blood trickled from Reed's nose and mouth—all over his new shirt. *Fuck!* He better get reimbursed for the shirt when it was all over. "Thing is, now I've stood the guy up, he might not even talk to me again. That's going to make it a lot harder to retrieve the map."

Supachai steepled his hands, chin resting on his fingertips, and stared at Reed for a moment before replying. It was a corruption of the traditional Thai *wai*, or greeting, and the subtle insult wasn't lost on Reed. It was Supachai's way of saying Reed didn't merit any hospitality at all. Not that Reed hadn't already figured it out—his hands and ankles were cuffed—but it was particularly galling since he understood the slight better than most *farangs*. He'd been in Thailand long enough to be familiar with most of the niceties Thais offered one another as a matter of course.

"Fine. You have two days to make up with your new boyfriend and get me the map. I have men heading up to the caves, ready to start the excavations as soon as we have the exact coordinates, and I don't want to pay them to sit on their asses or fuck the local girls and boys while you play around Bangkok trying to get in this *farang*'s pants. Two days or you will be sorry. Or dead." Supachai flashed a polite smile that turned cruel. "Or *wish* you were dead." Supachai laughed and it echoed around the large room for a moment before he continued. "It's up to you, but I am watching you so don't think you can sell the map to someone else, or run off to retrieve the Buddha yourself."

"Furthest thing from my mind," Reed said, speaking truthfully for a change.

"Joke all you want, my friend. But I'm deadly serious." Supachai exhaled and Boontung cracked his knuckles in preparation for a physical reminder. "No, Boontung. Snakebite." Supachai nodded toward the second goon, a compact, hard-muscled, serene-faced man Reed had never seen before.

Snakebite slowly rolled up a sleeve, exposing an exquisitely detailed tattoo. A green serpent coiled around his right arm, the colors iridescent in the low light. Reed marveled at the artist's skill rather than steeling himself for the blow. He watched as the fist, covered with a perfect depiction of a snake's head, down to the fangs along the fingers, came straight at him.

The next thing Reed knew he was on the sidewalk next to his motorcycle, half a block from the restaurant where he was supposed to meet Trent. He had no idea what time it was or how long he'd been kept at Supachai's before being dumped back on the street.

Trent! Oh, damn, could he still be there waiting? Reed picked himself up from the pavement and as soon as he stood up he fell again, clutching at his bike for support. He glanced at his watch but the numbers swirled. His head was thick and throbbed from the punches and possibly some drug Supachai had given him. He stumbled and fell back to the sidewalk.

He woke again at dawn, surprised he hadn't been arrested or robbed—or much worse. He had to clean up and get to Trent's hotel and apologize, sooner rather than later. Trent better have the map or the beating Reed would get from Supachai would make his treatment the night before seem like foreplay.

6

AS SOON as the first streaks of daylight filtered through the window, Trent got out of bed, eager to start a new day. He'd tossed and turned all night despite the reasonably comfortable bed. *I have to stop beating myself up over Reed.* As soon as he got out of bed, the ache in his head instantly reminded him how much Mekong whiskey he'd consumed the previous night. Less than if Phaibun hadn't been there, but far more than he should have.

He gulped down nearly a full bottle of water and crawled back into bed for another hour.

Feeling almost human again, Trent headed down the hall for a quick shower, then threw the few things he'd unpacked back into his suitcase and headed down the stairs only ten minutes past the time Phaibun was supposed to pick him up.

"Leaving already, Mr. Trent?" The desk clerk, Chakri, looked up from the television, which still emitted the sounds of shouts and gunshots from another program that commanded his attention until Trent walked up. "You aren't happy with Pink Tiger Hotel?" Chakri pouted slightly. Yesterday, he'd seemed perky and cute, but today Trent couldn't appreciate his impish charm. "More hot guys checking in today!"

"No. Yes. I mean, it's fine. I'm leaving Bangkok for a few days, heading to Kho-somewhere—"

"Khorat?"

"I think that's it. But I'm not sure where I'll stay when I return."

"Your room is paid for the whole week, sir." Chakri's sassy smile faded again. "You want a refund on your payment?"

"Just keep it." Trent turned and headed out of the hotel, dragging his suitcase behind him as Chakri *wai*-ed him furiously.

Phaibun and his tuk-tuk were waiting in front of the hotel. Phaibun looked as bright and fresh as he had the day before at the airport, despite the early hour and the previous late night. Trent had never been so glad to see anyone. The kind Thai was the one familiar face he could trust here. He hopped in the backseat as Phaibun stowed the suitcase in the back of the tuk-tuk.

Even at seven a.m., Bangkok could give the LA or San Francisco traffic a run for its money, but Phaibun took backstreets and they arrived at the bus station more quickly than Trent had expected.

What seemed like hundreds of buses idled at several terminals, concentrating the smoke and exhaust even worse than the usual Bangkok haze, making Trent cough. It certainly would be nice to get out of the city and into some fresh air.

Phaibun parked the tuk-tuk at one end of the station and helped Trent with the luggage.

"Wait here and I buy ticket," Phaibun suggested when they got inside the terminal.

Trent pulled some Thai money out of his pocket and handed it over. Phaibun took a few bills and returned the rest. He came back five minutes later with a pink slip of paper printed in both Thai and English: *Nakhon Ratchasima.* Hadn't Phaibun called it something else? He tried saying it, just to make sure it was the right place, and stumbling over the second word.

Phaibun nodded and smiled. "Good Thai! Bus leaves from spot number fifteen every hour. VIP bus very nice." He pointed to one of the doors leading outside.

"Thanks. I really appreciate your help with everything." Trent tried to hand more money over, but Phaibun waved it away with his usual smile.

"You have any problem, call me! I promise Miss Beth and Mali to take care of you."

"You have taken good care of me. I'll be sure to let Beth know." Trent felt a slight pang of fear as Phaibun began to turn away. He wasn't sure about being alone again, but he couldn't let what happened with Reed affect him any longer. "Bye!"

"Goodbye, Dallas!" Phaibun turned and walked toward the exit.

Trent's stomach rumbled. He needed food badly. If he missed his bus he'd only have to wait an hour for the next one. It was supposed to be about a four-hour journey, so he wanted to eat before he left. He wandered outside to a row of food vendors he'd seen when they'd driven in and chose a busy stall where he bought a helping of whatever everyone else was eating. He quickly gulped down a bowlful of rice with vegetables in a tasty sauce and headed for stall number fifteen.

A bus sat idling at the stall and the driver shouted something out the door and began to close it before Trent could get on.

"Wait!" Hopefully the driver or someone standing nearby understood English. A man closer to the bus rushed over and banged on the door, which opened for Trent.

"*Khob khun krub.*" He thanked the man with one of the few Thai phrases he felt confident about, and pulled his ticket out of his pocket to show the driver.

Waving Trent's ticket away, the driver came down the steps and opened the luggage compartment under the bus and stowed Trent's suitcase. Trent hopped on the bus and looked for a seat.

He wasn't quite sure what a VIP bus was but he was in Thailand, so he didn't really expect much.

The bus was unlike anything Trent had ever experienced before. He didn't mind being the only foreigner on the bus. The other passengers were polite, *wai*-ing and smiling and making small talk even though they knew he didn't understand. The tiny woman sitting next to him offered to share some of her lunch with him, and it smelled so good he nearly took her up on it.

In fact, during the first part of the journey he barely paid attention to his stomach. It was hot and humid, and the bus was full. All the windows had been opened and the slight breeze produced did little to cool the air. The back of Trent's shirt soaked through quickly and the green vinyl seat stuck to his back. The seats were so close together his legs extended into the aisle. It wouldn't be much of an issue until they stopped and passengers needed to get past him.

Despite the discomfort, he had no idea a Thai bus would be such an adventure. Once out of Bangkok, the road narrowed to two lanes. In addition to the driver, there was an assistant whose main job seemed to be hanging out a rear window and occasionally slapping his hand against the side of the bus. It took Trent a few minutes to work out the code between the assistant and the driver. Apparently the goal of a Thai driver was to pass as many vehicles as possible. The assistant watched the road and signaled when it was clear enough for the driver to pass, before oncoming traffic got too close.

The other passengers got into the game, shouting or gasping or sighing with relief after each successful pass. Once over his initial shock at the obviously unsafe driving practices, even Trent joined in, conceding the driver was quite skilled and avoided what Trent would have considered near misses. Best not to look out the front window, Trent decided after a couple of close calls that nearly made his heart stop.

With all of the excitement, Trent didn't have a chance to think about Reed. Or at least it kept him from thinking *exclusively* about Reed. It had been ridiculous to hope to meet someone on this trip. It should have been a snap to hook up for some casual sex but Trent had managed to fail at even that. No wonder his agent and publisher were less than thrilled with what he'd written lately.

I'm not going to let Reed ruin the rest of my trip. Trent turned back toward the window and watched the scenery rush by, occasionally scribbling his observations and thoughts in his little green notebook—the one for everyday, neutral observations. The blue notebook with the more X-rated thoughts was safely tucked in the bottom of the pack. The woman sitting next to him smiled and watched him writing, though he knew she couldn't read it. Half the time, he couldn't even read his own writing, and the jarring motion of the bus didn't help his penmanship.

When his stomach finally growled in protest, his seatmate offered him some of her lunch. It took three tries before he gave in, gratefully, and accepted a few pieces of grilled chicken. They made several stops on the side of the road to pick up or drop off passengers, in addition to the regular stops at bus depots. Outside of Bangkok, the bus stations seemed tiny, with one or two benches and a couple of food vendors sitting in the shade.

After about four hours Trent glanced at his watch. Certainly he'd enjoyed his journey so far, between the antics of the bus-slapping driver's assistant and the reactions of his fellow passengers, and the beauty of the scenery they passed. But he'd expected them to arrive at Nakhon Ratchasima by now. His seatmate had gotten off at the last town, which had been the largest so far, and only a handful of passengers remained. Tentatively, Trent approached the nearest passenger, an elderly man with hair that was still nearly entirely black, save for a few random silver strands. Deep wrinkles in his face gave away his age, and Trent wondered why he hadn't gone completely gray—or bald.

"Nak… khon…. Rachi… something?" Trent struggled with the syllables, suspecting he'd mispronounced it.

The man nodded vigorously and pointed over his shoulder.

"We passed it already?" Trent guessed at the man's pantomime.

"Khorat!" the man repeated and pointed behind him.

"No. No. I'm going to Nakhon… something." He pulled the ticket out of his pocket and showed it to the man, who read the Thai script and continued to point toward the back of the bus.

"Same same. Khorat short name." Another passenger with some grasp of English explained. Several other passengers repeated the name and pointed toward the back of the bus.

"Fuck!" Trent immediately covered his mouth apologetically but his gesture was met with laughter and smiles.

"You get other bus at next city. One hours more."

Trent frowned but thanked everyone so they wouldn't think he was angry with them. He dug the guidebook out of his daypack and, sure enough, Khorat *was* Nakhon Ratchasima. He'd been paying attention at every station, but once out of Bangkok there wasn't much written in English, only in curly Thai script, and it was more than likely he hadn't recognized the name of the town if the driver announced the nickname. It was his own fault for believing he could make his way around a country in which few people spoke English.

On the other hand, he was supposed to be having an adventure, and so far he was in one piece. The worst that had happened was he was starving, and a few hours away from where he wanted to be. *It's not like I'm on a schedule*, he reminded himself. He decided to just relax and go with the flow. He certainly had plenty of details to use for a new novel, and he went back to jotting down descriptions and impressions of the bus journey in his green notebook.

He had his head down, writing in the book, when he heard the screech of tires and the entire bus shuddered and veered violently. The few people still on the bus began shouting or screaming as the bus barreled off the side of the road and down a slope before coming to a stop with a loud crunching sound and the tinkle of broken glass.

7

Reed had cleaned himself up in the bathroom of a restaurant near where Supachai's men had dumped him off. He didn't want to take time to go home before trying to explain to Trent what had happened the previous night, and maybe if Reed looked battered he'd have more chance of having his apology accepted.

Bangkok's morning rush-hour traffic made the journey longer than he would have liked, and he'd arrived at Trent's hotel to discover he'd checked out only minutes earlier. Thankfully, he'd told the desk clerk where he was headed, and Reed managed to pry the information out of Chakri. Supachai's men hadn't done any permanent damage—just enough to provide aches and pains and a black eye that made him look like a troublemaker. He'd been lucky the clerk had even told him where Trent had been heading. A handful of baht and some heavy-duty flirting hadn't hurt, but it probably cost him more than if he hadn't looked like a thug.

On the chance his luck had changed, Reed again slipped up the rear staircase and headed for Trent's room. Maybe he'd thrown it away, not realizing what it was, and certainly not needing a map written in Thai. The door had been left open but the room hadn't been cleaned yet. The only thing in the trash can was a folder full of Web printouts titled "Bangkok Sex Resources, courtesy of Mick." "Try and use the whole box of condoms" was scribbled just below.

Reed wondered what kind of friends Trent had back home, and shook his head. He was almost glad the map wasn't here, so he could go after Trent and apologize. After he got hold of the map.

It had been difficult navigating the bustling Mor Chit bus station and by the time Reed had arrived at the area where the buses for Northeast Thailand departed, he saw Trent getting into a bus, which drove off almost immediately. He decided to follow the bus until Khorat and catch up with Trent when he arrived, rather than trying to get him off the bus any sooner. Quite honestly, Reed was happy to get out of the city—and away from Supachai's henchmen—for even half a day.

Reed was only slightly surprised Trent didn't disembark at his intended destination, and kept following. But when the bus went over the embankment, Reed panicked immediately. Bus crashes were commonplace in Thailand, thanks to the Thai bus drivers' penchant for "white line fever" and the need to pass any vehicle ahead of them on the road. Not to mention the flagrant disregard for speed limits.

The incline wasn't particularly steep, but Trent and the other passengers could still be seriously injured. Reed pulled to the edge of the road, left his bike, and ran down the slope toward the bus. People were already streaming out when he arrived at the bottom. The bus was still upright, but its tires were mired in mud and it would take heavy equipment to get the vehicle back to the road and driving again. Likely it would need some repairs. The bus driver had restarted the bus and his attempts to move it only dug the wheels in more deeply. He gave up, cursing, and exited the bus.

But Trent hadn't come out yet. Reed's heart did a flip in his chest and he rushed toward the door, only to come nearly face-to-face with Trent, who had been helping an elderly man retrieve his luggage.

"Trent, are you okay?" Reed asked.

Trent just stared at him, completely dumbfounded, mouth hanging open. For a moment he didn't say anything, and Reed reached a hand toward Trent's shoulder.

"What are *you* doing here?" Trent batted the hand away and finally found his voice. "Are you some kind of psycho or something? A stalker? Everywhere I go, you pop up. I wouldn't be surprised if you caused the crash."

Reed cringed slightly at Trent's understandable anger. He *had* stood the guy up the night before, and now he certainly acted like a stalker. The bruises hadn't garnered any sympathy after all.

"You sound okay." Reed chuckled, hoping to avoid more of the condemnation he knew he deserved.

"Physically, I'm a little shaken up. With regards to you, I don't want to see or talk to you." Trent went back into the bus, and called out, apparently checking seats for anyone who might still be on the bus, injured. When he got to the back of the bus, he turned around and came back out, stopping to pick up his own backpack and sling it over a shoulder. He glared at Reed and pushed past him, climbing down from the bus again.

"Look. I wanted to apologize about last night."

"You followed me for four hours to apologize?" Trent's disbelief was palpable, and so was his anger. The few passengers who hadn't climbed back toward the road were staring. They might not understand the words, but Trent's tone and body language left little to the imagination.

"Something like that." Reed grinned, knowing Trent wouldn't believe him. But it was true. Or mostly true. In fact, Reed had been so focused on catching up with Trent and apologizing, he'd forgotten about the map, but he couldn't let Trent get away again.

"You must have one hell of a good excuse." Trent's tone was still skeptical, but slightly bemused. "People kept warning me away from you since I got off the plane, and I should have listened. Go away and leave me the fuck alone!"

"Would it make any difference if I told you I got mugged last night? Some guys jumped me near the restaurant, or I would have been there. See?" Reed pointed toward his bruised cheek and swollen eye.

Trent glared at Reed and looked him up and down, concentrating on his injuries. Reed did his best to look sincere and in pain. Both were true, but it was unlikely he'd get any sympathy from Trent. But telling him the truth about what had happened was not an option.

"You don't really look like you got mugged."

Reed felt along his eye and realized the swelling had gone down considerably. For the first time in his life he wished he didn't heal quickly. He untucked his shirt and lifted it up. There were still several ugly bruises along his ribs.

"See?" Reed lifted his shirt higher so Trent could get a good look.

Trent looked him over for much longer than necessary to come to a conclusion. A good sign.

"Okay, I believe you. Those bruises look pretty bad. But I haven't changed my general opinion of you and I'm not forgiving you or anything. Trouble just follows me when you're around, doesn't it?" Trent grabbed his suitcase and started to make his way up the slope toward the road, muttering under his breath. "My backpack gets stolen. My room gets ransacked. My bus crashes. Should've listened to all those warnings. I'm better off without you."

Trent's words hit Reed's brain. "Your room got ransacked? When?"

"While I was at that restaurant, letting you stand me up. When you never showed up, I figured you planned it. Only nothing was missing."

"They didn't take anything. Are you sure?" Double fucking *fuck*. What if Supachai's men had somehow found Trent and gotten to the map already, completely bypassing Reed? *Triple* fucking fuck!

"No. I checked. Everything was there. Or at least I didn't notice anything missing. But why does any of that matter now?"

"You're right. It doesn't." Reed thought about this a moment. It fucking meant everything. He resisted the urge to rip the backpack off Trent's shoulder and check for the map. He'd have to be far more subtle than that now. But he had to get Trent off the fucking highway first. "Look, I've got a motorcycle. Let me at least give you a ride back to Bangkok or wherever you want to go," Reed shouted after him, and sprinted to catch up.

That was true enough when Reed said it, but as he got to the road he saw someone drive off on his bike.

"Fuuuuck!"

"Your bike?" Trent scoffed. "Thanks for the offer of a ride. Trouble!"

Clearly Trent's sarcasm hadn't been injured in the crash. He sat down on his suitcase and glared at Reed again, making Reed feel about two inches tall. No matter what he tried to do regarding Trent, somehow it got fucked up. The fates were aligned against him, for some damned reason. Reed was usually much more effective than this, and he was starting to get a complex. Either that, or Trent Dallas was the biggest—albeit hottest—bad-luck charm known to man.

By now the remaining passengers, thankfully none of whom were injured, had reached the road and started walking in the direction of the nearest town. A few of them glanced back toward Trent and Reed, but most likely assumed the two *farangs* would sort their issues out and make their own way to wherever they needed to go. Within a few minutes they were alone on the road.

"Let me help you, Trent."

"So, you think I need rescuing or something?"

"Apparently, you do."

"I don't need your help; I can take care of myself."

"You didn't manage to get off at the right city, now, did you?" Reed's voice was harsher than he intended.

"You are stalking me? Just how did you know where I was going?"

"The hotel clerk told me."

"When?"

"I got there just after you checked out."

Trent harrumphed, but he stopped glaring. Maybe Reed was having some success in proving he wasn't as big a dickhead as he appeared.

"I don't need your help, Reed. I don't want your help or a ride, or for you to carry my suitcase. I don't want anything to do with you. I'm perfectly competent to take care of myself!" Trent stood up dramatically, grabbed his suitcase, and strode off. He took two steps, tripped on a rock, and crashed down to the road as his right ankle twisted and buckled. He rolled a few yards down the gentle slope, clutching at his ankle before coming to a stop. He sat up and threw his hands up in surrender.

"Yeah, Scarlett O'Hara, you're perfectly fine on your own." Reed made sure not to laugh, though he really wanted to. Trent was tall and muscular, and the sight of him crashing down was particularly humorous. But he might actually be hurt.

Reed knelt next to Trent and felt his ankle carefully. If only the first time he got to touch Trent were under different circumstances, but at least Trent let him examine the ankle. Reed gently rotated Trent's foot to determine the extent of injury, and Trent winced.

"It's not broken. It'll swell, but at worst you might have sprained it. I don't think so, though. Let's hitch a ride to the next town, where we can have a doctor check it out," Reed suggested. The other bus passengers had already begun to walk along the road, and cars were slowing down to pick them up.

"No way!" Trent shook his head. "I am not getting in another vehicle driven by a Thai. They're crazy! I'd rather walk. Alone. On a broken ankle."

"Your ankle is not broken. Stop being a fucking drama queen."

Trent made his opinion of Reed clear with a rude gesture, but he didn't start walking. He continued to sit on the gravel with his head in his hands.

"Trent, are you okay? Did you hit your head in the crash?"

"Yeah. No. I just need a minute to gather my thoughts." Trent sounded exhausted and Reed wished he could do something to help, but at this point, any offer would be rejected. Reed deserved that.

"I'm heading to the next town to report my bike stolen." Reed moved down the slope. "There's a path along this stream here, probably a shorter distance than the road."

"You think so?"

"Yeah, the road twists and turns more, and it's safer down here."

"Well, I might as well go along with you," Trent conceded and he began to follow Reed.

THEY'D been walking in silence for about twenty minutes when a sudden rain shower erupted. The hot, heavy raindrops did nothing to cool them down. Soon Trent was moving even more slowly, his damp jeans making it more difficult to cover the rough terrain.

"Take your pants off."

"What?"

"You heard me. Take 'em off!" Reed told him sharply. He was tired after a night when he'd been kidnapped, beaten, possibly drugged and had slept it all off on a filthy sidewalk. He couldn't wait to get somewhere dry to see if the fucking map was even in the backpack.

But Trent just stared at him. "What the fuck?"

"Suit yourself."

Reed pulled a knife from his pocket and flicked the blade open. With the other hand he grabbed at a fold of fabric on Trent's thigh and stuck the knife in, blade side out, and sliced across the thick wet fabric. Deftly he removed the excess fabric so now Trent wore half a pair of shorts.

Maybe the cut was a bit high, Reed admitted to himself, as a piece of Trent's boxers came away in his hand. He hadn't noticed because his eyes had been drawn to Trent's thick, muscular thigh.

"Purple underwear?" *Jesus, this just gets better and better.*

"Not purple. *Lilac*," Trent corrected him with a pout, with wide-eyed surprise as he watched Reed repeat the process on the other leg of his jeans.

"Oh, sorry. *Lilac*," Reed mocked as he stripped away the rest of the excess fabric. Yeah, he definitely had made them a bit short, but Trent could move more easily now. And Reed did enjoy the view. He could just see the outline of Trent's cock and remembered how it had looked as Trent jerked off in the shower back in Bangkok. With a grin, Reed contemplated reaching out and rubbing it, wondering if it would harden and lengthen and peek out under the edge of those ridiculous purple boxers like some sort of obscene genie. He fought off the urge to test his theory.

"Do you know how—"

"How much they cost? No. I don't care and you won't either, I promise. But now you'll be more comfortable. Next time, stick to lightweight pants like I'm wearing. They're cooler, and they dry faster if you do get caught in the rain." He picked up the wet remnant of Trent's pants and stuffed them in his pack. He hated to litter.

Trent had started to roll his eyes but by the time Reed finished his little lecture, he just nodded, and they started moving again.

The rain stopped as suddenly as it started but they were both soaking wet and the mud made it difficult for Trent to roll his suitcase. He was moving ever more slowly and Reed modified his pace so he didn't leave him behind.

"Hurry up. It'll be getting dark soon," Reed called over his shoulder when he realized Trent wasn't keeping up even at a snail's pace.

"I'm trying."

Reed stopped and turned around to see Trent limping, favoring his right ankle. Maybe it was sprained after all. Pain was evident in the way Trent's mouth tightened each time he put any weight on his right leg, but he hadn't said a word or asked Reed to stop. That was a big surprise.

"Hey, let me see your ankle."

"See?" Trent lifted his foot up for about two seconds and put it back down again, like a lazy Rockette.

"I'm serious." Reed knelt down and examined the now-swollen ankle but Trent pulled away again when he reached out to touch it. "Let's stop for a while."

"I'd rather just get somewhere I can stay the night, and I don't want to end up sleeping in the middle of a muddy path."

Reed looked ahead on the trail, hoping to see some sign of a town, but all he saw were a few huts in the distance.

"Let's try one of those. I'm sure whoever lives there will let you rest. Thais are very welcoming."

"Sure, as long as they don't offer to give us a ride somewhere." Trent got up and started walking, suitcase trailing, practically before Reed had even finished talking. The suitcase bounced on the rough trail and Reed sped up and took the handle from Trent. He got a look of grateful relief from Trent, but it was mixed with the same suspicion he'd voiced at the crash site.

They passed several fallow fields and dilapidated huts before discovering one that was still intact. Just in time, because the rain had started again. Reed knocked and shouted a Thai greeting. When he received no response he tried the door, which opened with a heavy push.

Reed hoped the ramshackle building wouldn't come crashing down on him once he got inside. But it seemed sturdy enough to at least let them get out of the rain for a little while so Trent could rest—and Reed could get a look in that backpack. He went inside and Trent reluctantly followed him.

"Looks like no one's farming these fields yet this year and this hut's abandoned."

"No surprise. Smells like something died in here."

Reed wrinkled his nose at the damp, half-rotten smell inside. It was a toss-up between being soaking wet or suffocating. He'd vote for staying out in the rain.

"Well, Lilac, I'll leave it up to you. Inside or out?"

Trent glared at him in the dimness and chewed at his lower lip, probably biting back whatever he wanted to say. Reed chuckled softly as he watched a spectrum of expressions cross Trent's face, from surprise and anger to indignation and finally resignation and refusal to respond to Reed's taunt.

"There's bound to be a few more huts along the river somewhere, so if you're up to a bit more hiking we can find a place where the rats have a better standard of housekeeping."

"Fine. Here's fine. I don't care." Trent's voice sounded weary and the way he tightened his eyelids and raised his upper lip told Reed he was fighting the pain in his ankle. He could tell Trent didn't want to appear weak. That simple act of trying to brave it out hit Reed. He wished he hadn't given Trent such a hard time after the crash and vowed to look after him better, even if he was so fucking frustrating it made Reed want to scream at the top of his lungs or deck the guy. Or both. Hell, Reed's grandmother was more rugged than Trent. All those muscles were just for show, probably obtained with the assistance of a pansy-assed personal trainer at some expensive gym where they did pedicures and seaweed wraps. And used fancy body wash.

"Have a seat while I see if I can't clean out the really foul-smelling stuff." Reed flicked his lighter and scanned the room. It wasn't nearly as bad as he'd expected. The cement floor was slightly damp in spots from the leaking roof, but otherwise it was pretty clean. There was a mattress on the floor against one wall, a table with two chairs, and a few boxes stacked in a far corner.

Best of all, there was a gas lantern on the table, and once Reed lit it, the weak light it shone made the hut more pleasant and tolerable.

"Thanks." Trent sounded genuinely grateful as he sat on his suitcase and rubbed at his ankle.

Reed gathered up a pile of old papers and what appeared to be part of a broken chair and lit a small fire. The door was still open and allowed the smoke to clear the hut. The fire soon brightened the atmosphere and Trent looked like he was drying out and relaxing slightly. Reed scooted closer to the fire and pulled his shirt off, fanning it in the direction of the fire in order to dry it out. He unbuckled his ankle holster, sliding it and his gun into a corner where Trent wouldn't notice it. Then he moved his chair closer to the fire and draped his shirt over it. He slipped off his pants so they could dry out too. As he stripped, Reed could feel Trent's eyes on him. He enjoyed the appreciative look he saw there.

"You want to get out of those wet things? You'll be more comfortable."

"I, uh. Yeah." Trent slipped off his shirt and the remains of his expensive jeans, tossing both to Reed, who didn't hide his interest in what lay beneath Trent's designer facade.

When he turned his back slightly to Trent, he heard the sharp intake of breath and groaned inwardly.

"Reed, what happened to your back?"

Reed counted silently to five before replying. "Oh, that."

"What do you mean, 'oh, that'? It looks like—like…." Trent gave up.

"I got into some trouble a while back. Had something someone else wanted and they went to extreme measures to get me to tell them where it was." It seemed to be a trend, Reed mused wryly, pushing away memories and focusing on Trent.

"You mean they *tortured* you?" The fear and pity in Trent's voice was unmistakable but for some reason it didn't annoy Reed the way it usually did when he heard it. Something about Trent was just so damn sincere he believed it.

"So, Lilac, why don't you tell me what you do for a living?" Reed had to change the subject. He couldn't let Trent know any more about what had happened to him and, quite frankly, Reed didn't want to think about it. He wanted to put the memories behind him, but he knew by the way his heart was pounding at the recollection, he wasn't close to putting those demons to rest just yet. He cursed himself for feeling so comfortable around Trent he hadn't been more careful when he'd taken his shirt off. *Focus. Focus on the map.*

Trent seemed to sense he should back off and thankfully didn't pursue the subject of Reed's back or the circumstances surrounding it.

"I'm a writer." Trent finally broke the silence.

"A writer. Now why doesn't that surprise me?"

"What's that supposed to mean?"

"Nothing." Reed's mouth curled in a wry half smile. At least he'd gotten Trent to forget the scars on his back, but he wished he hadn't sounded quite so insulting. It was too late to take that back.

"It's not 'nothing' or you wouldn't have said it. I've noticed you don't waste words."

Trent had gotten that part right.

"It explains why even though you have the body of an underwear model, it's all just skin deep. It's all fake; just like writing. All fiction. Those muscles are from a gym, not real work. Why do you bother getting yourself in such great shape?"

"What's wrong with looking good?"

"Nothing, if there's some substance to it." Reed took the opportunity to look Trent's body up and down. Twice. "You seem comfortable with letting people judge the book by its cover." He indicated Trent's body with a sweep of his hand. Damn, it was such a shame Trent had turned out to be shallow. Why had Reed hoped for more? There was no point expecting anything from Trent; he had become part of this job—just a small detour from the big picture and nothing more. Reed couldn't waste time or mental energy on him. While Reed might enjoy the cover, he couldn't afford to get into the book right now anyway.

Maybe that was why he was suddenly so critical of Trent. He had to keep himself from actually *liking* the guy.

The hurt look on Trent's face made it clear Reed's remarks had insulted him. Trent turned away. Probably pouting. But then again, he looked so damn adorable when he did. Reed couldn't help his physical reaction to Trent. He could stick to the original plan of a no-strings fuck and leave with the map while Trent was sleeping.

"Okay, so what have you written? Should I have heard of you?" Reed attempted to make up for his unnecessarily harsh comments.

"I don't think so. I write gay erotic—"

"Erotic?" That got Reed's attention. A guy who writes smut for a living? *Perfect.* And given how much his clothes and luggage cost—not to mention how much he must shell out for his gym and treatments— Trent must be doing well at it.

"Yeah." Trent had a slightly ironic expression on his face.

"Got any of your books with you?" Not that Reed wanted to read a book at the moment, but he was curious what kink Trent had dreamed up for his stories.

"I do, actually." Trent grabbed for his backpack and Reed's heart skipped a beat. He watched as Trent pulled a sheaf of papers out and dumped them on the mattress before withdrawing a small leather case.

Reed's gaze zeroed in on the papers, and he thought he saw what he was looking for: a thick folded paper that could be his map. He let himself relax a little and turned his attention to Trent who was holding a cream-colored object about the size of a thin paperback. He handed it to Reed and stuffed the papers back into the pack before Reed could get a better look.

Reed took the thing and looked at it, turning it over and wondering how a piece of plastic with a gray screen like a PDA could be a book. "What's this?"

"An e-book reader."

Reed's expression must have given away his utter lack of comprehension.

Trent took the device back and switched it on. "The books are files and you can carry hundreds of them on here. Perfect for traveling."

Reed nodded. He understood the concept even if he was unfamiliar with the technology. He had been away too long. With a surprisingly clear and concise demonstration, Trent explained how to use the device and access his books. Reed handed the reader back.

"If I can't sleep I'll check one out." Reed did want to read one, but the last thing he wanted was to have Trent watching him while he got down to some one-handed reading. He certainly hoped it was going to get him hot and horny. Given the slim pickings in Bangkok for the kind of men he liked, Reed was used to taking his pleasure where he could.

"Up to you. I won't be offended if you don't read one."

"We're going to need food and water. Let me see what's in those boxes."

While Trent sat on the bed watching his ankle swelling, Reed looked through the boxes piled in one corner.

"Found a little propane stove here and some noodles." Reed glanced around for a pot, and when he found it he held it up in triumph. "I can make us something to eat."

"Good. I was starting to get hungry."

"Your stomach's been growling since we got here." Reed chuckled, glad to find something to do so he could avoid the inevitable questions Trent would ask about his own line of work.

"Oh, yes! Now we're talking!" Reed pulled an unopened bottle with a familiar yellow label out of the last box he looked in. He held it aloft for Trent to see. "Mekong. It's Thai wh—"

"Thai whiskey. Yeah, I know." Trent let out a sigh Reed couldn't interpret. One night in Bangkok and he'd already come across Mekong? Apparently Trent hadn't taken their broken date so badly, after all, and had managed to find other entertainment. Best not to think about it; though if the night before had been any good, Trent wouldn't have left Bangkok so early this morning. Reed wondered why the thought of Trent with someone else the previous night upset him, but it did.

"Want a swig? I don't think there are any glasses in here." He rattled the remaining items in the box just to verify. "Nope. Just bowls."

"No, thank you." Trent's tone negated the politeness of his words.

"Suit yourself." Reed cracked the cap open and took a long swig, thankful for the burn tolerable even in Thai heat and humidity. With the back of his hand, he wiped a few drops of whiskey, and got a condescending frown from Trent in return. *Well, isn't someone a bit prissy?* Reed took a few more gulps. Tonight was going to be long, no doubt about it. "There's probably a fresh water tank outside. Let me go and check. Then I'll make the noodles. Stay here and keep off that ankle."

Reed almost welcomed the glare he got in return for the potshot at Trent's usefulness. Without bothering to dress, Reed went outside in his boxers. Who was going to see him? At least it had stopped raining. It was still so hot nearly all traces of the sudden rain shower had already disappeared. As expected, he located the tank and filled the pot with water after testing it, finding it clean and fresh. He'd refill Trent's water bottle, too, once he started the water boiling.

Their meal consisted of a shared plate of plain rice noodles topped with the spices and condiments Reed found in the box. He'd never been in a Thai house without at least two bottles of chili sauce, and this abandoned hut was no different. The meal was filling enough for tonight, but tomorrow they'd need some real food when they got to the next town.

"Hey, did you say you had some maps?" Reed's gut clenched just bringing up the topic. "I want to figure out exactly where we are."

"Yeah, in my pack." Trent leaned down behind his chair and handed the pack to Reed. "In the outer pocket."

Reed pulled the maps out, noting with exquisite relief that his map—on thick, glossy paper and printed in Thai—was indeed there. Ignoring it lest he give his interest away, he pulled out an English map of Thailand and spread it over the table.

He pointed and Trent leaned closer to look. "We're in this general area and there looks to be a town about ten K away." He traced the route on the map and paused. "Six miles or so. Less than an hour on foot, unless you're injured."

"It's not hurting so much now. I think by morning I can manage."

"Good. Just rest up now. I'm going outside to wash the bowls and bring back more water to wash up, brush teeth, whatever."

"Okay. Thanks, Reed." Trent sounded genuinely grateful. "I'm going to write for a while." Trent pulled a little blue notebook out of the backpack and threw Reed an uneasy glance before settling onto the mattress. He rolled onto his side, back to Reed, and began scratching away, never even looking up.

He was still in the same position when Reed returned and sat down at the table again. Not that there was anything wrong with the view:

Trent's perfectly sculpted ass looked delectable in those pretty purple boxer-briefs, which clung to every contour.

"You might as well read something now, instead of staring at me." Trent spoke over his shoulder and motioned toward the e-reader, still sitting on the table. Did he have eyes in the back of his head? Or had Reed been that obvious?

Something about the way Trent could focus on whatever he was writing impressed Reed. It also depressed him. They'd had such good chemistry the day before and now Supachai had interfered and ruined any chance Trent would trust Reed again. What a waste of a night together stranded in the middle of nowhere.

He picked up the e-book reader and started one of Trent's books.

8

"YOU'RE not gay; you're a fucking woman!" Reed had been reading fairly quietly and sipping whiskey out of the bottle until he suddenly shouted and pushed the reader across the table in apparent disgust.

"I am, too, gay!" Trent didn't like Reed's tone, or the interruption, now that he'd gotten into the groove of writing.

"Well you're not a gay *man*, that's for fucking sure."

"I only sleep with guys."

"So do straight chicks. You might just possibly be a woman trapped in what I will admit is one fucking hot male body, but you are a chick. You dress like a chick. You smell like a chick. And you write like a chick. Look at your books!" Reed waved the e-reader around as if it were tangible proof.

"What's wrong with them? They're very popular. I sell a lot of books."

"You said it was 'erotica.' Where's the fucking?"

"There's no 'fucking.'" Trent mimicked Reed's snarky tone. "It's not erotica; but it is erotic. I write erotic *romances*."

"Ah, well that certainly explains some of it. I was half expecting these guys to run toward each other across the parking lot or something." Reed guffawed, and Trent's cheeks burned. Some people just didn't get it, and he'd given up trying to explain it, but Reed's disapproval burned worse than usual.

Trent sat up on the mattress, feet back on the floor, posture defensive. "My characters make love, they don't f—"

"I get it." Reed nodded smugly. "I understand perfectly: *you've* never fucked. At least not properly." Reed's voice was condescending and almost spiteful, and Trent wanted to smack away the smirk on his face.

"Well, I—" Trent looked at his feet in order to avoid Reed's piercing and apparently all-seeing, all-knowing gaze. *How the hell did he figure that out so easily?*

"Haven't you ever been somewhere, like a club, out on the dance floor, then you see a guy across the room and your eyes meet and suddenly you're so hard you think your pants are going to rip and your cock is aching, you practically feel it leaking. And you just have to go and catch up with him and you end up fucking each other senseless?"

"Sure, I've wanted to—"

"But, you didn't get to the fucking part?"

"No," Trent admitted, eyes still downcast. He could tell his cheeks were pink. He kicked a perfectly innocent rock about six feet and watched it skittle over the rough floor and come to a stop less than a foot away from Reed's worn, muddy boots. Trent's gaze moved from the boots, up Reed's nearly perfect—and perfectly mouth-watering—body. Trim waist, firm abs and pecs, and those huge nipples that stood out even in the heat. Trent had already thought about how it would feel to have them harden in his mouth. Hell, he'd written about it—in the blue notebook. Twice. He forced his eyes to Reed's face but had to look away. It was still too long because once again, Reed had read Trent's mind.

"I could help you out, just so you know what it's really like," Reed offered with a sexy grin with just enough invitation in it to cancel out the smirk Trent knew was really behind it.

"Help me out?"

"With some fucking…."

"*What?*"

Reed didn't reply, just kept smiling at Trent in a way that was quickly melting Trent's defenses.

"You'd fuck me for *research* purposes?"

"Sure, call it research. I like to be helpful."

Trent remained silent for a moment. He had been thinking about Reed—and his body—practically since they'd met. And almost constantly since Reed showed up to help him after the bus crashed. But could he really sleep with Reed now? Trent *wanted* to; he just wasn't sure he *should*. Especially after Reed had offered in such a patronizing manner.

"Maybe." Trent had no idea how the word had popped out of his mouth. He didn't want Reed to think he liked him or anything. Because he didn't. He *certainly* did not. Reed was pushy and rude and acted like he was an expert on everything. Plus trouble followed him around like a shadow. But that didn't mean Trent didn't want Reed's *body*. That was the point, after all. "But it's just for research. Nothing else. It's just sex."

"Agreed. Just sex. Nothing else." Reed's eyes glinted and his dimples deepened, if that were possible.

Trent had a feeling Reed could tell exactly what he'd been thinking. He tried to glare at Reed, but he couldn't pull it off.

Reed got up and walked over to Trent, hovering over where he sat at the edge of the mattress. Reed's boxer-briefs were snug enough that it took no imagination for Trent to get a good idea of what was underneath. He had to keep from licking his lips in anticipation.

"Because you really need to get fucked properly, Trent. I can tell."

Reed's words stopped Trent in his tracks and broke the spell. He needed to be fucked? Talk about insulting and arrogant! He leaned backward, away from the heat of Reed's body and the delicious manly scent of him.

"Need? I'm not Scarlett O'Hara, and you're no Rhett Butler!" Trent pushed Reed away, fingertips against smooth, hard, warm abs. God, it was even better than he'd imagined to finally touch Reed. Trent couldn't remember the last time he'd been this close to someone who got him this hot. Cassandra's words about needing a mindless fuck to "reboot his system" rang through his mind. With Reed this close, it was certainly all systems go, but still Trent held back.

"Yes, you need this," Reed repeated, his voice no more than a whisper as he moved in again and let his fingertips play along Trent's jawline. With a slight pressure of fingers under Trent's chin, he beckoned him to stand. Agonizingly slowly Reed's fingers traced down Trent's throat to his collarbone with just enough pressure to drive Trent's body wild, though his brain fought desperately for control.

I am not giving in to this! No matter how good it feels or how hard I am right now. Trent attempted to talk himself out of it as fingertips trailed along the deep groove between his pecs.

His eyes followed the fingers. It was safer than looking into Reed's eyes or realizing those lips he'd fantasized about—even jerked off thinking about—were only an inch from his own. Heat emanated from Reed's body and his whiskey-tinged breath whispered against Trent's cheek. Gentle, knowing fingertips circled one nipple, which peaked and ached, and the touch left a burning trail. Trent might have actually whimpered with the effort to keep his desire in check.

"Just let me know if you *want* it," Reed added in a gravelly, irresistible voice and let his lips just brush against Trent's before he leaned back and started to move away, taking his lips and fingertips off Trent's aching and now fully aroused body.

Oh, God, how he wanted this. Wanted Reed. Wanted anything and everything Reed might want to do to him. He'd left it to Trent to take the next step, put the ball firmly in his court. But Trent wasn't about to let himself be manipulated and seduced like this! The arrogance of Reed Acton was infuriating. But not as infuriating as the man in front of him was desirable, and all Trent had to do was to give in and ask for it.

Why not?

Trent couldn't remember the last time he was with anyone who had such a profound effect on him, someone who evoked such pure sexual longing in him. Reed's attraction was purely physical, something Trent fully admitted had been lacking in his life and his writing. It had never been like this with anyone before—not even Marc.

If only Reed wasn't such a dick. He didn't deserve to have Trent.

Or did he? Reed had followed him from Bangkok, after all. He certainly looked like he'd been beaten up, and he'd been dressed as if for their unfulfilled date. He'd stayed with Trent, found a place for him to sleep, and even cooked him dinner. Didn't that count for something?

Trent's cock sent him signals that it definitely counted for something. Counted for everything, as far as it was concerned.

"Yeah, I want it. But not from *you*." Again, Trent wasn't sure how the words had formed themselves. Had he really refused what promised to be an incredibly satisfying and memorable sexual experience?

As soon as he spoke, everything changed. The corners of Reed's mouth sagged and his brow creased, not just in what Trent took for surprise but actual disappointment. The cockiness was gone, replaced with what Trent might have interpreted as hurt in anyone else. Whatever it meant, Reed no longer controlled the situation, and that made all the difference to Trent. Now it really was his decision.

Yes yes yes! his throbbing cock and aching nipples chimed in and tipped the decision, but it was completely Trent's choice now, not Reed's.

Reed took a half step backward, almost in surrender, and Trent noticed the much more distinct outline of his cock and the tiny damp spot. The flickering light of the lantern emphasized the dark bruises along the ribs of his left side, and the dam broke. Trent let his own desire loose, suspecting he'd never wanted anyone or anything as much as he wanted Reed to fuck him into that mattress.

Reed reached toward the table and took another pull at the whiskey. Before he could put the bottle down, Trent grabbed it away and put it back on the table and reached for Reed's elbow. Trent pulled him back in until their lips touched again. Letting his mouth fall open as Reed's lips brushed his, a moan escaped into Reed's mouth as he took possession of Trent's with as much desire and power as Trent had hoped for. Whiskey stung Trent's lips and he licked hungrily at Reed, seeking more of the sharp flavor.

Reed's arms circled him and pulled Trent against firm, hard flesh, cock pressed against Trent's thigh, letting him know Reed wanted this as much as Trent did. Their mouths nearly crashed together with the force of their combined need. Reed's tongue took over Trent's mouth, not simply exploring, but as if he already knew its contours and exactly what Trent enjoyed.

Reed's hands were everywhere, stroking Trent's back, cupping and squeezing his ass, pulling him closer and deeper into Reed's magic. Tentatively, Trent let his fingers play along the ridges on Reed's back, unsure if he might be causing pain, but Reed barely noticed.

Reed let go of Trent and stepped half a pace away to slip his boxers off. Trent looked him over. He wasn't as muscular and bulky as Trent, but Reed's body was lean and hard. A body made hard from physical work. Large, dark nipples stood out clearly, just as Trent had imagined. His cock was perfectly proportioned and rock hard, jutting out from Reed's body so invitingly that Trent reached down to take hold of it, his hand moving up the shaft so his fingertips could trace the contours around the head.

Reed groaned and moved to push Trent's boxers down his hips, his fingers skimming their way along the waistband, further igniting Trent's skin. The shorts slipped down to pool around his ankles. Reed stepped closer and maneuvered Trent onto the mattress and lay next to him.

They continued to kiss for a few delicious minutes as Trent's body took control away from his brain and he let Reed and his instincts take over. Fingers and mouths traveled along firm planes of muscle and Trent bent to take one of those beautiful nipples into his mouth. He circled with his tongue, sucking, feeling the nub grow even larger. Reed let out a husky moan and arched into Trent's touch.

"Condom?" Reed asked when Trent's kisses moved lower.

As fantastic as the kissing and sucking felt, Trent was far too close to delay. He rolled over slightly to grab condoms and a tube of lube from his backpack. Then he pushed the pack off the other side of the mattress before handing the supplies over to Reed.

Reed slicked a few fingers with lube—strawberry, from the smell of it—and took hold of Trent's cock with his other hand, slowly and loosely stroking him as he started the prep. The very first touch of Reed's fingers set Trent's body on fire again. He focused on the mixture of concentration and desire on Reed's face as he slipped a finger inside. It had been far too long since he'd been with anyone who excited him this much. Reed's fingers circled and pressed and quickly, but carefully, worked as Trent rolled a condom onto Reed.

"Hands and knees." Reed slid his hand along Trent's hip, gently moving him over as Trent repositioned himself. Reed moved between his legs and used his fingers before Trent felt the tip of his cock press against his hole. He wished he could see Reed's face, but this was supposed to be about getting off and not about making a connection.

Any rational thought Trent had disappeared the second Reed entered him. Forcefully but carefully Reed pushed inside, and Trent's entire consciousness focused on their single point of contact. Reed made a couple of shallow thrusts before burying himself deep inside of Trent in one hard fast motion that nearly knocked Trent off balance.

Steadying himself by gripping Trent's hips, Reed pushed in deep again and again, grunting softly with each stroke before switching to a shallower thrust that brushed the magical spot inside, and Trent wasn't sure how much more he could take. He wanted more, much more, but his body neared its limits, shuddering as he groaned, and pushed back into each thrust. Gently, Reed took hold of Trent's cock, and the slight touch nearly sent him over the edge. Two pulls and Trent started to come, Reed catching most of it in his palm.

The hard deep thrusting resumed. Reed pounded deep into Trent, who was weak on his knees, head dropped down to the mattress and ass high in the air. Reed dug his fingers into Trent's flesh almost painfully and grunted his own release before pulling out and flopping back onto the bed.

Trent collapsed and lay unwilling, and probably unable, to move, eyes closed, listening to their breathing gradually resume a normal cadence before he let the world back in again. When he'd recovered, he rolled over toward Reed, who lay propped up on one elbow, watching him, apparently for some time, based on his expression.

"You were certainly vocal. And loud."

"What?" Trent didn't remember saying anything.

"During."

"You're lying." Fuck Reed! He had to ruin everything.

"I liked it." Reed's voice was playful but sincere. Not a trace of his earlier sarcasm remained.

"What did I say?" Trent dreaded the answer.

"Nothing special."

Trent lay back and drew his arm across his face, blocking out the light and Reed so he could think. Despite the brevity of the encounter, he had undoubtedly just had the best orgasm he could remember, definitely among the best in his life. It had been rough and hard and fast, and unlike any experience he'd ever had. It had been exactly what he wanted.

But now, he didn't know how to react. Was he supposed to thank Reed for fucking him like that? He hadn't expected tenderness or post-coital cuddling and he hadn't gotten any, but Reed's attitude seemed somehow different.

Even though he knew better, Trent hoped there would be more fucking. He definitely needed more research, didn't he?

"That *was* one hell of a lesson," Trent said finally.

"Pretty much sums up what you were saying. Let me know when you're ready for lesson two." A little bit of Reed's cockiness had crept back into his voice, but it sounded like he wanted another round as much as Trent.

"I'm ready when you are."

Reed moved closer to Trent, who found his heart already racing in anticipation of Reed's hands on him, Reed's cock filling him up. As soon as Reed's lips brushed his, Trent felt himself getting hard again. This time the kisses lasted longer, Reed still in control and Trent content to give up as much as Reed wanted to take. Reed was a fantastic kisser: not too wet; and he paused now and then, almost instinctively knowing when Trent needed to take a breath.

As they kissed, Reed's hands traveled along Trent's body, caressing here, pinching there, squeezing until once again Trent thought he'd explode with need before Reed ever got around to fucking him.

Trent played with Reed's cock and balls, discovering he was extremely sensitive and somewhat ticklish, but he loved the sounds Reed made as he stroked and squeezed and tugged. *I'm not the only one who's loud.*

Reed felt around the mattress for another condom and the lube, handing the condom to Trent, while he applied more lube. Still slick from the first time around, Trent didn't need much prep, and once he'd rolled the condom on Reed he started to roll over.

"Not this time." Reed reached out to press Trent's shoulder back toward the bed. He slipped into Trent smoothly and Trent wrapped his legs around Reed's waist. Like the first time, Reed pounded deep inside, rough and just this side of pain. He took what he wanted, how he wanted it, eyes half closed. At one particularly pleasurable jolt Trent let out a moan, or maybe he said something, but Reed's eyes opened and he looked down into Trent's. Their eyes locked and Trent thought he saw a look of wonder in Reed's gaze. The thrusts slowed and became shallower and Reed leaned down to catch Trent's mouth in a long, deep, incredibly sensual kiss.

"I'm close," Trent whispered when they broke for air.

Reed nodded and shifted position, so each thrust brushed Trent at just the right spot inside and, almost before he realized, he came, spurting hot and thick across his own belly and chest. Reed stilled his movements, leaned down, and licked at the come on Trent's chest and nipple, whatever he could reach while remaining inside Trent. Each stroke of his tongue sent aftershocks of pleasure racing through Trent. Then Reed lay back down, pressing tight against Trent and almost gathering him up in his arms. With just a few stutters of his hips, Reed came with a soft sigh.

This time Reed didn't roll off of Trent but remained half on top, holding him close enough that Trent could feel Reed's heart beating. They lay like that for a while before Reed got up to get rid of the condom. When he turned back toward Trent, still on the bed, the look in his eyes made him seem a different man than the one who had so upset Trent the previous night and infuriated him earlier that day.

TRENT looked at the raised stripes on Reed's back with a mix of disgust and curiosity. Tentatively he reached out and slowly traced one with a fingertip just hovering above the skin. Reed's body radiated heat and Trent was compelled to touch him, feeling the hard ridge of skin and imagining the pain Reed must have endured during and after a beating that still marked his body and very likely his soul. He felt Reed tense beneath him, but Trent didn't stop his gentle stroking. Eventually he felt Reed relax and give himself up to the feel of Trent's hand on his back. Trent leaned down and brushed his lips from one shoulder to the middle of Reed's back and wished he could kiss away the memories of this and the other horrific experiences Reed must certainly have endured.

But Trent still didn't know how Reed had gotten mixed up with the people who tortured his body—who still tortured his mind. It scared Trent more than a little bit because he had no idea who Reed really was. There was time enough to learn, though. Tomorrow or the day after, or the day after that. So far, Reed had seemed to be there to protect him or help him through the unexpected dangers which turned out to be so prevalent in what he'd thought was a safe and peaceful country.

REED woke well before sunrise. He hadn't intended to fall asleep, just to wait for Trent to and then take the map and leave. It wasn't the only thing he hadn't intended to happen.

Now, nearly morning, Trent slept facing Reed, one arm with its large paw of a hand draped across his chest. God how he wished he could just snuggle up into Trent's heat and comfort and simply enjoy being together. But he couldn't. Reed's obligations were bigger than his personal desires or needs.

Heart heavy, he rolled out from under Trent's arm, padded silently over to the backpack, and found the map. He quickly stuffed it into the back pocket of his pants and proceeded to dress as he watched Trent sleeping peacefully. Reed crossed to the door and allowed himself one final glance before he walked out of the hut and jogged along the riverbank, knowing he'd eventually come to a town. He'd contact Supachai from there and make arrangements to deliver the map and put the next phase of his plan into action.

He'd send someone to retrieve Trent while he went off with Supachai because there was no way Reed was going to bring Trent on the final search for the Buddha. It was far too dangerous. Hell, it was dangerous for Reed, and he was properly trained. Trent had sprained his ankle walking across the street, for God's sake. Reed couldn't leave him to find his way to transportation injured and alone. It was much better to send someone else to pick him up and make sure he got to Khorat—or wherever he wanted to go—safely.

The night before didn't really change anything, did it? As much as Reed had imagined the answer to be "no," he soon found he couldn't get the images, the memory, or the sensations of making love with Trent out of his mind, even as he jogged slowly along the riverbank in the heat, oppressive in late morning. If his calculations were correct, he'd be in a town well before noon. He could have Trent rescued and back on his way before Supachai even showed up to collect Reed.

"Just sex." Trent had set the ground rules. In the end it hadn't been "just sex" at all, and both of them knew it. At first Reed had let physical need for release and his undeniable attraction to Trent take over; he hadn't bothered to hide the unbearable hunger. That seemed to be all either of them wanted, until Trent called out Reed's name with a mixture of desire and tenderness that pierced Reed's consciousness, and he no longer saw Trent merely as a body giving him pleasure. That simple act had turned Trent into a lover, a person with whom Reed could connect on more than a physical plane.

Trent wanted *Reed*, not just anyone to fuck him, research or not. Reed hadn't been desired by any of his sexual partners in a long time. Whether he'd paid for it or not, he'd simply been responding to physical need, and that was all he'd been able to satisfy. Trent reminded Reed how much more fulfilling the experience could be.

It hadn't taken long before they'd both felt the connection; the way their bodies blended together so perfectly, each of them somehow sensing exactly what the other wanted or needed. Sure, they'd fucked at first, but then their movements became slower, more tender, and their kisses sweeter. They'd tired each other out and slept for a while, then held each other and whispered about everything and nothing.

They'd been lying together, gathering strength and energy after the second round, when, to Reed's horror, Trent began to trace the long scars on his back. It had been the first time anyone had ever touched them and he flinched at first, but Trent's gentle strokes soon relaxed him and the care and tenderness in the touch brought a lump to Reed's throat. Trent snuggled close, spooning against Reed's back and wrapping his arms across Reed's shoulders, enveloping him in a cocoon of warmth and affection that he hadn't realized how much he'd missed.

It had all felt so comfortable and—

Reed stopped himself right there. *Comfortable? What the fuck?* He sounded more like one of Trent's books than Trent's books did, and that had to stop right now. He had a job to do and as much as he'd enjoyed the time he'd spent with Trent, he had to move on and finish the job. A lot of people were counting on him, and he wouldn't fuck this up.

Deep down he knew he wanted to see Trent again. But first Reed had to get to the town and get Trent rescued. If Reed could wrap this up quickly, there might still be a chance to explain everything to Trent and get to know him properly before he left Thailand. Maybe the connection would still be there. Reed hoped like hell it would.

And then what?

Reed realized he'd unconsciously decided this would be his last job. He wasn't going to do this again. Money had never been an incentive. Truth was, Reed was too tired and he didn't need the kick from danger anymore. He'd discovered, even for a brief period of time, what a kick there could be from making someone else happy, from letting someone make him happy. He had no idea how goofy, fastidious, fussy Trent had managed to affect him so quickly, but he had, and Reed knew he wanted a chance at more than the little slice of happiness they'd shared over the past day.

TRENT woke up alone, body aching from the crash, the uncomfortable mattress, and Reed. He glanced around wildly but noticed almost immediately Reed's clothing was no longer draped near the burned-out ashes of the fire. Maybe he was outside and would be back soon.

As the minutes passed, eventually Trent had to come to terms with the truth: Reed had left.

Closing his eyes, Trent tried to recall every detail of the previous night, if only to convince himself it had really happened. The way Reed had felt and tasted and smelled. He looked down at his skin, marked here and there by the proof Reed had really been with him and had wanted him, even if it was only for a temporary pleasure.

"Just sex." Trent's words came back to him harshly, and he wished he'd never made that qualification. He didn't know why or how but sometime during the night, "just sex" had become a whole lot more for him, and he thought he'd felt the shift within Reed as well.

I'm a fucking great judge of men. Left alone again. It wasn't like Reed had gone out to get Starbucks, the *Times*, and a dozen pastries. He'd gone for good. Trent sighed and let his eyes wander the room again. He spotted his backpack on the table: unzipped and the flap half open. Last Trent remembered, it had been next to the bed when they'd gotten condoms and lube from it.

Had Reed taken something? Trent hobbled over to check. The cash was all still there in his money belt, along with credit cards, passport, and traveler's checks. Maps were scattered on the floor. Trent had put away all the maps but the one Reed had used to ascertain their location the night before. What had Reed been looking for? Trent gathered up the maps and was about to shove them back in when he realized the odd Thai map on the thick glossy paper was gone.

Reed's attentiveness hadn't been about Trent or sex, or even money, at all. It had been about something inside that backpack. The realization washed over Trent like a cold wave, leaving him nauseated and depressed. Phaibun had been right that very first morning. Reed had just been after something else all along. Now Trent couldn't even enjoy the memories of the way their fucking had slowly turned into something more tender and emotional. He'd been used. That's all Trent could think about, and he hated Reed more than he'd ever hated anyone before—even Marc.

Except possibly himself. How had he let himself get his hopes up like this only to be hurt?

THE first trace of habitation Reed came across was more a village than a town. No pay phone, no cell phone signal, no real communication, and no vehicles, unless you counted a couple of oxcarts. It was another hour beyond that before he found modern communication and transportation. As soon as he thought he was in range of cell service, he powered up his phone. It beeped immediately, indicating voice mail.

Reed sat at a street stall, ordered grilled chicken, chugging a few glasses of cool water as he listened. Six messages from Supachai, with exponentially increasing levels of anger, culminating in a death threat. He considered his next move. He had to call Supachai and he had to get someone to Trent. But Trent wasn't in any danger, except possibly from himself, so Reed called Supachai first.

"It's about fucking time!"

"Sorry. I had a crash and I just made it to a town with cell service. I'm about fifty K past Khorat."

"I know. So am I. Where shall we meet?"

What the fuck? Supachai was nearby? *Already?* How the fuck had he known where Reed would turn up?

"Give me an hour to eat and take care of a few things and you can pick me u—"

"Make it five. Five minutes to finish that chicken and then we talk." Supachai nearly growled into the phone and hung up.

Reed looked down at the plate of chicken the stall keeper had just placed in front of him. He looked around, taking in the details of the street, the people walking by, the cars, everything. He was well-trained and this should be second nature. Supachai was watching him at that very moment, but none of Reed's experience or instinct had warned him. He'd let his guard down while he'd tried to decide how to take care of Trent, and now he was trapped. The location wasn't of his choosing: too out in the open and too many ways he was vulnerable. As he slowly chewed his lunch, he tried to get the lay of the land and plan how he'd deal with Supachai. He had a terrible feeling their partnership was about to come to a very ugly ending.

Reed finished eating in about five minutes and got up, leaving a wad of cash on the table for the woman. Much more than he owed, but he was in a hurry. He managed to make it off the main street and into a back alley before his phone rang. He ignored it, knowing Supachai was trying to distract him, and knew exactly where he was.

"Acton!" Reed spun at the sound of Supachai's voice behind him. "Thought you could keep the map and cheat me? Sell it to the Yakuza or find the Buddha yourself and cut me out of the deal?"

Supachai certainly jumped to conclusions, but then again, that was probably the safest way to do business if you ran half the Bangkok mob. "It's a damn good thing I put that tracker on your bike. I'm not about to let you out of my sight until you hand it over." No wonder Supachai's men had jumped him so easily at the restaurant in Bangkok and apparently found him here in the middle of nowhere. It meant his bike couldn't be far.

"No, Supachai, not at all. I have the map with me. Well, not on me at the moment. I hid it." He was lying but he was good at it, and there was a fifty-fifty chance Supachai believed him. "The deal's still on and I'm ready to go with your men to retrieve the statue."

"Let me see the map. I want to know you didn't already sell it to someone else."

Supachai walked up to Reed and pulled a knife on him. Reed had a knife and a gun but he didn't want to fight. Unfortunately negotiation and chatting were moot at this point. Everything was unraveling right now and Reed couldn't risk it. He kicked at Supachai's blade, a roundhouse that knocked the older man off balance, but Supachai held onto the knife. Reed expected Supachai's men to pour into the alley to help their leader take him out and get the map, but so far there was no sign of them.

"You came alone?" Reed tried to stall, hoping to distract Supachai long enough to catch him off guard.

"Some things I like to take care of *personally*." Supachai gave Reed a chilling smile as he said the final world. "Killing you will be one of them. I look forward to watching your blood drain from your body as you contemplate your own death. It will be very satisfying."

The blade was against Reed's neck now and any slight pressure would slice through his jugular. "But you don't know where the map is. You'd be a fool to kill me before you get it."

"Killing you would give me almost as much pleasure as finding the Buddha. This is true."

"I have no incentive to tell you once the blood starts draining from my body." Reed took a risk of further annoying Supachai, but it was a calculated risk and it worked.

"This is true."

Supachai moved the blade back less than a centimeter and Reed saw his opportunity. He shoved the man hard and reached for his own knife, but Supachai slashed at his arm, ripping a gash that didn't hurt until well after Reed saw the blood begin to flow and drip. It didn't stop him from retaliating. Supachai might be older, but he was in good shape and adept with the blade. Reed couldn't get close enough again to disarm him or to injure him though he earned another wound in the arm for the attempt. Supachai had plenty of scars on his arms and a couple on his face, but he was still alive. That proved his expertise with the blade; definitely better than Reed could hope to be, but after a few minutes of sparring, Reed's youth got the advantage as the older man began to tire. Reed moved in close enough to get him swinging and leapt out of the way in time to avoid another blow, but he was effectively tiring his opponent.

Eventually Reed was able to kick Supachai's knife out of his hand, leaving the older man clutching his stomach as he straightened himself up. This time he had a gun in his hand. Instinct took over and Reed reached for his own. In one smooth motion he aimed and fired, hitting Supachai in the right shoulder. The man fell to the pavement, groaning and cursing Reed in Thai. Supachai managed to grab hold of his gun again, but this time Reed shot him dead with a bullet to the head.

Fuck! He rifled through Supachai's pockets, grabbing his wallet— and any way of identifying the body—and took off. He ran from the alley, ripping off one shirttail and wrapping it around his bleeding arm, which now hurt like a million tiny blades slicing into his flesh rather than one sharp one. The deal with Supachai was as dead as he was. Now Reed didn't have a clue how the fuck he was going to manage the second part of the deal.

Walking fast enough to get away from the alley before anyone found the body, but not fast enough to attract attention, Reed retraced his steps. He needed to find transportation and get the hell out of there, and then what? How the hell could he salvage this?

He still had the map.

Without Supachai in the deal anymore, Reed decided the best alternative was to get the statue himself and connect with the buyer in order to bring the whole thing to a close. He'd invested too much time— nearly three years—to let it end like this.

All he had to do was to get to the caves before Supachai's men caught up with him. He knew they couldn't find the Buddha on their own, but they had a general idea where it was, and they could intercept him. It was a risk he had to take.

But then there was Trent. Reed couldn't leave Trent in that hut or struggling on his own along the riverbank toward town. There were far too many ways for him to get into trouble, and Reed didn't want to be responsible for that too. He'd already caused Trent enough problems and possibly heartache, and the last thing he wanted was to make it worse. He'd find someone to go and get Trent and bring him to town.

Reed pulled out the wallet he'd taken from Supachai's pocket and discovered a thick wad of currency. More than enough to hire someone to fetch Trent. But Reed didn't know if he could trust anyone in this town. Chances were most of them were honest, but what if the person just kept the money and didn't go to get Trent? The potential bad karma might not be enough to deter everyone. Supachai had known where Reed was as soon as he'd arrived here, and Reed suspected someone in this little town wasn't trustworthy.

Could he manage to get Trent and still reach the caves in time? Reed glanced at his watch, closed his eyes, and took a deep breath. Why the fuck did it have to come down to a decision like this? Should he go after Trent or should he salvage two-plus years of work and his reputation, possibly his life? That reminded Reed: one of Supachai's men might be watching him right now. He just might end up getting himself and Trent killed.

But at least he was going to try. Instead of retracing his steps, he ducked into an alley in search of a vehicle to hotwire. To his surprise he came across his own motorcycle. The thug who'd stolen it from the scene of the bus crash must live in this town, and he'd taken the easy way out after the crash by stealing Reed's bike. Thankfully the helmet was still hanging from the handlebars. He shoved it onto his head, climbed onto the bike, and raced out of the alley, scattering a few slow-moving residents and a couple of loud chickens as he headed for the main road.

Once he got there he paused before turning. To the left were the caves, the Buddha, Supachai's diggers, and his big payoff. To the right was Trent and most likely more than an earful about being abandoned after they'd spent the night pouring their loneliness and longing into each other. Reed knew he'd be lucky if Trent spoke to him again after leaving before dawn without so much as a note. Was there any point trying to explain why? Trent wouldn't forgive him again, especially because Reed knew he had to tell him about the map. Fuck it all!

Reed kicked the bike into gear and turned right.

9

"I DON'T need a babysitter. I'm fine all by myself. Why did you even come back? I can see there's something more important than I am, and I'm okay with that." Trent's lower lip quivered slightly and it was plain to Reed he was *not* okay with that.

"I came back to get you, not to babysit you. I was worried. Look. I brought food." He'd only gone a quarter of a mile before he'd turned around and gone back to town. At the first street stall he came to, he stopped, bought some of everything she was serving, and then headed back to the hut for Trent.

Reed held up the bag, from which delicious aromas emanated, but Trent waved it away dismissively, so Reed put it down on the wobbly table.

"If you were so worried about me, why'd you leave in the first place?"

It was a valid question, but Trent's gaze dropped to his feet and he avoided Reed's eyes. Obviously, he didn't want to hear whatever bullshit excuse he expected Reed to tell him. Reed decided not to give him an excuse. He'd tell him the truth.

"I had an appointment to keep."

"Out in the middle of nowhere? With who?" Trent glanced up and met Reed's gaze.

"Whom."

"What?"

"With whom. You're supposed to be a writer; you should know how to use English properly, shouldn't you?"

"Fuck you. I don't need grammar lessons from some stupid tough guy who thinks with his dick and not with his brains."

"Fuck you!" Reed stopped himself from saying anything else, or this would turn into an infantile shouting match. He didn't want to argue with Trent; he wanted to fix what he'd broken when he'd left that morning.

"So, what happened?" Trent's voice betrayed concern, though the expression on his face remained aloof. Reed knew it was all for show, and it broke his heart to see the conflict of emotions inside of Trent. But it convinced Reed he'd made the right decision to come back for Trent before heading out to find the Buddha.

"Nothing happened."

"How can you say nothing happened? Look at all that blood! It is your blood, isn't it?"

"Some of it."

"Your arm is still bleeding."

"It's fine." Actually it hurt like fuck, but Reed was used to that sort of thing. Occupational hazard.

"It's bleeding. How could you be fine? Let me see it!"

"You don't know how to fix a wound, just keep your paws off me."

"So you *are* wounded? What happened?"

"My appointment didn't go so well."

"You're big with the understatement, aren't you?"

"As the saying goes, you should see the other guy." It had never been truer, and Reed couldn't help laughing even through the pain searing his entire arm now.

"You think joking around does any good?"

"I don't like to dwell on this sort of thing." Reed preferred not to think about some of the things he'd done or endured. A manicured-and-moussed-guy like Trent couldn't understand and would probably judge him harshly. There wasn't time to explain the details about why he'd done what he'd done.

"Oh, I get it. If you pretend it never happened, then you're fine? Because you're not fine. You need help and there's nothing wrong with asking for help. Or letting someone help you when they want to!"

"Why do you want to help me?"

"Because *you* need it." Trent stared straight into Reed's eyes as he threw Reed's words from the previous night back at him.

The corner of Reed's mouth curled up in acknowledgment that this round went to Trent. The guy was two-and-oh. Maybe there was more to Trent than was obvious at first glance, and the guy had some balls to stand up to Reed. Even offering to help was unexpected. No one had ever offered to help Reed before.

Wait a minute. Reed stopped that thought in its tracks. It wasn't so much that no one had offered to help him as he had never *let* anyone help before. Never let on he needed any help—or anything, for that matter— from another person. He used to think he did that to protect people. Reed knew he was stronger and could handle everything on his own. The job didn't give him much choice. But now, as Trent worked to stem the bleeding and patch him up, Reed realized he'd never let his guard down long enough to accept help from anyone before. Was it weak to accept care and kindness from someone else? Why not open up and take what someone else offered now and then? It was frightening and unfamiliar to admit being wounded and vulnerable, and even more surprising how damn good it felt to have someone else take care of him for a change. Reed closed his eyes while Trent cleaned the wound.

"Damn you, that hurts! Any whiskey left?"

"Good idea!" Trent went across the room, kneeled next to his now much-battered suitcase, and pulled out the bottle. A couple of inches of golden liquid remained. He fumbled around for a moment. "Aw, fuck!"

"What?"

Trent tossed the contents of the case around, evidently looking for something.

"I know I had two," Trent mumbled, more to himself than to Reed.

"Bleeding here and in pain…" Reed reminded him.

"That's what they took! I had two bottles of body wash and now there's just one."

Reed shook his head and waited for a translation.

"When they broke into my room, that's the only thing missing!"

Reed burst out laughing. Trent had attracted a thief even gayer than he was. It was priceless and took Reed's mind off his injuries and predicament for the moment.

Trent kept muttering and cursing and eventually pulled out a shirt. Even from across the room Reed could tell it was another handmade, perfectly tailored number. Trent seemed to have an unlimited supply of them. He brought the shirt and the bottle over to Reed.

Reed reached for the bottle but Trent didn't hand it over. Instead he poured some onto Reed's wound. Reed howled in a mixture of surprise and pain.

"God-fucking-damn-you. I wanted to *drink* it!"

Only then did Trent offer him the bottle. Reed grabbed at it, eyeing Trent warily, and then gulped down the remainder of the whiskey. While he did so, Trent sat down next to Reed on the bed.

Reed let the bottle slip from his hand as he watched in disbelief as Trent proceeded to rip his shirt into wide strips. "You just destroyed that fancy shirt of yours."

"It's the closest thing to clean bandages we've got, and I can't think of a better way to keep the wound from getting infected."

"How do you know so much about dealing with knife wounds?"

"One of my characters got into a knife fight and he needed to get patched up." Trent smiled. "I like research! So sue me!"

Reed couldn't help but laugh at Trent's need to justify his knowledge. He also was grateful Trent did know what to do and went about it rather efficiently. Reed wouldn't have been able to patch up his arm by himself and he might have lost a lot more blood.

The whiskey started to kick in and the nice warm feeling in his belly competed with the throbbing of the knife wound. He watched Trent clean up the blood-soaked towel and the remnants of his shirt. Damn, he really had liked that shirt.

"Want some food?" Trent asked, holding up one of the bags Reed had brought.

"Not hungry. You go ahead." Reed didn't want Trent to know he'd already eaten. He lay back and watched Trent pick at the food at first, until hunger overcame his manners and justifiable anger and he stuffed his face like a sumo wrestler, clearly enjoying the meal.

Reed's own mood had improved dramatically, and he didn't bother to hide the fact he was enjoying the way Trent's ass looked in those cutoff shorts or noticing the muscles straining against the sheer fabric of his shirt. Neither the whiskey nor the ache of his arm deterred Reed's cock from fully appreciating Trent, and it didn't take long before Trent noticed Reed's erection.

"Oh no. You can just forget about that. Not now."

"Why not?" Reed flashed a crooked, half-drunk, and very horny smile.

"Try and sleep. You need rest."

"I need comfort." Reed smiled and pushed his lower lip out slightly. "Just come over and sit here with me."

"No sex." Trent gave in and sat down at the edge of the bed, but it sounded as if he were trying to convince himself as much as Reed.

"I'm pretty harmless like this. See?" Reed weakly raised his injured arm and the resulting sting made him wish he hadn't.

Unfortunate but true. It would be difficult if not impossible to do much to Trent, and more than likely he'd hurt himself just trying. Trent could suck him off but it wasn't what Reed really wanted at the moment. He craved intimacy more than sex, and it had finally dawned on him Trent had already given him more in just one night than Reed could remember ever feeling.

"I think you're a lot more dangerous than you look."

"You're safe. Just sit with me until I fall asleep?"

"Okay." Trent sounded wary, but he settled next to Reed on the mattress, their legs and hips pressed together. Trent turned slightly toward Reed and smoothed his fingers along Reed's good arm, trying to comfort and relax him. Reed quickly dozed off.

When he woke, he noticed the sun's mid-afternoon slant. Trent's head rested on Reed's good shoulder. As soon as Reed shifted his weight, Trent awoke with a start but settled back against Reed's body with a faint sigh.

"Trent," Reed whispered.

"Hmmm?"

"Your cock is digging into my side."

"Mmmm?" Trent mumbled again. Then he opened his eyes. "Oh, sorry."

"Don't apologize, you big tease."

Trent tried to sit up but Reed used his good arm to lay him back down.

"It'd be a shame to waste a perfectly good hard-on, wouldn't it?"

"I thought you were too injured to fuck. Have you recovered already or did you have something else in mind?" Trent sounded skeptical, but there was a hint of a smile in his eyes Reed could see even in the dim room.

"Why don't you do the fucking this time?" Reed didn't usually bottom and he couldn't honestly remember the last time he had. But he knew he suddenly liked the idea of having Trent's beautiful and impressive cock inside of him. He trusted Trent enough to take care of him and make it good for them both.

"What?" Trent still sounded a bit groggy from his own nap.

"How about if you kiss me while you think about it?" Reed leaned forward and pressed his lips to Trent's, feeling Trent's mouth fall open with only slight initial resistance. But once he started kissing back, Trent was quickly caught up with mounting excitement that had Reed hard again almost instantly. He nearly forgot about his injured arm until he tried to embrace Trent.

"Careful, Reed. I don't want you to get hurt."

"Be gentle with me, then." Reed's tone was playful and Trent moved in for another passionate kiss, this time taking care not to jostle Reed's arm.

"You're probably best on your stomach, with your arm out to the side." Trent began to pull off his shirt. As he stood to remove his shorts, Reed laughed at how easily Trent had changed his mind on the matter of sex.

"Sure."

Trent helped him roll over and placed his arm out of the danger zone. Then Trent stood and went over toward his backpack. Reed watched him dig around in the pocket containing the lube and condoms. "Use the piña colada one this time!" he teased.

Trent shot him a sharp look over his shoulder, but it quickly melted into a dark gaze that revealed his desire.

Trent came back to the bed and stood behind Reed. Even over his own now ragged breath, Reed could hear Trent slip his boxers off. The bed dipped with his weight. Trent leaned across Reed's body and, using hands and mouth, he touched and licked and kissed Reed until he'd built up a need so strong and aching within Reed that he was practically fucking the mattress with anticipation and impatience. Trent had been sucking on a particularly sensitive part of the back of Reed's neck, and now began to kiss his way agonizingly slowly down Reed's body until he reached the small of his back.

There Trent lavished kisses and feather-light whispers while his fingers explored the curves of Reed's ass, only occasionally straying between his legs or nearing either his hole or ghosting across his balls. Damn, Trent knew how to drag this out. Reed wanted him so badly he moaned and grunted and pushed his ass toward Trent.

"Patience," was all Trent said and he didn't speed up his caresses. Finally Reed sensed Trent's weight shift as he reached for the lube. He heard Trent open the tube and the telltale wet sound as he squeezed some out. A moment later a cool, slick fingertip pressed tentatively against his hole while Trent used his other hand to spread Reed's cheeks apart. Suddenly feeling uncomfortably exposed and vulnerable, Reed tensed up and Trent let go of him.

"Do you want me to stop?" Trent's voice held a mixture of worry, disappointment, and gravelly desire, but it was the last emotion that made Reed's decision for him.

"No, keep going." Reed relaxed as Trent's huge hand smoothed along the curve of his ass for a moment before the fingertip again tickled his entrance. It circled once, twice, then a third time before just the tiniest tip breached his hole and stopped. Trent pushed his finger in more carefully than Reed imagined possible and he relaxed around it, getting used to the long-unfamiliar sensation of being filled. Damn, Trent had long—and thick—fingers! When Trent finally began to move the finger slowly out and in again, Reed groaned with the unexpected pleasure of the movement. He could hear Trent's sigh of relief, and the tempo picked up slightly.

Trent gradually worked Reed open while still managing to keep him fully aroused, and by the time Reed heard the telltale ripping of a condom wrapper he was aching for release, fucking his hips down into the mattress as he groaned his impatience.

But the fingers were nothing compared to the sensation of Trent's thick, rock-hard cock as he slowly filled Reed up, moving past the initial ring of resistance and stretching Reed wide as he gradually worked most of his length into Reed as carefully as he had worked his fingers.

Reed could feel Trent's breath hot and steady on his back and Trent took his time and obviously paid extra care not to take Reed too far too fast or to brush his injured arm. Reed wondered if he'd ever been as careful with anyone as Trent was with him, and while a part of him longed for Trent to just fuck him into the mattress, he knew he'd regret that as soon as he felt a stab of pain.

"Oh, God, Reed," Trent panted against Reed's back. "Feels so amazing." Trent let out a few grunts as he began to thrust ever so slowly and carefully. The heat of his skin and the weight on Reed's back were new sensations for Reed, and he gave himself over to them as Trent's cock filled and emptied him, occasionally dragging over his sweet spot and causing him to shudder uncontrollably with pleasure, which radiated throughout his entire body before settling back into white-hot need that made his balls ache.

Suddenly, Trent pulled out, leaving Reed empty and wanting in a way he'd never felt.

"Can you turn over? Onto your back?" Trent asked, sounding ridiculously polite, given the situation.

Reed immediately complied, while Trent pulled the pillow out of the way and helped Reed onto his back, careful of his injured arm. He welcomed Trent back inside and tightened his legs around Trent's waist, bringing him as deep as possible. *Deeper.* Reed couldn't control his own shudders or the way his hips instinctively moved to meet Trent's thrusts. Real-life Trent fucked way better than his characters did, and Reed wanted—needed—more.

One of Trent's hands came up to stroke Reed's cheek, an oddly gentle caress when all Reed wanted was to be fucked within an inch of his life. Reed saw Trent gaze into his eyes before he squeezed them shut as another tremor of pure pleasure pulsed through him, and he lost track of everything but the man in and around him.

Trent's hips stuttered wildly and his teeth dug into Reed's left shoulder. The next thing Reed knew he was shouting into the mattress as his cock exploded and shot rapid jets of come all over himself, splashing up to his neck. Wave after wave of heat washed over him and he only faintly heard Trent's own pleasure echoing in his ears as Trent came deep inside of him, cock pulsing and throbbing while Trent's powerful arms tightened around him.

Carefully, Trent eased himself down, half lying on Reed, half on the mattress, his body slick with sweat. Reed lost himself in the peace and contentment of strong, corded arms snaked around his body. Hot breath puffed into Reed's ear, ruffling his hair slightly, and he turned to face Trent. Only inches apart, Reed looked directly into Trent's gray-brown eyes with their wide-blown pupils and wondered if Trent felt the same way he did now.

10

WHEN Reed woke again, the sun was low and the last rays of daylight were streaming in through the small window. Trent sat fully clothed on the edge of the bed next to him, watching him.

"Reed, what did you take from my backpack?"

Reed had been dreading this conversation. He tried to sit up and pain shot through his injured right arm again. He groaned but Trent showed no sympathy this time. "Backpack?"

"Don't lie. You're not as good at it as you think."

I used to be an expert at it. Did it for a living. What about Trent had changed that? And how had it happened so fast?

"It's complicated."

"Then go slowly so I can try and wrap my thick skull around it." Trent practically sneered. The afterglow of their reunion had faded, and he wanted answers. He deserved them. Deserved the truth. Only Reed didn't want to have to get into the whole thing right now. He wanted to get Trent somewhere safe and soon.

"A map." Reed got up and went to his pants and pulled the map out of the pocket. He handed it to Trent, whose eyes shone with recognition.

"This is just a map of Thailand. What's so special about it?" Trent unfolded the thick, glossy map, eyes scanning it.

Reed took the map from Trent and drew his attention to a corner. Very slowly he separated the layers. It was, in fact, two thin maps carefully glued together with the "treasure map" sandwiched in between. He exposed just a small portion, enough for Trent to see a piece of the aged paper. When he handed it off to Supachai's second it would be better if he didn't let on he'd seen the location of the Buddha.

"Wow, just like a spy movie." Trent's voice held a mixture of fascination and skepticism. "But what is this map to and how did it end up in my backpack? And how are you involved with any of this?"

"It's the location of a Buddha statue. A golden Buddha inlaid with rubies, called, not surprisingly, the Ruby Buddha."

Trent looked Reed up and down, eyes lingering on his still-bruised face and the blood-soaked makeshift bandages wrapped around his arm.

"Are you some kind of smuggler? Oh no. No, no, no. I don't want anything to do with this. Or you." He tossed the map back at Reed and grabbed for his backpack. Then he started toward the door.

"Trent! Wait!" Reed sprang up after him, grabbing at his elbow. He couldn't let Trent leave now, with this misapprehension. "I'll start at the beginning. It's not as bad as it seems. Well, not quite as bad. Just give me a chance, okay?" Reed's voice rose in supplication. He didn't understand why the idea of Trent walking out on him made him feel so miserable. But it did. He didn't want Trent to leave.

"Reed, someone beat you up the other night and you just got stabbed."

He doesn't even know I killed a man a few hours ago.

"I don't want to get involved with anything like this. Anyone who does things like this. You." Trent stared at his feet and his shoulders drooped in disappointment. Reed knew *he'd* been the disappointment. "Even if it's just a few days while I'm on vacation, I can't be with a criminal." Trent spat the word like daggers ripping into Reed's chest.

"I'm not a criminal. I'm a federal agent."

Trent's head shot up and his eyes widened.

"Yeah, right. What's a federal agent doing working in Thailand?" The skepticism was back in full. "Why should I believe you?"

"Give me five minutes to explain. Please?" Reed knew he was pleading again but this time Trent listened and sat back down. He still had the backpack slung over his shoulder, so he hadn't completely committed to staying yet. Reed knew this would be the most difficult— and most important—explanation he'd give in a long time.

"Five minutes." Trent glanced at his watch, then turned his attention on Reed, but his face was dark. Reed had his work cut out for him.

"I'm part of an international task force to stop transnational criminal activity in Asia. I'm undercover, working to link a prospective Chinese buyer to a Thai ring that smuggles antiquities, among numerous other illegal activities. This map is a key item in the sting operation."

"Sounds more far-fetched than one of my books. Assuming it's true, how did I get involved?"

"This map should have been given to another agent who would pass it to me, but it got put into your bag by mistake."

"Who put it there and when?"

"A customs agent—one of our local contacts—in the airport in Bangkok. I was supposed to retrieve and hand it over to the Thai mob boss."

"So you came up to me in the airport only because I had your map, and when I didn't go with you, you followed me around?"

"Yeah. Something like that."

"And our date?"

"That was real." Reed tried to swallow but there was a hard knot in his throat. "I wanted to spend time with you. I had to get the map, but I didn't think it could hurt to try and get to know you at the same time."

"Then why didn't you show up at the restaurant?"

"Supachai—the mob boss—sent some thugs to 'invite' me to a little meeting to find out why I hadn't given them the map yet."

"They're the ones who beat you up?" Trent looked and sounded worried again. Reed hoped it meant Trent actually cared about *him*, and not just that he was starting to believe the story.

"They knew if they killed me they wouldn't get the map. Only I knew who had it at that point."

"So you followed me on the bus to get it?"

"Yes, or they would have made things very unpleasant for me, and it was necessary to put the next phase of the operation into play. I wasn't just worried about my own skin. I have a job to do and three governments are relying on this plan working out."

"I don't understand how you can be so calm about the possibility you might have been hurt even worse, or killed."

"It's not the first time I've been in a dangerous situation." Reed paused, recalling the last time. *Feeling* the whip again. The scars burned but he knew it was only his imagination.

"Your back...." Trent let his words trail off.

Reed didn't like to dwell on the subject—or the memories—and he certainly didn't like to talk about it. He'd spent some time in a Buddhist monastery when he first came to Southeast Asia. It had taken all of the meditation techniques he'd learned in order to survive what happened later. He employed them whenever the terror of that ordeal came back— as it threatened to do now. He hoped Trent wouldn't press the issue.

"It's part of the job." Reed closed his eyes for a moment while he focused on his breathing and heartbeat.

"So what happened when you left with the map this morning?"

"I made it to the nearest town where I could get a phone signal and called Supachai, but he was already there. I think he must've had a GPS tracker on my bike because I found it there too. It can't have been just coincidence. Anyway, once he knew I had the map on me he tried to kill me. Accused me of trying to cut him out of the loop and deal directly with the buyer. I think he had another buyer lined up."

"But you got away?"

"Yeah, I got away." Reed glossed over the truth. Maybe he wouldn't have to reveal the details.

"What will you do now? Isn't he part of the plan?"

"I have to think about the next step. Supachai is supposed to provide the men for the excavation. I hadn't planned a scenario where I took out—" Reed bit his lip. "Had to cut out a key player. I need to figure out a Plan B."

"How far is the Buddha from where we are?"

"Couple hundred miles or so. It's hidden in a cave, in fairly untraveled territory. Supachai knew which general area, but not exactly which cave it was in. That's why he needed me and the map, or his men would be digging up caves for years before they found it."

"So how much is it worth, the Ruby Buddha?"

"Nothing."

"What? You're risking your life for *nothing*?"

"The map leads to a fake. There is no Ruby Buddha. It's a myth. A millennium-old Khmer-Thai legend. There are plenty of people who'd pay a fortune for it if it did exist, but it doesn't—at least not the genuine Ruby Buddha. The Thai government had a replica made that would fool anyone but an expert."

"It seems like a lot of risk to take to catch antiquities smugglers. Why aren't you chasing drug dealers or the ones who traffic weapons or people?"

"We are. The statue is bait for the real fish. The big fish. Kao Lung."

"Kao Lung? Doesn't sound Thai. Sounds more like Chinese food. Kung Pao." Trent grinned.

The Chinese-food joke amused Reed, but he questioned whether he should continue. He glared at Trent. "Why should I bother explaining if you can't be serious?"

Trent had the kicked-puppy look again, but he took a breath and stared back at Reed. "Look, this is a lot of new stuff for me: Thai gangsters, Chinese triads, lost artifacts. I might make stuff like this up when I'm writing, but it's helluva a lot to take in, in real life. So cut me some slack." Trent's expression turned somber again. "Keep going."

Reed liked how Trent stood up to him. He had been expecting far too much from him. It was a lot to deal with even for someone with Reed's training.

He hadn't expected Trent to need this much detail. "Many Thai gangs are affiliated with Hong Kong triads, others with Japanese Yakuza families. Kao heads one of the most insidious triads in Hong Kong, with influence all over Asia. He happens to also collect Buddhist antiquities."

Trent nodded, then shook his head. The pieces hadn't quite fallen together for him.

"But the Chinese government is afraid to arrest Kao, so the Buddha statue was designed to get him out of China where he's safe. If he comes to Thailand, we'll arrest him on antiquities trafficking. Taking him out of play will disrupt their entire organization enough so the Chinese can go in, mop up the rest, and shut it down."

"Kind of like getting Al Capone on tax evasion with a major domino effect?"

"Good analogy." Reed smiled. Trent was definitely a smarter cookie than he'd given him credit for.

"How do you know the big fish is going to come to Thailand? Wouldn't he know it's a risk and just send someone to pick up the statue?"

"Another good question." Reed was impressed Trent had grasped the most salient points. "This guy is fanatic about his collection. The magnitude of this discovery is off the charts, and he'd want to see it personally before money changes hands. Kao has three passions: Buddhist art, golf, and racehorses. I'm pretty sure he'll make the trip when he can satisfy two of them at once. The meeting is supposed to take place at one of the best golf resorts in Thailand."

"Sounds like you've thought of everything."

"I've been working on this operation for nearly three years, so, yeah, I hope I've thought of everything." *Everything except what happens when I kill one of the main players.*

"I suppose you can't possibly have made all that up just to convince me you aren't a crook." Trent seemed to have relaxed. He slid the backpack off his shoulder. He was staying.

Reed let out the breath he hadn't realized he'd been holding.

"So what do we do now?"

"There is no 'we.'" Reed stood and paced around the room, his back to Trent. He didn't want to see rejection cloud Trent's face. This wasn't personal, at least not yet. But it was dangerous. "You're going back to Bangkok, or on to Khorat if you prefer. You'll be safer there than with me."

"You're not coming back with me?" Trent's disappointment cut Reed just to hear it. Oh God, how Reed wanted to go with him. But he couldn't. Not yet.

"I have to get the next part of this operation going, with Supachai's men and the buyer. Then I can get back to you in Bangkok when it's wrapped up."

"Let me come with you?"

"No way. You saw what they did to me. I don't want to be responsible if anything happened to you. I want you somewhere safe where I won't have to worry about you."

"You've got that Superman thing going again, and I don't need saving. I can handle myself. Just because I missed my bus stop doesn't mean I can't help you out with this."

Reed doubted that, but he wouldn't dream of saying it and hurting Trent even more. "Trent, I know you could help, but I'd never forgive myself if you got hurt. I...." *Care about you too much*, Reed wanted to say, but didn't. This wasn't the right time or place. Hell, Reed couldn't even understand what he felt about Trent, much less share that with him.

"So what are you going to do after I go back to Bangkok?"

"Try and get in contact with Supachai's men and start the excavations and then let the buyer know when it's found."

"Why go through the whole thing of digging it up? Why not just present the thing to this Chinese dude in the first place? It's all so dangerous and complicated."

"Two reasons. We can't just try and sell a fake statue to someone. That's entrapment. The case might get thrown out. If we *facilitate* the transaction it's not an issue. That's the legal side, or a simplification of it. Different countries have different regulations but that sums up the basic situation." Reed paused as he watched Trent absorb the logic behind this. "On the practical think-like-a-criminal side there's also the matter of trust and reputation. Because the buyer doesn't know me or any of the agents we've got undercover, he wouldn't trust us with a purchase of this value. We didn't have time to build up a strong-enough rep for an undercover agent as the seller, and this way we get to nail the Thais involved as well. Kao Lung had trusted Supachai—from his very well-earned reputation— and now...." Reed stopped when Trent cocked his head and looked at him sideways.

"Trusted Supachai? *Past* tense?"

Fuck. Trent was definitely too sharp for Reed's own good.

"What happened with him?" Trent's voice wasn't much more than a whisper.

"He's not part of the operation anymore," Reed said, biting off each word carefully, hoping it would signal he didn't want to discuss this particular issue any further.

"That's his blood on your shirt? He tried to kill you, didn't he?" Realization dawned in Trent's eyes. "Did you... kill *him*?"

Reed nodded slowly and looked away from Trent. He couldn't bear to see the disgust and accusation he knew he'd find there. It was exactly why nothing could work out with them, even for a few days of fun. Reed wasn't on vacation; he had a mission to finish. He didn't have time for fun now, and to be honest, he suspected he wanted more from Trent. But Trent could never deal with the realities of what Reed's job forced him to do.

To his great surprise, Trent rushed over and wrapped those long, strong arms around him, as if a hug might possibly comfort him over taking someone's life. Reed hadn't killed many people over the years, but he took some degree of consolation knowing each one had been in self-defense. It didn't make it any easier to deal with afterward. This time, he'd had Trent's well-being to worry about. Focusing his energy on something positive and good took the sting of killing away. There was too damn little of "positive and good" in Reed's life.

"Reed, I'm so sorry. So sorry I didn't understand all of this. All the pressure you must be under." Trent pulled Reed in close, and for a moment Reed wondered whether he could simply relax into the embrace and block out the world, block out the reality he'd nearly died and only saved himself by killing someone else. Was the result worth the sacrifice? Reed had to consider the lives saved if the triad was taken down. Supachai probably deserved to die for the crimes he'd already committed, but it should be up to a court of law and not for Reed to play the role of executioner.

And for a few minutes, Reed let go. He let Trent practically scoop him up and lay him down on the mattress, sheets still crumpled and stained from the last time they lay here together. He let Trent ease his body and his mind. It would take a lot more to erase the darkness from his soul. But one thing became crystal clear: This was Reed's last mission. As soon as he'd wrapped up the deal and locked up whoever they could implicate, he was quitting. Leaving Thailand, probably leaving the Bureau. Life was too short to already regret so many things by the age of thirty-two.

He glanced over at Trent, who sat at the edge of the bed watching him with intense concern until he simply lay down next to Reed and wrapped him in those long, strong arms, corded with muscles he could feel gliding beneath the smooth delicious skin. Reed smiled as he remembered the way Trent's skin tasted. The smell and feel of him, especially now that he was close again. This time Trent lent his strength to Reed instead of the other way around.

For the first time in a long time—maybe the first time ever—Reed let someone hold and comfort him. Trent stroked Reed's hair and face and shoulders, as he lay against Trent's chest, listening to the strong steady heartbeat. Reed never opened up or let his guard down. He'd never before had anyone there to prop him up like this. Just more proof he wasn't cut out for this job anymore. Was he getting too soft? Or did he finally understand just what he'd been denying himself all these years, using work as his excuse?

His biggest regret wasn't anything he'd done. It was what he hadn't done. The time he hadn't taken to live his own life. He couldn't fathom how Trent had affected him so much so quickly, but it had started the day they met in Bangkok. Something had changed in Reed. He should have focused on the job—getting the map—and what had he done? Planned a date instead of stealing the damn thing, even if he had to hold the guy up at gunpoint. He wouldn't have had to hurt him, just scare him enough to give up the map. Simple. He'd done it on more than one occasion. Is that why his first sight of Trent had caused him to make such a mess of retrieving the map? Had that touristy innocence reminded Reed of so much he'd been missing?

He didn't know and, for a little while, he didn't care. Let Trent make the decisions for the both of them, just for an hour or two. Soft caresses and the rhythmic beating of Trent's heart combined with the comforting heat and Reed let himself doze off.

WHEN he woke, Reed could see the light beginning to gather outside the eastern-facing window. Dawn was near. Had he slept the whole night? He'd intended to get the hell out of Dodge under cover of night. He needed to get Trent to the nearest bus station and away from the danger that surely would soon catch up to Reed. By now Supachai's cohorts would know something had happened. It had been what, twelve, fifteen hours since Reed had killed him? His cohorts must have noticed he was missing. Someone had probably discovered the body in the alley. Reed was probably the only *farang* in town, and the woman from the food stall would have remembered. Two strangers showing up in a small town and one of them turning up dead: it wouldn't take Sherlock Holmes to figure out the connection. Both the police and Supachai's second-in-command would be looking for him. As pleasant as it sounded, Reed couldn't hide here with Trent forever. He had to find the Buddha and get Kao Lung to Thailand.

Trent was spooned up behind Reed, breathing softly against the back of his neck, one arm wrapped around Reed's waist so he was pinned in the bed. He did his best to move slowly, but as soon as he stirred, Trent woke as well.

"Mmmrn."

Reed took that for a good-morning greeting and rolled over to face Trent. Before he could say a word, Trent's arms closed around him, pulling him back into comfortable, delicious heat. He inhaled Trent's scent and immediately felt himself getting hard. Time enough for that later. He willed his cock to obey and got up.

They washed up and Trent gave Reed a clean shirt. Between Reed's knife and Trent giving Reed shirts, the poor guy would be nude in a few days. Reed chuckled at the thought as Trent gathered up and packed the remainder of his belongings. Today he wore a pair of lightweight cargo pants. Apparently Trent hadn't completely ignored what Reed had told him that night in the rain; that was a very good sign.

Reed cut strips from what remained of Trent's jeans from the day of the bus crash and wrapped them around Trent's ankle, providing some support. Trent grimaced as Reed pulled the makeshift bandages tight, but with his injured arm he couldn't tighten them as much as he'd like. That should get him back to Bangkok, where he could have a doctor examine it and rule out any serious injury.

"Ready, Trent? I want to get you to the next town in plenty of time to get a bus back to Bangkok."

"Yes." The reluctance in Trent's voice was clear but Reed had to do it this way.

Trent was only a couple of steps behind Reed when he walked out of the hut to find a gun pointed in his face.

11

REED was face to face with Supachai's second in command, Boontung. He hadn't expected they'd have tracked him to the hut, since Supachai usually kept the specifics of a job—like the location of the tracker on a target—to himself. Why hadn't he planned for such a contingency? He'd been too eager to get back to Trent to check for the transmitter or remember to leave the bike sufficiently far from the hut to confuse anyone looking for him.

To make matters worse, Boontung hadn't come alone, either. He had half a dozen minions with him and several more arrived as Reed opened the door. *Fuck.* If he and Trent had left sooner they would have avoided this ambush.

If only they hadn't made love again the night before, they'd have already been gone by morning.

Made love? Reed shook off the concept. It was *fucking*, he reminded himself, not *love*making. At least that's what it was supposed to have been. But he couldn't even convince himself it had been merely physical. Trent had gotten to him in a way no one ever had. In any other situation Reed would be thrilled at the idea of meeting someone special. But this wasn't any other situation. This was work. Dangerous. *Life or death.* He'd let himself be distracted by the pleasure—physical and emotional—of spending time with Trent. It had filled so many empty places inside. Reed hadn't realized just how empty he'd been until just a couple of days ago.

Now he'd gotten Trent mixed up in it. Reed was prepared to take risks to do his job, but he absolutely did not want Trent to get hurt because he'd fallen down on the job of protecting them both.

"Change of plans?" Trent had come out of the hut, limping slightly, and he turned toward Reed with a surprisingly composed look on his face, despite finding half a dozen armed men gathered around Reed.

One of them turned his weapon on Trent. Reed's heart rate accelerated and blood pounded in his head as his stomach roiled about what might happen. Even worse, this was all Reed's fault. Not the best way to start a relationship, was it? *Relationship?* Where had that come from?

"Where's the map, Acton?" Boontung's guttural words snapped Reed out of his soap-opera musings. He waved the pistol menacingly at Reed for emphasis. Boontung's English was more heavily accented than Supachai's.

Trent glanced over at Reed again, but didn't say a word. The blank expression on Trent's face impressed Reed. Hopefully it would fool Boontung into thinking Trent didn't know what this was all about.

"Look, Boontung. I've got your map." Reed patted his pocket. "I'll hand it over and then you let us go."

"You know I can't do that." Boontung switched to Thai.

"Sure you can. You take the map and find the Buddha. I'm out of it now."

"I need you to contact the buyer. Supachai didn't give me that information."

Reed could see it pained Boontung to admit Supachai hadn't trusted him enough to share details of the scheme, but he tried not to show his amusement. In typical mobster fashion, Supachai hadn't told any one of his lieutenants all of the information, keeping them loyal— unless they all banded together to oust him, but none had the guts for that. Apparently Supachai hadn't revealed the buyer's name. Only Reed knew how to contact him. For once Reed wished he didn't have to follow through in order to complete the mission.

Wouldn't it be nice to just hand the map over and let someone else on his team finish the job? But Reed had to be the lone wolf, had to take on more than anyone else, and he'd signed on for a bigger role in the operation than his superiors had wanted. Now he was paying the price. With Trent involved, it seemed more like recklessness than duty. For once there was actually something to lose besides failing to lock up the bad guys.

Reed could handle anything Boontung or his thugs could hand out. He'd taken more than most men and lived through it. He glanced over at Trent, remembering his lilac boxers, the smell of his fancy body wash, and the way his lips felt against Reed's. There was no way on earth Trent could take any real physical abuse. Sure, he was strong, but he wasn't *tough*. Mentally, he definitely wasn't up to the challenge, no matter how brave a face he put on.

"Search Acton," Boontung said.

One man pinned Reed's arms behind his back, sending white-hot pain down the length of the injured arm. Another frisked him, immediately finding the gun and knife and relieving Reed of the weapons.

Boontung stepped toward Trent, who now looked appropriately worried. As one guard pinned him, Boontung stepped forward, first giving Reed a knowing grin, then searching Trent himself. Reed struggled against his own captor as he watched Boontung's hands all over Trent, taking his time with an unnecessarily thorough search. Hands traveled up one leg and across Trent's crotch, as he stood with a helpless expression that pained Reed more than the knife wound.

"Very nice," Boontung said with a lascivious grin that Reed wanted to punch. It would be worth whatever punishment he got. "We're definitely keeping him," Boontung added with a laugh, and stroked Trent's chest for emphasis. Trent kept his gaze focused on the ground and blinked a few times, but his fear was evident.

"Get them both into the truck." Boontung waved a gun toward a vehicle. Reed translated and Trent got into the truck bed as indicated, though one of Boontung's thugs gave him an unnecessary shove, sending him sprawling on hands and knees. Reed lunged at the guy but let go as soon as he felt the barrel of a gun against the back of his neck. When Reed turned toward Boontung, the other man slammed the pistol into his right temple. Twice. Cheek stinging, he silently climbed in beside Trent, and two thugs with rifles joined them.

"You okay, Trent?" Reed fought the urge to touch Trent, to comfort him.

"Fine." Trent brushed sand and blood off one knee and gave a pained smile that was far too familiar to Reed now.

Reed appreciated Trent trying to act brave, but he was worried. Boontung wouldn't kill Reed at least until after the buyer had been reached—or they force Reed to divulge the contact information. But now Reed had to worry about what they'd do to Trent. He'd become a pawn, Reed's Achilles' heel. If Boontung threatened Trent, Reed would give in and do just about anything. Reed could take being tortured, but he couldn't watch someone else being hurt, especially not someone he'd begun to care about.

"How about you?" Trent reached up to touch Reed's cheek just below where Boontung had hit him and Reed flinched slightly. Trent pulled his hand back and looked like he was the one who'd been hit.

"I'm tough. I can handle these guys. They don't have much imagination from what I've seen so far. It's their boss who was the really dangerous one." Reed kept his voice low, just in case the men guarding them understood English. He hoped Trent would figure out why and do the same.

"The one who's… dead?" Trent only mouthed the final word, clearly understanding not to advertise Reed had killed Supachai, in case his minions hadn't already figured it out.

"Yeah." Reed glanced over at the two men who sat across from them on the wooden benches in the back of the truck. One was already half asleep and the other watched the scenery fly past. Neither seemed to be paying much attention to Reed or Trent, but it was best not to take chances or underestimate the danger of the situation. That's how Reed had gotten them into trouble in the first place.

Reed's cheek throbbed from the blow and he could feel blood trickling from the wound. Best not to even pay attention to the pain. He wished Trent hadn't touched him. Not because the gentle caress and the concern it conveyed was unwelcome. Reed didn't want Boontung's thugs to realize there was anything between Reed and Trent. Maybe they'd be too dense to figure out they could use Trent to get Reed to do what they wanted.

Reed glanced over at Trent, who was still watching him intently. Much to his surprise, Reed didn't see fear in Trent's eyes. Instead, it was concern, worry; but not for himself. It seemed he was more concerned about Reed than what was about to happen to them. Reed wasn't sure if he should be relieved or more worried. It certainly made him feel worse about dragging Trent into this mess.

If only he'd managed to get the map that first day and hadn't screwed around so he could meet Trent or hook up with him. Reed realized this whole mess was due to his own selfish needs and attraction, but Trent would likely be the one to pay in the end. The sting operation might or might not work out, but the success or failure wouldn't depend on whether or not Trent was involved. It had more to do with what happened once Boontung found the Buddha and whether Reed got Kao Lung to come to Thailand for the sale.

The ride to the caves took about four hours from the hut. Boontung let the trucks stop a few times along the way for food, water, or other necessities, and both Reed and Trent were allowed to eat and drink, under close guard.

One of the men stood guard a few feet from Reed and Trent as they ate, but not close enough to overhear them, even if he could understand English.

"This is really delicious. What is it?" Trent waved a forkful of chicken in Reed's direction.

"Some local dish. I don't know what it's called; I haven't spent much time in this part of the country."

"I was wondering whether or not they'd let us eat," Trent mumbled around a mouthful of food. They hadn't eaten that morning before they'd been captured and they were both starving by the time they did get some food. Both Reed and Trent had been shoveling it in, just in case they got dragged back into the truck at any moment.

"One thing about the Thais is that they do have a sense of fairness and karma. They rarely mistreat anyone."

"You don't call beating you up the other night in Bangkok or hitting you with the gun 'mistreatment'?" Trent paused, a quizzical expression spreading across his features. He motioned toward the swollen knot on Reed's cheek. "So, is that what they call pistol-whipping?"

"Yeah. That's pistol-whipping." Reed nearly laughed at the way Trent had asked. But even smiling hurt; he'd have to remember not to. "Gonna use it in a book?"

"I don't know. Maybe." Trent shrugged slightly, then broke into a shy smile, once he realized it took more than pistol-whipping to get to Reed.

"I'm glad this is educational for you." Reed smiled wryly while Trent had the good sense to look sheepish. "As for the Thais, they won't harm another person unless there's a good reason. There's no reason to starve us. They've gotten their message across, so they figure we won't escape."

"What makes them think that?"

"Boontung and Supachai think I'm too greedy to disappear before I get paid. That's the good part. Boontung knows he needs my help to find the Buddha and contact the buyer. He was Supachai's muscle, not part of upper management, so he's out of the loop without the contacts to pull off a deal like this."

"So, you're in no danger." Trent grinned, not mentioning that left his own fate uncertain.

"Trent, you're fine as long as I do what they want—or at least appear to. They're keeping you around to keep me in line."

"Ah." Trent looked into Reed's eyes with an expression of concern and pity. He quickly shoved another forkful of food into his mouth.

Reed could tell Trent was probably thinking about the scars on his back and wondering how much Reed could or would take. There was a hint of guilt in his expression as well; he was probably assessing his responsibility for the situation they were in.

"You better do what they say, then." He tried to grin as he spoke with his mouth half full, but the tone of his voice belied strong emotions beneath the surface.

"Don't worry." Reed couldn't meet Trent's eyes. He looked down at his plate of food. "I won't let anything happen to you."

"I know." Trent sort of gulped out the words and put his fork down. He'd only eaten half the food on his plate but he pushed it away and blinked a few times.

"Trent, it's not your fault."

"Yes it is. If you'd given them the map sooner then they wouldn't have come looking for you and then I wouldn't have gotten in the way and delayed you and you wouldn't be stuck here with me. You'd still be free and part of their team and not a prisoner."

"Who knows? They may have taken me prisoner again once they got the map."

"You're just trying to make me feel better." Trent managed a half laugh.

"Is it working?"

"No."

"You better eat the rest. Who knows when we'll get our next meal."

Trent nodded and resumed eating slowly, as if the food had lost its flavor and appeal for him.

For most of the meal, Reed managed to keep his injured arm on his lap, so neither Trent nor any of the Thais would notice it had started bleeding again. When he poured another glass of water, he instinctively used his right hand and a few drops of blood splashed onto the table.

"Reed! You're bleeding again!" The stridency in Trent's voice caught Boontung's attention and he came over to see what the problem was.

Boontung took hold of Reed's arm and unwrapped the now bloody cloth, seeing the raw gash.

"What happened?" Boontung growled in Thai.

"I cut my arm working on the bike before you showed up this morning." Reed hoped Boontung wouldn't notice the straight, clean edges of the wound—telltale signs of a knife wound and not an accident.

Boontung gave the wound a cursory glance. He had plenty of experience with knives, but Reed knew he didn't pay attention to details. Precisely why he'd hit his own glass ceiling in Supachai's organization. "If it's still bleeding that's bad."

Reed had to agree. He hadn't lost a huge amount of blood, but given the less-than-sanitary conditions, the risk of infection was a bigger concern.

"There must be a doctor around here," Reed suggested, not expecting Boontung to care much about his health. He was about to remind Boontung that if he died before he contacted the buyer, they'd be SOL, but he didn't need to.

"Find a doctor!" Boontung shouted to one of his men, who immediately went up to the food stall keeper.

Trent watched, wide-eyed, until Reed explained what was happening, though he didn't translate everything.

"This guy hurt his ankle." Reed pointed to Trent. "If you expect to get any work out of him, you might want the doc to check him out too."

"Good thinking." Boontung nodded, almost without thinking. Reed had earned back some trust, though he hoped he wouldn't need to appear to turn on Trent just to get on Boontung's good side. There would be time enough for explanations later.

Boontung and one of his men accompanied Reed to the doctor, while another guard walked more slowly with Trent. A cut this deep was going to require stitches. It was doubtful Boontung would let the doctor wait long enough for any anesthetic to kick in and it would be better if Trent wasn't around for the procedure. Reed could handle it. It wouldn't be pleasant, but he'd survived far worse.

The doctor's office wasn't far and he took Reed in immediately. Triage generally allowed for the person bleeding the most to move to the front of the line, even in the Thai boonies.

To Reed's surprise, the doctor refused to allow anyone in the room during exam or treatment. He made sure Reed had sustained no major nerve or muscle damage. Twenty stitches later Reed was bandaged and released with some painkillers and details on follow-up care. As if Reed was going to be in a situation where he could follow the doctor's instructions. He swallowed a couple of pills before the doctor released him and took Trent into the exam room. This time Boontung insisted on staying, and Reed had to act as translator for Boontung, since the doctor chose to speak with Trent in passable, if heavily accented English, and refused to speak with Boontung directly.

Trent's ankle had suffered only a slight sprain. The doctor said staying off it for a few days should be sufficient for it to mend on its own. Reed played up the severity of the injury to Boontung. It would keep the guards from worrying about Trent getting away. The doctor gave Reed a quizzical look, fully understanding he hadn't accurately translated.

Boontung's men were in the waiting room reading old Thai gossip magazines and appeared to be arguing over the attractiveness of some film stars. As soon as they saw Boontung emerge from the treatment area with Trent and Reed, he told them in rough, vulgar Thai to stop acting like grannies. They sheepishly put the magazines away and hopped to attention. Even Trent could understand the gist without need for interpretation by Reed.

Boontung paid the doctor's charges. In Thailand, the person of the highest standing traditionally pays for those of lower standing, even at the doctor, and apparently even when they are his prisoners.

After lunch the convoy got back on the road, and this time two different guards climbed into the back of the truck with Reed and Trent.

"At least they didn't split us up," Trent remarked. He stayed quiet for a while, as the truck bounced and jarred them.

"You know, Reed, if it wasn't for these guys hitting you I would have sworn this had all been set up by my friend Beth."

"… the fuck?"

"My friends thought I needed some adventure in my life, which is why I'm in Thailand in the first place. Beth's a bit extreme when it comes to… well, everything. She booked me into that guesthouse instead of a real hotel. She even hired a tuk-tuk driver for me to make sure I had a real Bangkok experience."

"You're kidding me." Reed was glad he didn't have friends after all; he had enough trouble to worry about. "So if I wasn't bleeding, you would have chalked the whole thing up to her?"

"Unless of course she's paying you extra to let those guys beat you up, but I don't think even you would do that for money."

"What do you mean 'even you'?" Is that all Trent thought of Reed? That he'd do anything for money? Maybe he'd misjudged Trent after all. "You would believe I'd fucked you just because Beth paid me?"

"No. I'd suspect my other close friend Mick paid for that. It's exactly the sort of thing he'd do." Trent paused and he seemed to realize he'd insulted Reed. "Sorry, I guess it came out wrong." Trent pressed his lips together in a thin line and entreated Reed to forgive him with a sad puppy-dog look Reed was already unable to resist. "I meant if you are with the FBI, then you probably aren't the kind of guy who'd do something like that for money. You seem to have strong principles."

"Thanks." Reed's voice was even and Trent still looked worried he hadn't been forgiven. Didn't he believe Reed's explanation about the operation to catch Kao Lung?

As the afternoon heat grew, Reed was glad for the tarp covering the back of the truck. The sides were rolled up to allow for cooling airflow while the top canopy kept the blazing sun off them. One of the guards offered Reed a water bottle; he let Trent drink first before taking some for himself.

The heat and exhaustion finally overcame Trent's fear or anxiety, and he fell asleep slumped against Reed's shoulder. The soft, even breathing reminded Reed of the two nights they'd spent together. Despite the heat, Trent still smelled like his shampoo, and Reed felt another frozen part of his heart melt, wondering how just a few days with Trent had changed him and his entire outlook.

Before they'd met, Reed could only think about his mission and how best to achieve it. Now, he couldn't wait to get the whole thing past him to the point he'd actually considered escaping and letting the whole sting fall apart just to keep Trent safe. He'd always tried to keep civilians out of harm's way, but what he felt for Trent was different. More than getting Trent out of danger, Reed wanted to protect him in an entirely different way.

Trent mumbled something in his sleep and Reed had a ridiculous fleeting worry that Trent could tell what he was thinking. The truck hit an uneven section of road and the resulting sharp swerve woke Trent.

He looked dazed and slightly embarrassed at having fallen asleep as he wiped at his mouth with the back of his hand.

"You okay, Sleeping Beauty?" Reed did his best to inject some humor into his tone.

"Um, yeah." Trent gave Reed a slightly disgusted look, probably at being called "Sleeping Beauty," which let Reed know he was as okay as possible given their predicament.

"Shh. The guards are asleep. Don't wake them up."

"Think we could push them off the back of the truck? Or jump off and escape?"

"That's not a half-bad idea, actually." Reed was surprised Trent had even suggested escaping. Maybe the guy wasn't as fragile as Reed originally suspected. On the other hand, it may only be a writer's imagination for an idea that sounded good on the printed page but he'd never try in real life. Whatever the reason, it gave Reed some degree of confidence they could carry out a plan to get away. But now wasn't the time or place.

"We're not the last vehicle in the convoy, so the men behind us would see and we'd be followed pretty quickly if we tried to get away on foot. Even if your ankle was one hundred percent, I don't know this area very well, so we have no advantage in terms of shortcuts or hiding places."

"Oh, I didn't think of that." Trent looked defeated.

"No, you had a good idea, but not a good plan at the moment. Keep thinking, and between the two of us we can come up with something we can work with."

"Really? That was a decent idea?"

"Sure it was. I'm kind of impressed you even came up with it."

"A backhanded compliment if I ever heard one." Trent pouted slightly but not enough to indicate his feelings had really been hurt.

Reed was glad to see Trent's spirits were still strong enough to joke around. And it meant he trusted Reed enough so he wouldn't panic or disintegrate into a puddle of terrified jelly. If only he didn't look so damn fuckable with his lower lip pushed out. Reed forced himself not to think about Trent's lips. Or fucking. And especially not about both of them at the same time. He also hoped Boontung didn't really want Trent for himself, because that would be a real problem.

"It wasn't meant to be." Reed flashed Trent a smile and a tiny wink. Trent's resulting grin cheered Reed up immensely. Such a bright, wide smile, and he hadn't seen it since they'd walked out of the hut and right into Boontung's clutches. Too bad. If they weren't here.... Reed forced himself to shut out the images of them on a clean hotel bed ripping each other's clothes off. If they weren't here, Trent would be back in Bangkok and Reed would be riding in the front seat of one of these trucks with Boontung, as one of the team and not as his prisoner.

"So, what is the plan?" Trent whispered, glancing sideways at the snoozing guards.

"I'll have to see how many men they have at the dig site. I helped to hide the Buddha, so I know the caves and the terrain around there like the back of my hand. There are places we can hide if we can get away from these guys."

"Like after they go to sleep tonight?"

"Not tonight. They'll probably have someone guard us until they think I won't try to run. Boontung needs me to help them sell the statue, but he won't expect me to run and risk losing a big payout." Reed took a slow breath as he considered the options. "No, it will have to happen later. Can you hang tight for now?"

Trent nodded.

One of the guards shifted on the bench and slowly opened his eyes, elbowing the other guard until both were wide awake again, staring menacingly at Reed and Trent.

The truck stopped while Boontung spoke with his men, clearly discussing a plan. Reed did his best to try to overhear Boontung's words, hoping it would give him a clue as to how to arrange their escape.

12

AS THEY drove, the villages got farther apart and smaller. Some were little more than a handful of ramshackle huts scattered along the side of the increasingly rough road. In every tiny hamlet Trent noticed one constant: one building in good repair, usually with the familiar steeply sloped roof that signified a temple. Even in the far-flung reaches of Thailand, the people held the same reverence for religion as in the capital.

They stopped again at a small village where Boontung and another of the men got out of their truck and struck up a conversation with the first person they saw, a dusty middle-aged man wearing drab khakis and a frayed shirt that might have been white at some point.

"Can you understand what they're saying, Reed?" Trent kept his eyes on Boontung, not caring if the guards in the back of the truck overheard their conversation.

"Boontung wants to hire men to guide them around the caves and to help with the digging."

The local man shook his head violently and rushed away.

"Doesn't look like he's having much luck."

"The man said the caves are sacred ground. Anyone who goes there will be cursed. I can't tell exactly since he's using a local dialect I'm not familiar with. They seem to be particularly superstitious in this village."

"Is that good or bad for us?"

"I'm not sure. Probably good. If they don't get a local guide, they'll rely more on me, especially since I obtained the map." Reed squinted in the dusk as he tried to follow the conversation as Boontung approached another man, this one slightly younger than the first. This man also rushed off, and Boontung and his lieutenant strode away from the trucks, clearly in search of less superstitious locals.

"Those older men are going to be more easily spooked than the younger generation" Trent observed. "Probably easier to sway the younger ones with money too."

"Good point. Yes, the younger generation—even in a remote area like this—are aware of and want the same modern devices and toys as the city kids have." Reed nodded and his expression held a look of respect that somehow made Trent feel a sense of satisfaction he'd actually impressed Reed, rather than merely amused him. Reed's approval meant a lot to Trent. He wanted to be appreciated for more than just the way he was able to please Reed physically. It was obvious Reed didn't trust or respect many people, so earning his approval was difficult and significant. Trent smiled.

While they waited for Boontung to come back, his men stretched their legs, staying close to the vehicles, leaning against them smoking and chatting. Cigarette smoke drifted into the back of the truck and Trent wrinkled his nose as it mingled with the other prominent scents of this village: cooking, trash, and the ever-present aroma of incense wafting from the direction of the tiny temple a hundred yards down the road from where they'd stopped.

"Stay here; I'll be back." Reed mumbled a few words to their guards, who had jumped out of the back of the truck and sat on the back bumper. One of them responded and Reed joined them on the ground.

Trent watched as he took the cigarette one of the men offered him and lit it. Reed inhaled deeply, blowing smoke out of his nose, the wisps disappearing into the deepening dusk. Reed smoked? He was full of surprises, clearly not all of them good. As he smoked, he chatted with the guards. Then he wandered over to one of the other vehicles and spoke with the men who hovered around it.

What is he doing? Trent couldn't help wonder why they'd let Reed loose and why Reed hadn't taken him along. He stood and stretched his own legs, which were slightly cramping after sitting in the back of the truck on the uncomfortable bench for hours. One of the guards at the back turned around and shouted at him in a warning tone, but quickly went back to conversation with his compatriot.

IT WAS late when the little convoy—including another dozen men they'd managed to collect at various villages on the way—arrived at the caves and Boontung quickly ordered the men to set up camp. Several men unpacked the digging equipment from the back of one truck while others put up tents. They'd brought a generator and soon strung up lights between the tents. Trent couldn't help but think the makeshift village reminded him of the 4077th compound on *M*A*S*H*, a favorite show from his childhood. He wondered if he'd ever watch it—or anything else—again.

Trent and Reed weren't expected to help and, clearly, cuffed together at the ankles as they were, they probably wouldn't have been able to contribute much to the task of making camp.

"Why do you suppose they cuffed us now, when they left us free before?"

"I don't know."

This was the first time Reed had admitted to not knowing something. Trent wasn't sure if he should be glad to discover Reed wasn't perfect, or whether he ought to worry Reed wouldn't be able to keep them both safe.

"They wouldn't kill us, would they? Not after they dragged us here to the caves. I mean, they could have killed us a lot sooner." Trent searched for explanations to cheer himself up.

"Boontung needs me to contact the buyer, so he'll keep me around. Don't worry."

"But he doesn't need *me*." As soon as he spoke, Trent remembered the overly personal pat-down he'd gotten from Boontung and hoped he was right.

"He's probably figured out if he does anything to you, I'm less likely to cooperate."

The thought cheered Trent for only a moment before he realized Reed might have to take a lot more abuse to keep him safe. He certainly didn't want to be the cause of Reed getting injured any more. Trent already knew most of the unfortunate things that had happened since his arrival in Bangkok had been his fault. Reed getting caught and beat up that first night, Reed chasing after the bus, and the fight with Supachai…. Trent gulped when it sank in that Reed had to kill a man because of Trent's stubbornness.

Sure, Supachai was a gangster and probably deserved it, but Trent could tell killing him had taken a personal toll on Reed, and that was far more painful for Trent to contemplate than a dead Thai crook.

They sat on the hard ground in silence and watched the activity around them.

Someone brought them water bottles and spoke briefly to Reed.

"They have beds for us in one of the tents," Reed translated.

The man watched as Trent and Reed got to their feet, awkward and clumsy as they tried to get accustomed to the cuffs binding their ankles together. The Thai laughed softly as he watched them struggle. Then he walked off toward one of the tents while Reed and Trent attempted to synchronize their steps to follow him.

When Trent thought of Reed and handcuffs, this was definitely not the image that sprang to mind. At first they bumped into each other and brushed together, and even the slight awkward contact got him slightly aroused. Not particularly appropriate given the danger they were in, but a pleasant distraction.

The Thai held the flap open and Reed was about to duck in when Boontung walked up. He spoke briefly to the guard, who rushed off on some more urgent errand. Reed didn't bother to translate, so Trent assumed it wasn't important.

Boontung motioned them inside the tent. It was low-ceilinged and dim, the only light coming from the half-open flap at the entrance. Two cots lined the opposite wall and a case of bottled water stood in the center of the tent. The place smelled like dirt. It was really no worse than the hut, but it made the Pink Tiger Hotel seem like a palace.

A silent nod from Boontung indicated they were expected to sit down on one of the cots while he sat on the other, facing them from across the tent. With slightly better coordination than before, Reed and Trent managed to sit down without falling or doing another Abbott and Costello impersonation.

As they settled themselves, the Thai who'd brought them to the tent returned with Trent's backpack and suitcase. He sighed with relief at the sight and held out a hand, but the man handed the pack to Boontung, turned on his heel, and left.

Boontung spent a few minutes acquainting himself with Trent's belongings. Even in the low light Trent could easily make out the smile on his face, and accompanied as it was by occasional laughter, it was clear the man was enjoying himself. Trent chewed the inside of his lower lip and racked his brain for what could possibly be so amusing. Next to him on the cot, Reed stayed silent, but the firm pressure of his leg, thigh to knee against Trent's, was warm and reassuring.

Boontung tossed the pack aside and walked over to Reed and Trent. Trent noticed him glance at the chain connecting their cuffed ankles and hoped he was going to remove it, but he didn't.

Instead, he grabbed Trent's wrist and, with one swift movement, he had cuffed Trent's arm to one of the metal bars on the cot's frame. He stepped back a pace and chuckled as Trent rubbed his wrist, now smarting from the roughness of Boontung's treatment. Reed still hadn't said a word and Trent glared at him, hoping Reed could read his mind again.

Boontung took a step toward the exit, then glanced at the water bottles. He kicked them closer to the cot, so they were within Reed's reach. On his way out he picked up the backpack, pulled something out, and examined it for a moment. Trent couldn't see what it was but he tossed the item to Reed, who caught it easily since both his hands were free. Boontung muttered something and laughed like a hyena before departing.

"He's leaving us alone until morning," Reed translated, and handed Trent the item Boontung had left them.

The tube of piña colada lube.

Trent felt himself blush so furiously he worried his face and neck might illuminate the entire tent.

"We said we were going to use it next time, didn't we?" Reed's tone was entirely too cheerful for Trent, and Trent glared again. Even in the dimness, there was no way Reed could miss it.

"You mean he knows we… we're…."

"Of course he does. That wasn't an act when he gave you that extra personal pat down before." Trent blushed again at the memory of Boontung's rough hands on him when they'd been captured. He hadn't realized Boontung had been feeling him up until now.

"Anyway, why does it matter? I thought you were out."

"I am, but this is different."

"Why?"

"He's a Thai mobster!"

"You haven't been in Thailand long, but surely even you've noticed they're fairly laid-back about anything remotely sexual in this country."

"I guess...." Trent paused for a second as he absorbed the implied insult. Then he decided to ignore it.

"Besides, if anyone is going to be unhappy about Boontung knowing, it's me." Reed chuckled again and Trent's anger flared.

"Why?"

"Because he also made a few comments about what he'd like to do with your cute little ass. He'd already have had a go at you if his own boyfriend wasn't around."

"God, no!" Trent gaped at Reed and pressed his knees together. "What boyfriend?"

"Yeah, the guy driving the truck Boontung was riding in. Are you going to tell me you didn't notice?"

Trent shook his head. "No. But then again I was really only paying attention to you."

"You do know how to flatter a man, don't you? Don't worry, though. I'll protect you."

Trent huffed, expecting another Scarlett O'Hara remark from Reed but none came. Instead, Reed shifted on the cot next to him and leaning in close, face and body so close to Trent, but not touching. Trent waited for a touch, a brush of lips, his body anticipating. Craving.

Nothing.

Trent only had to move a millimeter to close the gap, lips brushing Reed's. Oh, God, even the minimal point of contact ignited every nerve ending in Trent's lips and kept going, all the way down toward his cock, each one firing a burst of excitement and relief. He needed to feel Reed close and hard and comforting. Then Reed increased the pressure on Trent's mouth, his stubble a pleasant counter to the softness of his lips. Trent opened up to let Reed in and the kiss deepened.

Sharp pain seared its way from Trent's wrist to his shoulder as he tried to embrace Reed. *Fuck.* He'd forgotten he was shackled to the bed. In any other circumstance handcuffs would be exciting, but right now it reminded him they were in danger, prisoners of a Thai thug with enough guns to arm a revolution in a small third-world nation.

"Careful." Reed pulled back and rubbed Trent's wrist, easing the pain away. "You're probably better off if you lie down. Then you can keep your arm at your side and it might be more comfortable."

"Okay."

"No argument from you?" Reed planted a soft kiss, half-missing Trent's mouth in the dark. "That has to be a first."

Trent bit back a reply, wanting Reed's touch more than a quarrel, and let Reed take control. He hadn't forgotten his arguing about being sent to Bangkok had gotten them in this situation in the first place.

"Just stand up for a minute and let me see...." Reed walked toward the other cot, pulling Trent along with him until he could just grab onto it with his fingers and drag it back toward the other. It took a minute of rearranging cots and limbs until they were lying side by side on a surprisingly sturdy double-wide cot.

"Now, where were we?" Reed rolled up against Trent and resumed kissing.

Reed's lips ignited all his pleasure points again and he was lost to the power of his own incredible attraction to Reed. Even if his brain told him it was madness to attempt any sort of lovemaking handcuffed to a cot—and Reed—while being held prisoner, his body quickly took over and was running the show.

Reed pressed up close and Trent felt his erection against one hip, further inflaming his own desire. He opened his mouth to welcome Reed's tongue and let out a soft moan. Reed wrapped his arms around Trent, and they kissed for a long time. Unconsciously, Trent thrust his hips toward Reed, seeking more contact, friction, and he groaned in frustration as his clothing became an obstacle to his release.

At this, Reed lifted his head and rolled to one side of Trent.

"Don't stop."

"I'm not."

Trent hadn't realized he'd spoken.

"Just going to get some of these clothes out of the way, okay?"

"Yes." It was more a groan than a word and Trent could see Reed's cocky grin, now his eyes had gotten accustomed to the dark. The man never changed, did he? Even in a dangerous situation like this he played it cool, as confident and aware of his effect on Trent as he had been when he'd offered to fuck Trent in the name of research. Trent couldn't help laughing at how much had changed in such a short time. Had it only been two nights ago?

Deftly, Reed peeled back Trent's shirt, then his own, before going to work on Trent's pants. These new accommodations were similar to the hut, though they were no longer alone, and no longer free. But they were together and that counted for so much more than Trent could have imagined only a day earlier.

Reed's fingers brushed along Trent's abs and electricity spiked through his body. He lifted his hips to help Reed slide his pants down and waited impatiently for Reed to slip as far out of his own pants as their cuffed ankles would allow. Reed lay back down, and his weight was welcome pressure on Trent's body. He sought the heat and the hardness of Reed.

Luckily his arm was in a position where he could carefully reach and stroke along Reed's hip and the curve of his ass as he lay on top of Trent, the heat from his smooth skin burning. He resumed kissing until Trent's grunts and increasingly insistent bucking made it abundantly clear Trent wanted much more than kissing and foreplay, no matter how good it felt.

Reed settled himself on his knees between Trent's thighs, ankles touching where they were bound together, and located the lube. In the dimness, Trent could just see the way Reed's cock jutted out from his body, wonderfully hard and thick. He sighed at how fantastic every touch of Reed's hands or lips or body made him feel. Reed leaned forward and sucked a nipple, and Trent forced himself to swallow the moan that nearly escaped his lips. When Reed licked a hot wet stripe along the underside of Trent's cock, he nearly lost it right there, and he fought for control of his body. When Reed swirled his tongue around the head of Trent's cock, then took him deep, it was the end. Pleasure and relief crashed through Trent's body and rolled like waves over him and he didn't even attempt to stop it from happening.

After Reed had swallowed every drop of Trent's release, he gently licked and kissed his way down Trent's cock and nuzzled at his balls, prolonging the wonderful sensations. All the while he stroked and caressed any part of Trent he could reach with his good hand.

It didn't matter a single iota that Trent hadn't lasted very long. With anyone else he would have been mortified not to hold on longer, but Reed neither said nor did anything to make Trent feel self-conscious.

He simply leaned forward, kissed Trent deeply, letting Trent taste himself on Reed's lips and tongue.

"Thank you." Reed's whisper was husky.

"Shouldn't it be the other way around?"

"No."

Trent was getting used to Reed's cryptic replies even if he couldn't yet interpret them. He also knew he never felt happier or more desirable than he did at that moment, though he couldn't explain precisely why.

Much to Trent's surprise, Reed didn't immediately slick his fingers up and prep Trent. Instead, he kissed his way back down Trent's body, paying special attention to each nipple, licking and sucking until they budded and stiffened in his mouth and he had Trent moaning and squirming beneath him again. Trent watched with wide-eyed joy as Reed seemed to get as much pleasure from every touch and kiss and caress as Trent did.

It didn't take long before Trent's body had recovered and again taken control away from his brain and he found himself as hard and impatient as he had been before Reed had sucked him off. When Reed's finger finally pressed inside, he was ready for more and his body welcomed the stretch and pull. He groaned "yes" and "hurry" more times than he wanted to admit and eventually Reed slipped on a condom he pulled from his pocket and entered Trent slowly and carefully.

Reed filled Trent up, moving exquisitely slowly, though in the end, he didn't last much longer than Trent. At one point he stopped moving completely, settling back on his heels, still inside of Trent, while he used his hands to bring Trent to orgasm again before allowing himself to come with a muffled sound resembling a sigh more than a groan. Afterward, he lay on top of Trent, stroking his throat and collarbone.

With one arm useless, Trent could only caress Reed's side and back, and in the dark his fingers traced along the raised ridges of scar tissue crisscrossing Reed's back like a road map. He imagined the path Reed had taken in his life to end up here with Trent.

13

"WHO'S Marc? You said his name in your sleep." Reed watched Trent rub his eyes as he came fully awake.

"Marc?" The look of near terror on Trent's face told Reed he'd hit a touchy subject, but it was too late to un-ask the question.

"My… uh… boyfriend. Partner." Trent rolled away from Reed and huddled at the far edge of the cot, as far from Reed as he could get, given his limited mobility.

Reed hadn't expected his stomach to drop ten stories at Trent's response. Boyfriend? *Partner?* The words cut deep into the unexpected contentment Reed had experienced since he'd met Trent.

"I was under the impression you were single." Reed swallowed but the lump in his throat still threatened to choke him. "Is he in LA?"

"No." Trent's voice was so soft Reed could barely hear the reply. "He's dead."

"Oh, God. I'm sorry." Reed hated himself for the sense of relief he felt. But even a dead lover was competition if Trent hadn't completely gotten over his loss. "You don't have to tell me. I won't ask again."

"It's okay. It happened two years ago."

Trent sounded so forlorn Reed wanted to put his arms around him and make him feel safe, but it didn't seem like a good idea at the moment. He needed to let Trent control the rest of this conversation.

"I'll tell you. I want to." Trent rolled back toward Reed, eyes red-rimmed and full of pain.

Reed reached out to stroke Trent's shoulder and got a small smile in return, but a couple of tears spilled out of Trent's eyes.

"Marc ran an art gallery in LA. He was very successful but he always complained it was boring. He'd travel sometimes for work, and I'd go with him, but most of the time he was at the gallery sucking up to rich people—as he put it.

"So, for excitement, he bought a motorcycle."

Reed thought he knew where this was going, but Trent hadn't objected to the prospect of Reed taking him on the bike.

"No, he didn't die in a motorcycle accident." Trent had read Reed's mind. "After a while the bike wasn't enough and he needed something else: hang gliding, off-trail skiing, bungee jumping, skydiving. None of those are particularly dangerous if you do it right and you take safety precautions. I even did some of it with him, until fear outweighed the fun for me."

"You jumped out of a plane?" Reed couldn't keep incredulity out of his voice.

"Yeah, with the instructor—not on my own. Still, I didn't worry about Marc until some of his skydiving friends got him talking about BASE jumping. That's where you jump off of something instead of out of a plane."

"I've heard of it. It's a lot more dangerous."

"Right. A lot of people get hurt when they crash against the cliff or building. Well, Marc went with these friends to jump off some cliffs in Mexico." Trent paused and Reed realized he'd been holding his breath, dreading the predictable conclusion to Trent's story. "I couldn't eat or sleep or write, waiting for him to call to say he was okay after they'd jumped."

Reed swallowed, waiting for the inevitable.

"Eventually he called. He was fine. Not a scratch on him." Trent laughed, a wry, bitter sound. "Maybe he thought he was invincible after that. The week after he came back, he went skydiving at his club—a fairly routine jump he'd done dozens of times." This time Trent's pause was tellingly long. "His chute failed and by the time he pulled the reserve, it was too late and he hit the ground too fast. They think he didn't check his equipment properly."

"Damn." There wasn't really a lot to say.

"I don't think it was just the equipment." Trent looked Reed in the eye for the first time since the subject of Marc had come up. "I think he hesitated on purpose, trying to make the jump more exciting. That's what he'd always say: 'I want more excitement.'" This time Trent looked away again. "I wasn't enough to keep him happy and he had to seek 'excitement' elsewhere. I just wasn't exciting enough."

"You can't possibly blame yourself for that!" Reed instantly hated Marc for making Trent so insecure he'd thought Marc's death was his fault.

"I figured that out after a while, but I've had a kind of aversion to excitement since then." Trent let out a feeble laugh and a weak smile. "I've been lying low, avoiding almost anything new, like I'd be safer if I just did the same things and ate at the same restaurants. I let myself stagnate because I was too afraid to take any risks."

"The last few days must have been really tough for you." Reed understood now why Trent was so timid initially, and he was even more impressed with the way Trent had handled himself since Boontung had taken them.

"It was at first, but... but with you, I felt safe." Trent shrugged and closed his eyes. More tears spilled out.

Reed leaned forward and took Trent in his arms, kissing his hair and stroking his arm and back as sobs wracked his body. The thrill from taking risks was familiar to Reed. He'd taken on jobs just because other agents considered them too dangerous. Maybe it was for the excitement or because he didn't think he had much to lose, even if he got killed. But Marc had been selfish and that was completely different. Marc left Trent behind, blaming himself. If Reed had someone like Trent waiting at home, he would have done so many things in his life differently.

DURING the second night, Trent tossed and turned on the cot next to Reed, and Reed couldn't sleep either. He put out a hand and stroked Trent's shoulder. Trent rolled over to face Reed, causing his cot to creak and nearly overturn. Reed leaned forward and ran his fingers through Trent's unruly locks. "What's wrong?" Stupid question, considering the guy was cuffed to a cot in the middle of nowhere in Northeast Thailand.

"You." Trent let out a sigh.

Not what Reed had expected and he wished now he hadn't asked. He was starting to sound like one of the guys in Trent's books. And so was Trent. Reed wondered if he didn't prefer fucking to lovemaking after all. So much less emotional crap to deal with.

"Don't you ever get scared? Getting beat up. Guys pointing guns at you. Knife fights."

"Not really."

"That's just not normal. That kind of stuff should scare you, even if you're a....trained to deal with it."

Reed let out a breath. He'd worried Trent might say "FBI agent" or something that might be overheard and understood by one of Boontung's people. But Trent seemed to grasp the danger in their situation. "It's not a question of normal or not. I can't let any of it scare me or I can't do my job."

"But why?"

"Why what?"

"Why do you put yourself at risk like this? To stop some guy from smuggling a chunk of stone or whatever that statue is made of? How is that worth anyone's life?" Trent reached out for Reed's hand and took it in his. "How is that worth *your* life?"

"Because Kao Lung isn't just an antiquities smuggler, and he isn't just a drug dealer. He smuggles people, mostly young girls, young boys and they end up like slaves in the sex trade, in Hong Kong, Taiwan, Singapore. Used up, addicted to drugs and dead before most American kids get their driver's licenses. In comparison, the drug trafficking is inconsequential. Sure, he gets people addicted, and I'm not saying it isn't a huge problem, globally. But what he does to these kids, who're just trying to find a better life, thinking they'll be maids or houseboys, and then end up as some pervert's toys. That's worth risking lives."

Reed stopped to breathe, and because Trent's face had gone pale.

"I didn't have any idea. When you explained about the antiquities and the golf, and the race horses, it didn't sound so serious."

"It's deadly serious and very important. But if I ever hesitate or wonder if I should just give up, I try to put myself in one of those kids' shoes. How scared is he or she? What's his life going to be like if I don't do my job?"

He thought about the photos he'd seen, of the kids he'd met who'd told their stories. He never tried to put those images out of his mind. In fact he did his best not to forget a single face or one detail of their stories. He'd never tell Trent half of what he knew; Trent couldn't handle it, and Reed liked how Trent hadn't seen the worst in life. "I can't let Boontung or Supachai or even Kao Lung scare me. I just have to think faster, be smarter than they are, stay one step ahead. Or I could end up like one of those kids." Or worse. The scars on Reed's back stung in recollection.

Trent let out a sad little sound. "I guess I fucked that strategy up. I—"

Reed put a finger against Trent's lips, enjoying the warmth and the expression of surprise that crossed Trent's face.

Reed almost agreed with Trent but he stopped before a reply left his mouth. The look on Trent's face was so despondent. Like he felt personally responsible not just for getting them caught back at the hut but for the fact that Kao Lung was still breathing.

Trent gave a bitter smile. "I think I finally get it. Get *you*. I thought you were like Marc, chasing the danger for the thrill. And yeah, I was mad you got me caught up in it. But now, I see why you do it. I just don't know why you came back to the hut, once you got the map. It ruined your plans."

"Good. So promise me, when the time comes, you'll listen to me, follow my directions to the letter."

"I can do that."

"You trust me?"

Trent looked directly into Reed's eyes and nodded. "Yeah, I trust you."

Now, for the first time in a very long time, Reed *was* scared.

LATER that night they made love, quietly and awkwardly on the cots.

Reed slid off of Trent but stayed close, their bodies tightly pressed together despite the heat and humidity. The need for closeness and Trent's touch was far stronger than any desire for comfort. He made sure to stay away from Trent's shackled wrist and instinctively chose a position that made it difficult for Trent to reach his back. He'd come to terms with the scars on his body and how he'd gotten them, but he still preferred to keep that part of his life separate from what he shared with

Trent. One miscalculation on Reed's part had left Trent prisoner rather than safe on a bus to Bangkok, and it was more than Reed could handle. Fear that Trent might end up with even one scar to show for the ordeal terrified him.

He listened as Trent fell asleep. Thank God he could sleep despite the mess they were in. Reed knew Trent trusted him, which terrified Reed even more. He hoped he could keep Trent safe. One reason Reed preferred to work alone was to avoid having to worry about another agent. This was worse in so many ways: Trent was no trained agent and Reed had already come to care far too much about him to be able to simply do his job without concern for potential collateral damage.

Trent. Their lovemaking hadn't lasted long tonight, but it had left Reed even more content and satisfied than he'd been after an entire night of passion like the one they'd shared only forty-eight hours earlier. Reed had never before felt this way, and a weight like a boulder sinking deep in his gut warned him he was unlikely to feel this ever again.

Feel? Reed didn't allow himself to have feelings; he had *duties,* responsibilities.

Trent, on the other hand, was nothing but feelings and emotions. Every look or movement gave away whatever he was thinking at any moment. But that was what drew Reed to him. He was so refreshingly ingenuous, innocent. So real.

Reed had spent too many years with people pretending to be one thing or another: his father, his fellow soldiers, his first partner, his Thai associates, the scum he had to work with to accomplish his missions. It got easy after a while. The first time you shoot a man, or let a complete stranger take possession of you—body or soul—was the worst. That was gut wrenching, soul crushing. Reed reminded himself of this whenever he thought of those kids that Kao Lung and his triad destroyed, bought and sold like sacks of rice. Used up and replaced just as easily.

With practice, you could get used to anything. Reed was an expert at that. The last thing he wanted was for Trent to end up like him.

AFTER the first two days, Boontung didn't bother to keep Trent cuffed, though most of the time someone guarded them. Even Boontung had figured out he wouldn't leave without Reed, and Reed wouldn't leave before he got his cut—once the buyer paid. It certainly made lovemaking much easier, though Trent admitted he had enjoyed discovering different positions necessitated by the restraints. Reed filed that information away for later use.

There was a spring near the camp that afforded a place to bathe, and Reed convinced Boontung to let him and Trent clean up. Reed's bandaged arm made bathing difficult, but Trent was happy to wash him, a comforting, intimate experience, though the presence of their guard kept it from being completely enjoyable. At first Reed protested as Trent's hands soaped his back, but he eventually relaxed. He had nothing to hide anymore; Trent had seen the scars even in daylight and they hadn't scared him off.

Because his good arm was unusable, Reed couldn't shave, but Trent gladly offered to do that as well. He spread shaving cream—coconut scented, of course—on Reed and slowly pulled the razor across his cheeks and jawline, using one hand to reposition Reed's chin as needed. Like the bathing, this was done in such a loving way, the scrape of blade against skin was a profoundly sensual experience, and Reed found it far too arousing given the presence of the guard.

Back in the tent, Trent gently toweled Reed dry, this time in complete privacy, and Reed fully intended to follow through on every lustful thought he'd had back at the spring.

"Hey, what're you doing?" Reed pulled away when Trent smoothed something cool and fragrant on his back.

"I just thought this lotion would help. It's got all sorts of healing herbs and essential oils in it. Maybe make the scars less noticeable. I know you don't like them, and I thought you'd feel better if they went away."

"It won't help," Reed nearly barked, his original intentions forgotten, and Trent backed away, hurt-puppy look on his face. That wasn't strictly true. Reed had never considered treating them. He assumed they were there to stay and he tried to forget about them. "Now I smell like—"

"Like a girl?" Trent sounded like a dog that had been kicked. "I fucked up. Sorry. I made a big mistake and I won't do it again." He got up and huffed out of the tent, the first time he'd been apart from Reed since they'd gotten here.

Reed swore in Thai. He was the one who'd fucked up. He had actually been about to say he smelled like Trent, intending it to be a compliment, but his lack of experience with compliments had left Trent feeling insulted. Damn. No wonder he'd so carefully avoided relationships and entanglements. Practically everything he said upset Trent. It was only when they were quiet and related on a purely physical level that Reed managed not to offend him. That Reed actually cared about Trent's feelings made him realize he had a lot to learn, which, despite his failures so far, he desperately wanted.

Trent barely spoke to Reed the rest of the day, and the Thais whispered and joked about it. Thankfully Trent couldn't understand, and Reed would never let him know. Even though the misunderstanding had been over something petty, Reed wouldn't push Trent for reconciliation. After what he'd been through during the past few days, it was no wonder something so slight had set him off. The amount of mental strain he must be under was staggering, and Reed cut him plenty of slack. They'd sort everything out when Trent was ready.

In some ways the misunderstanding was timely and could be useful. With a little emotional space between them, it would be that much easier to get Trent to leave on his own when it was time to carry out the plan.

While Trent lay on his cot that night—he'd pulled the cots apart in a not particularly subtle indication he was still upset—Reed concentrated on how to get Trent out of captivity.

"I've come up with a plan, and I put the things you'll need in the daypack." Reed spoke to Trent's back, knowing he wasn't asleep yet. "You'll keep your money and ID on you in the money belt."

No response.

"I know you're mad at me, but I need for you to listen while I explain everything."

"I'm listening."

"Your life could depend on this, Trent. Please don't let your anger with me put you in any more danger."

Trent sat up and faced Reed. He dug in his pocket for that damned little notebook and pen he carried everywhere and stared expectantly at Reed, pen poised.

Reed explained what each of them needed to do. Trent took it in and nodded as he made notes. When Reed had finished they discussed several aspects in greater detail until Reed was confident Trent trusted him and could carry out the plan to the letter.

All that was left undetermined was when they'd put the plan into effect, and Trent agreed to let Reed make the decision.

Almost as a reward, Trent pushed the cots together again, but when they finally got in bed together, he kept his distance and didn't encourage any physical contact from Reed.

Disappointed, Reed knew it was better if Trent was still a little upset; it would make it easier for the plan to work for Trent to escape on his own. And for Reed, the plan was designed entirely with the goal of keeping Trent safe.

14

"SO, LET'S just go tonight." Trent's voice held a mixture of excitement and fear. It was the third morning of their captivity. "Both of us."

"No. We need to wait until they find the Buddha. They'll be distracted and it'll be easier to get away. Trust me." How many times had Trent trusted him so far? Reed hated asking for so much faith from Trent, especially after the misunderstanding of the previous day. At first the fear of disappointing Trent or getting him hurt nearly paralyzed Reed, but eventually he'd come up with a solution, as long as Trent did his part. He had to remember they were both safer if Reed gave his full attention to the job.

"And you know I can't leave with you. I still have a role to play to get the real mission back on track."

Trent sighed and kicked at the dust with the toe of his shoe. Reed was in two minds about Trent's reaction: he needed Trent to leave when the time came, but he was glad to see Trent still wanted to be with Reed, regardless of Reed's verbal faux pas.

As luck would have it, the diggers came across the Buddha late that afternoon, gleeful shouts and hoots announcing the discovery. Boontung insisted on supervising the excavation once they unearthed a corner of the statue. He ordered Trent and Reed to help with the more delicate task of retrieving the Buddha, thinking they would be more careful than his burly thugs.

"Wow! Is that gold?" Trent asked when he'd first seen the glittering object still mostly buried. Even Reed would have believed Trent thought it was genuine.

They'd uncovered less than half—Buddha's head and part of one shoulder of the approximately three-foot-tall statue—when Boontung decided to stop for the day and celebrate the discovery. First he set three men to guard the statue.

Clever, Reed thought. *Three men can never agree on anything. It's a safe number to choose when you want to make sure they don't plot against you.* Maybe Boontung was smarter than Reed had given him credit for.

With the guard set, Boontung distributed a few cases of beer he'd been saving for the occasion and doled them out to the workers, while he shared a bottle of whiskey with a couple of his mobsters. He poured out two cups of whiskey for Trent and Reed, though they stayed near the edge of the circle as the Thais toasted their luck and future fortunes.

"GO, NOW. Run!" Reed spoke emphatically, but quietly, while shooing Trent away as unobtrusively as possible.

Trent stood there for a moment, unable to move. Now the time had come, he couldn't leave now, on his own. Reed had to come with him. It wasn't that he couldn't handle the situation without Reed; he didn't *want* to.

"No. I can't leave you here!"

"If you don't go now, we'll both be trapped. You promised to trust me on this. Get out of here, and let me do my part to get them in contact with Kao Lung."

Trent remained, fixed to the spot.

"Trust me!" Reed glanced behind him and must have seen Boontung's men coming, because he tried to wave Trent away again, like a stray dog. "You know how important this is, what's at stake."

Trent did know. He hadn't stopped thinking about it once Reed explained: stopping Kao Lung from harming anyone else. Trent wanted to help put him away, and he wanted Reed to be proud of him for doing his part, even if Trent's part was leaving Reed.

Reluctantly, Trent ran.

The plan called for Trent to hide in a nearby cave Reed had described. They'd passed it on the way to the digging camp, and Reed had drawn a map—which he'd forced Trent to memorize—and then destroyed it in case one of the Thais discovered it or their plan. Trent recalled the directions as he ran. He had the flashlight and some food he'd managed to hide in his pockets: a few handfuls of rice wrapped in a piece of cloth. It wouldn't last long, but it would keep him going until dark when he would make his way to the nearest village. Reed had taught him a few important Thai words and written them down, to help him communicate once he got there. Trent was to wait in the village until Reed could get away and join him.

He rushed off, struggling to remember Reed's directions in his fear and excitement. Right here, then left. Go straight until you see the fifteen-foot-tall boulder covering the entrance to the cave. According to Reed, the Thais wouldn't even notice the entrance unless they were looking for it. Reed would distract them with talk about the money they'd earn on the sale of the Ruby Buddha while Trent hid in the cave. By the time they realized he'd escaped, they wouldn't be able to find him.

Trent jogged quietly, keeping to the hillside and staying low so his movements wouldn't be so obvious in case anyone happened to be looking in his direction. His ankle had almost completely recovered, but at Reed's suggestion, he'd limped and favored it, lulling the Thais into thinking he couldn't run away if he wanted to. Soon, he recognized the huge boulder. Until he got right up to it he couldn't see the entrance to the cave. It was a perfect hiding spot.

Thank God Reed had helped select the hiding place for the fake Buddha, so he knew the area around these caves well. This cave wasn't even on the map; Reed had only noticed it when he'd come up here to hide the Buddha. It seemed Reed had planned for any contingency. Knowing someone as capable and resourceful as Reed was attracted to him still surprised Trent; it made him feel special.

He removed the backpack and began to squeeze through the narrow opening, wondering if he would fit. For the first time in his life, he wished he had a smaller physique. He entered the space between the boulder and the edge of the cave opening, the boulder hard and cool against his cheek as he attempted to slip between the proverbial—and suddenly literal—rock and a hard place. He exhaled completely, emptying his lungs of every molecule of air before he managed to slip into the cave. The ragged edges of the rocks tore his shirt and scraped his chest and back, but he barely noticed until he was safely inside. He reached into his pocket for the flashlight but it wasn't there.

Fuck! The flashlight must have fallen out as he struggled to squeeze through the narrow space. He got as close to the slit as possible and reached out a hand, feeling around on the ground outside the cave for the cold metal. Nothing. He got closer, craning his head at an angle so he could extend his reach, and his fingertips brushed the edge of the flashlight. He was so close, but he couldn't manage to pull it close enough to grab. He considered going back through the slit when he heard men running outside and shouting.

Looking for me! Damn it!

He couldn't go out now or he'd be caught. On the other hand, the flashlight on the ground near the boulder would be a sure sign he was nearby. He couldn't risk someone seeing it. Now his chest was heaving simply out of fear of discovery, and he couldn't get close enough to reach the flashlight. *Calm down or you'll get caught!* Reed would be calm and collected in the same situation, and Trent tried to pretend he was Reed. Just pretend you're *writing* this, not living it! A few deep calming breaths and he managed to snake his arm out again, very slowly, and hook his finger under the rim of the flashlight so it rolled in his direction.

Yahtzee!

He snatched the flashlight and pulled his arm back just as one of the men ran within a few feet of the slit. Thank God! He'd been worried his movement might catch someone's attention. Too close for comfort, but Trent sat on the floor of the cave, willing himself to calm down again. He turned toward the deep recess of the cave now, face to face with nothing but empty blackness.

At that moment Trent realized he was afraid of the dark. Not the kid-needing-a-nightlight kind of afraid, but a cold, deep fear of the unknown that lay somewhere in front of him. The sky was darkening and there was almost no light coming from the crack between the cave wall and the boulder. He couldn't see even the outline of his body anymore. He could still hear men shouting outside the cave and knew he couldn't turn the flashlight on just yet.

If Reed saw me now, he'd laugh his ass off and call me "Lilac" again. Trent let out a tiny nervous laugh, but just the idea of Reed saying those words was enough to distract him from the darkness. Instead, he closed his eyes. That way he couldn't see just how dark the cave was. He concentrated on the sounds outside and on his own breathing, like Reed had taught him, and eventually he could feel his heart rate slowing back to normal. He felt strangely calm and alert. *Maybe there's something to meditation, after all.*

He waited until he couldn't hear anything at all from outside before he took the chance of turning on the flashlight. Even when he finally did so, he made sure to point the beam down and away from the entrance, just in case. This cave may not be on the map, but if one of the men searching for him saw any type of movement, it would attract attention. Hopefully they would chalk it up to an animal and not investigate further. What kind of idiot would squeeze into a dark cave like this? Trent laughed again at the realization he was just that kind of idiot. The sound echoed softly from the heart of the cave.

Trent checked his watch. Only ten p.m. Reed warned him to wait until at least two a.m. before leaving the cave to walk five or six miles to the nearest village before getting a ride to a larger town where Reed would meet him. He had hours ahead of him to wait. The battery wouldn't last that long, so he'd have to use the flashlight sparingly. Maybe he could take a nap for a few hours? But what if he didn't wake up in time and slept past the safe time window for escape? That would be dangerous. Trent forced himself to conquer his fear of the dark and what might be in the cave.

He tried the meditation exercises again but it took only fifteen minutes before he was bored senseless by listening to the sound of his own breathing. How on earth did Buddhist monks meditate for hours or days on end? Maybe they were all insane.

Too bad I can't be writing! But he could. While he couldn't actually write, he could work on a mental outline of a new story. He remembered Cass's criticism of his last book: the plots were worn thin and repetitive and his characters sounded like the same two guys over and over. That was why she and Beth had conspired to send him to Thailand in the first place—so he could have an adventure.

Well, he'd had plenty of adventure so far! More than either of them dreamt when they planned this trip. He recalled the day he arrived: meeting Reed in the airport, the first ride in the tuk-tuk. He went over everything that had happened or he'd experienced in the smallest detail, willing himself to remember how he'd felt, how the food had tasted, how the streets had smelled. How Reed's lips had felt the very first time they had kissed.

Mmm… what a delicious memory. Well, maybe not their very first kiss after Reed had insulted him, but pretty much everything *after*. Trent tried to slot the pieces of his memory of people, places, and events into a story line. It was difficult at first without pen and paper to make notes—something he normally was never without. He did have both in the side pocket of his shorts, but he didn't dare use the flashlight to write. This would be a good mental exercise, he decided. Even if he didn't remember all his ideas later on, he'd still have something he could use as a basis for a new book once he got home again.

If he got home again.

He was glad he hadn't brought his laptop to Thailand, or he'd have lost everything. He'd left his suitcase back at the dig site with Reed, but he didn't really expect to see any of his belongings again.

And what about Reed? Would Trent see him again? He checked his watch. Midnight. Despite knowing Reed would stay with Boontung until the sale was arranged, Trent couldn't help hoping he might decide to leave tonight and join Trent here in the cave, and not days later in the village. Trent wanted to believe Reed would come back for him—again.

The past few days had brought them even closer and it had been even harder to leave than Trent expected. It had been one of the most difficult things he'd ever done. Not just because he'd been frightened—he fully admitted that to himself. Worse, he didn't want to leave Reed now that he was getting to know him, breaking through that hard G.I.-Joe-exterior to the living, breathing, man beneath. Had Trent been fooling himself that there could actually be something between them? Had Reed simply been trying to keep him safe, and there was nothing more than simple sexual attraction between them?

A sinking feeling started in the pit of Trent's stomach at the thought he might not see Reed again. Or if he did, what if Reed didn't reciprocate any of Trent's feelings? He tried to convince himself he was just hungry. He took one of the mashed-up balls of rice out of his backpack and nibbled at it in the dark. It tasted awful. Cold and lumpy and sort of linty from the cloth he'd wrapped it in. He didn't know when he'd get his next meal, so he tried to make it last.

He still had over an hour to wait. At least it wasn't completely dark near the entrance. The moon was full and bright and a tiny sliver of light filtered in so he could see his hands and get a general idea of the interior of the cave.

For some inexplicable reason, Trent wanted to venture farther into the cave. It was a mixture of curiosity and determination not to let the darkness get the better of him. He'd already been in more dangerous situations in the past few days than he'd ever experienced in his entire life. How scary could it be to walk into a cave when he had a bright flashlight? *Research*, he told himself.

The cave narrowed as he moved away from the wide chamber near the entrance, and he stayed close to the wall, deciding if the cave branched off, he'd take the left fork each time in order to make it easier to find his way back to the entrance. The last thing he wanted was to end up lost in the cave and die here, because there was no way Reed would even think to look for him here.

The cave did branch off, and Trent discovered there were some rooms off the left fork. He flashed the light around, but didn't dare enter any of them. The ceilings were low and the odor of dirt and something else he couldn't name permeated the heavy air. He wondered if any animals lived in these caves and realized he should have considered that possibility sooner. Ending up as dinner for some wild Thai wolf—or something worse—didn't much appeal to him.

He took two more left forks until he nearly tripped over a stone. He shone the flashlight on it and was surprised to discover it wasn't just a natural rock in the pathway. Half buried in the floor of the cave, it had even edges and looked like it had been shaped with a tool. *Someone's been in here before!* Trent was more intrigued than ever. He checked his watch again: 1:15 a.m. Still time to keep looking around in here.

Shining the light on the ground, he noticed several other stones buried in the hard-packed dirt. Was this some kind of marker or path? Trent ventured farther following these signs. He peeked into the chambers that opened off the main cave and discovered a small stone Buddha in one. The next one had a larger Buddha figure. Each one had the hands in a different position. Something he'd read in the guidebook came back: each Buddha represented a different concept, depending on the position of the hands.

Why had he remembered those details? Trent's friends were constantly ribbing him about his memory for details like this, calling him "Cliff" after the character from *Cheers* who always volunteered some incredibly useless piece of trivia on nearly any topic that came up in conversation. Well, they wouldn't be laughing at him now, would they?

Could there really be a Ruby Buddha hidden in one of these caves? Reed and his bosses had obviously used a real legend when they'd come up with this plan, but maybe it was more than legend. He hurried back to the first few chambers with Buddha figures. All together there were six chambers with Buddhas, each of which demonstrated a different posture. Which one would it be in, assuming it did exist? Trent walked into the first one, shining the flashlight on every surface, looking for a sign of something besides the small stone statue. The ground looked undisturbed, though would it still show evidence of digging even hundreds of years later? Why not, if no one else had been in here since then?

Again, he ran the meanings of the hand positions through his mind until he remembered the one where Buddha's left hand was facing palm out and the fingers pointed toward the ground. This position meant charity or boon-granting. Wouldn't a valuable Buddha statue be associated with this icon, rather than one depicting teaching or fearlessness? Or would they have hidden it with an image totally unrelated to its value, in order to protect it? Trent had no way to decipher what the ancient Thai-Khmer people would have been thinking, but he'd go with the most obvious to start. They'd put the statues here to worship, not to hide them.

He went back into the room with the "charity" Buddha and looked around the statue carefully for indications of digging or a hidden chamber behind it. The basic Indiana Jones search. Trent laughed as the thought went through his mind.

Suddenly, he heard noises from the main tunnel. Could Boontung's men have found him, or was it Reed here to join him after all? Fear gripped him for a moment as he listened for the sound of his name—that would be Reed—or stealthy footsteps of the Thai mobsters. The sound was familiar, though he couldn't place it until it was almost too late. Birds? No, not the flapping of *birds'* wings. He shone the flashlight toward the ceiling, and a mass of bats flew through the weak beam. He ducked as quickly as he could to avoid being hit by any of them.

Bats. Yech. His skin crawled as too many late-night horror movies flooded his memory. Dracula, vampire bats… did they even have vampires in Thailand? What the fuck was he thinking? There were no vampires, except in books and film. It was ridiculous to be more afraid of vampires than Thai thugs with guns. The men posed a much more dangerous—and real—threat to him.

Once the bats had passed, Trent went back into the chamber and resumed his search. He found nothing indicating another statue was buried here, but he hadn't looked behind the statue. He carefully held the flashlight between his teeth so he could see what he was doing and leaned down, trying to move the figure away from the wall of the cave. It was much heavier than he expected, considering the statue was fairly small, only about two feet high. He should be strong enough to scoot it away from the wall enough to see what was behind it.

He strained and finally the stone figure moved a tiny bit. He managed to move it a couple of inches but the exertion already had him breathing hard. He sucked in air and lost his grip on the flashlight. It clanked on the top of the statue as it fell. Then the light went out and he heard batteries scatter in the pitch blackness.

Triple fuck! If he broke the flashlight he might never find his way out of this cave. His pulse raced and his breathing became ragged gasps until he reminded himself he'd never get out of here if he didn't calm down and think logically—like Reed had told him. There's a way out of everything if you just calm down and take stock of all the elements of the situation.

Trent sat on the floor of the small chamber for a minute until he got control of his breathing. *I can do this!* Slowly and methodically, he crawled around on his knees feeling for the pieces of the flashlight. Nothing. Then a fingertip brushed it. At least he hoped it was the flashlight and not a skeleton or something. He'd have to stop watching horror movies.

It turned out to be the barrel of the flashlight. Within a few minutes he'd located the batteries and the cap and was able to reassemble the flashlight. He switched it on and nothing happened. The fear came back twice as quickly as when he'd first dropped the flashlight. Batteries. Maybe he'd put them in incorrectly. He repositioned them and this time the flashlight switched on.

A loud sound echoed through the tiny room and he realized it was his own sigh of relief.

He shone light on the Buddha statue and discovered the flashlight had chipped a piece off the statue when it fell. He peered more closely, worried he might have damaged some relic of cultural and religious importance and he was now going to whatever the Thai Buddhist version of Hell was. But what was under the stone?

As he shone the light again, Trent saw what looked like a flash—or maybe a reflection? Sure enough, under the surface of the stone was something that looked like gold.

Just the too-active imagination of a writer. He'd fallen asleep at the entrance to the cave and now he was dreaming. But he scratched at the stone with a fingernail and revealed a bit more gold! He would have stayed and tried to dig what might be the real Buddha out from under its outer shell, but the flashlight began to flicker, reminding Trent the batteries were running low.

Reluctantly, he worked his way back to the entrance, drawing a rough map on a scrap of paper he had in his pocket. He needed to follow Reed's plan or they'd never find each other again. Once they met up again, they could come back here and see if he really had found something valuable. A quick glance at his watch told him it was time to get the hell out of the cave. Trent had to come to terms with the knowledge Reed would not be joining him tonight and made his own way toward the village.

But Trent had faith in Reed and expected to see him the following days, in a village far enough away from the caves that Boontung's men wouldn't easily be able to follow their movements.

REED glanced up at the nearly full moon, wishing it wasn't so bright tonight. It would be easy for Boontung's men to find Trent if he hadn't made it to the cave before the search party found him. He glanced at his watch for about the thousandth time, silently praying Trent had followed his directions rather than try to improvise his own plan.

It was nearly two a.m. and Boontung's men had been gone for hours. If they'd found him, they would have come back by now, and Reed consoled himself with that knowledge. Six half-drunk men had taken guns and gone hunting for him almost as soon as they'd realized Trent had escaped.

But not before Boontung had given Reed another beating. He'd first asked nicely where Trent was and offered to bring him back. The longer Reed held out, the more vicious Boontung got. He'd surprised

Reed, who hadn't realized the pent-up anger Boontung must have been hiding as Supachai's second in command. Boontung had turned out to be a hothead and far crueler than Supachai had ever been. Supachai was first and foremost a businessman: he did nothing unless he expected a payoff. He'd never beat someone senseless, or he risked not getting the information he needed.

Boontung had come up through the ranks in the military and had learned the business from Supachai, but at heart he was a soldier—a warrior—for whom strength and violence were simply tools. Reed had learned that the hard way and had suffered for his failure to correctly anticipate Boontung's reaction to Trent's disappearance.

Now, Reed lay next to one of the trucks, one wrist handcuffed to a bar behind the front tire. He was again battered and bleeding and his body ached all over. He was able to ignore the pain. Instead he focused his mental energies on imagining where Trent was and what he was doing at that moment.

AT THE appointed time, Trent had left the safety of the cave and run as far as he could before he had to slow to a fast walk, gasping for air. He should have spent more time on cardio at the gym, but he never expected he'd actually need to run anywhere other than on a treadmill. Following Reed's directions and the scribbled map, he came to the little town he was looking for just as the sun came up, brightening his way as well as his spirits. He was supposed to keep going and find a hotel in the next town. He flagged down a tuk-tuk and rode the last few miles, exhausted and mentally drained from the events of the previous night.

He checked into the Sawatdee Hotel with no trouble. Reed said every town had a hotel called Sawatdee—"welcome"—and even though he'd never been in this town, he'd been correct. Trent took one look at himself in the mirror and realized what a mess he was: dirty, sweaty, clothing nearly as filthy and slightly ripped. Despite near-exhaustion, he wanted to get cleaned up and presentable while he waited for Reed to arrive. He found a small clothing shop across the road from the hotel and he bought a few shirts and pairs of pants. He couldn't remember the last time he'd been so excited about wearing clean clothing, something he'd taken for granted until a few days ago.

Back in the room, Trent turned on the shower—private, this time—as hot as possible and looked in his backpack for his shower gel. Then he remembered: Reed had packed the bag with the essentials for his escape, and Trent had added the body wash and a couple of other items. But apparently Reed had deemed the body wash unnecessary. *Just like Beth.* Trent realized with a start he'd barely thought about her or anything back home for days.

But, damn Reed! Trent wanted to be clean and smell nice for him, and whatever soap was in the bathroom was going to have to do.

It did just fine for cleaning up, and Trent spent extra time washing dirt and worry away before he crawled into the surprisingly comfortable and clean bed, ready for a very much-needed sleep.

Just one thing he wanted to get out of the bag first. He dug around at the bottom, expecting to find the secret blue notebook where he scribbled his most personal and erotic thoughts. But the blue notebook was gone too.

15

THE first day of waiting crept along and Trent's entire body ached with anticipation at Reed's arrival, or possibly from overexerting himself during the escape. Reed thought it was likely to be the second day before he showed up, as they needed to finish digging up the Buddha and get back into town to contact the triad leader, Kung Pao, or whatever he was called. Once the triad leader had been contacted and agreed to come to Thailand to inspect the Buddha, Boontung wouldn't need Reed any longer. The authorities would be able to make the arrest easily enough and Reed didn't have to be part of that, as long as they had the Buddha statue and the mobsters together. Then Reed would be free to meet up with Trent.

But Trent couldn't keep from hoping Reed would arrive early. He spent most of the first day in the hotel lobby, watching TV with Jaran, the day desk clerk, until one of a trio of silver-haired ladies playing cards came over and tried to recruit him as a fourth.

Despite the language gap, the ladies quickly adopted him and did their best to explain how the game was played, with some assistance from Jaran, whose own grasp of English was minimal at best. The ladies took turns checking his cards and showing him which to play. The rules of the game eluded Trent, and more than half the time he simply guessed, but it seemed enough for the women and it turned out to be an enjoyable way to spend the time. He managed to learn a few dozen new Thai words for various items of clothing, food, and body parts. From the way the women cackled as he repeated some words, Trent suspected the last ones were slang and not for general use. He'd have to check with Reed.

Late that night, Trent still sat in the lobby, watching yet another Thai film for which the ammunition budget far outweighed the wardrobe budget, reluctant to go upstairs to sleep. When he fell asleep on the battered leather couch for the third time, he forced himself to go to his room.

He ended up sleeping late and it was nearly lunchtime when Trent awoke and rushed downstairs. If Reed had arrived, he would certainly have come up; disappointment chilled him despite the heat.

What if Reed wasn't coming after all? The last full day they'd been together Trent had been such a bitch to him. Maybe Reed had decided he wasn't worth following. Reed could simply have arranged Trent's escape and figured he'd be safe and not need any more help.

The thought took Trent's appetite away and his gut ached. He sat outside on the porch watching every vehicle that passed, hoping Reed would get out, but he never arrived.

He was busy fighting off demands from the card-playing ladies when he heard the sound of trucks coming down the main street. He immediately recognized Boontung's truck with the huge dent in the driver's-side door. It went by slowly, and there in the back of the truck was Reed. His back was to Trent and he was chatting with two Thais sitting with him.

"Reed." Trent choked the word back, remembering he wasn't supposed to let any of Boontung's men find him or he'd be a prisoner again. Reed's body language seemed comfortable and casual and suddenly Trent doubted everything he'd been told. Reed hadn't been trying to get away at all. Maybe he wasn't even an FBI agent and really was part of the gang.

It was only when Reed turned to the side as the truck drove by that Trent saw the bruised and swollen flesh. He thought he saw a handcuff glint in the sun, shackling Reed's arm to the canopy frame.

It looked as if Reed was still a prisoner, and worse, he'd been beaten after Trent escaped. He wanted to run after the truck but he had no idea how he would help. Fear rooted him to the spot on the hotel porch. Mouth hanging open, he watched the trucks drive through town and disappear into the distance.

What the hell was he going to do now? Would Boontung kill Reed? If he'd been beaten, that was a real possibility. Once they'd gotten Kung

Pao on the way to make the purchase, no one needed Reed around. Before, that had been good news, but now it was the worst. Reed would have no value, and getting rid of him meant one fewer to share in the profits.

Fuck!

"AMERICAN Embassy." The voice was female and Thai, which made it so much more surreal than the situation already was. Didn't they have Americans working there?

"Uh, hi. I'm an American and...." *And what?* "I want to report another American, an FBI undercover agent, is missing. Well, captured by some criminals."

The words rushed out ahead of Trent's brain and he was shocked when he finished and the woman said, "Hold on," rather than simply hanging up on his maniacal rant.

He waited for several minutes before a male American voice came across the line. Older than the woman, with the timbre of authority. Suddenly Trent wasn't so sure he was doing the right thing.

"Can I help you? Have you been arrested here in Thailand?" The man sounded bored rather than concerned, and Trent knew the chances of anyone believing him had dwindled further.

"No. A friend of mine was kidnapped." That sounded more urgent. It didn't really matter who Reed was, did it? A kidnapped American ought to get some sort of response, and hopefully action.

"First off, what's your name?"

Trent's blood boiled at having to slow down for the basics. "Trent Copeland."

"Can you spell that?"

"Look, someone's been kidnapped, why does it matter how I spell my goddamned name?" Trent surprised himself. His mama would not be proud of his lack of manners right now and he didn't fucking care.

"Fine. Was there a ransom demand? This is a common ploy to get tourists to pay—"

"No. They don't want a ransom. I think they'll kill him." Trent's voice rose again and out of the corner of his eye he could see heads swivel in his direction. He was attracting attention. Too much attention. There was always a chance one of Boontung or Kao Lung's minions were around and might overhear. If it was one of Boontung's men, he'd probably grab Trent and bring him back to his boss in the hopes of getting a reward for finding the escaped *farang*. Trent only hoped *he* wouldn't be someone's reward. He remembered the way Boontung looked at him, touched him. The prospect made him shudder.

"Can you come into the embassy and explain what happened? We'll see about getting the Thai authorities to help you. We have translators and—"

"No!" Trent had to cut the man off again. He'd never heard someone as calm and impassive as this guy! Trent wondered what kind of training they had at the State Department if embassy personnel didn't find the mention of a kidnapped citizen about to be killed worth even the tiniest bit of concern or emotion.

"I'm not in Bangkok. I'm near Kalasin!" Trent practically shouted, but he remembered Reed and his Zen crap. He held his breath for a count of five before continuing more calmly. "And my friend is being taken to a golf resort to meet a Chinese triad leader. And he's an FBI agent. My friend, not the Chinese triad leader." *Oh, great. Now he sounded like a real loony.* "His name is Reed Acton." Maybe that specific detail would give him some credibility with the embassy lackey.

"Ah. Okay." The guy didn't sound any more credulous than before. "Sir, why don't you start from the beginning and hit the highlights. I'll stop you if I need more details."

That was an improvement at least. Thank God he'd bought the high-value phone card. Calmly, Trent explained what Reed had told him about the undercover mission and Supachai and the Ruby Buddha and the buyer from Hong Kong. When he had finished he realized he'd just summed up a plot worthy of a Hitchcock film.

"Can you please hold on?"

"My phone card is almost empty...."

"Let me get the number of the phone you're calling from. I'll call you back when I locate someone who can help you and your friend."

The man's tone reminded Trent of Nurse Ratched—calming, yet unbelieving—but he read the number off of the telephone. "Oh, can you tell me your name, in case I need to call you back?"

"Theodore Green."

"Thanks." Trent put the receiver down and took a few breaths, replenishing the oxygen his body needed desperately.

Would Theodore Green really call him back, and how long would it take? He sat down on one of the chairs near the front of the office where other people waited to receive calls. To make the time pass more quickly, Trent pulled out his notepad and scribbled some notes and details he'd want to remember at some point in the future when he got home and started writing again.

Home. Not once during the past few days, even when he'd been chained to the cot in Boontung's camp, had Trent missed home. When he sat in the dark in the cave he hadn't wished he was back in LA safe and comfortable watching DVDs with Godiva or sipping pometinis with Beth and Mick.

He hadn't wanted to be anywhere but here in Thailand, searching for some fake Ruby Buddha with an undercover FBI agent who made him weak in the knees. And now, maybe Trent was the only one who could help Reed. He only hoped the embassy could send help in time. There was always the chance they wouldn't want to jeopardize this sting operation, but they couldn't just leave one of their own to die without any backup, could they?

"Trent!" The guy at the counter shouted and Trent went up to take the call in one of the cabinets.

"Hello?" He couldn't hide the anticipation in his voice as he was connected to the embassy. "This is Trent Copeland."

"Hello, Mr. Copeland. I'm Thomas White from the U.S. Embassy in Bangkok."

White? Green? Had he stumbled into a Thai version of *Reservoir Dogs?*

"Yes. Can you help Reed Acton?"

"Your report states you believe Mr. Acton to be an FBI agent. I checked, and the Bureau has no record of an agent with that name. In fact—"

"Oh." Trent couldn't believe this. Then the explanation came to him. "It could be an alias, right? He's undercover so he wouldn't be using his *real* name, would he?"

"Well, Mr. Copeland, I'm afraid it's not quite as dramatic as that. You see, we do have Reed Acton listed on our roster of Americans living in Thailand and he's fairly well known to us." White spoke in the same officious, emotionless tone that Green used.

"So you do know him and you can help!"

"Well… Mr. Acton is also known to be closely associated with the local criminal element and he's been in trouble with the Thai authorities for one thing or another since arriving in the country several years ago. I have to warn you it's likely you've been the victim of some scam or fraud he's running, and I advise you to stay away from him and return to Bangkok. He's in no danger, but you may very well be."

"What?" Trent struggled to make sense of Thomas White's words. Was Reed a crook after all? "Are you sure of that?"

"Yes, I am confident this accounts for whatever you think you've witnessed. He and his group are very skilled con men."

Reed's whole undercover story *was* too preposterous to be true, and Trent must have been a complete fool to have been taken in. Not only had Reed fed him a pack of lies which he'd readily swallowed, but Trent had actually thought they'd had some sort of connection. Physical, emotional, even deeper. Reed had just used him, then let him go once he was convinced Trent wouldn't go to the authorities.

It explained why Reed hadn't come after him when he'd escaped. Why Reed seemed to go willingly with Boontung and Kung Pao or Kao Pung or whatever his name was. He wasn't cuffed or restrained. Those men had been part of his gang and they'd kept Trent with them so he wouldn't go to the authorities and report the antiquities theft. That Buddha they found was real, and Reed had used the whole undercover mission to disguise the fact they were stealing it. Maybe the Thai authorities were in on it too. He'd heard there was some level of corruption in the police.

Trent shook his head and inhaled slowly and deeply. Once again his overactive imagination had allowed him to be drawn into the ruse. Beth and Mick would find his gullibility incredibly amusing. He'd never hear the end of this. *If* he told them. He just wouldn't tell them.

Trent wandered the streets of the small town, dragging his feet while he decided on his next move. Completely deflated, he honestly didn't care what happened to him. He made his way over to the bus depot, and through some combination of charades and guesswork he learned the next bus to Bangkok wasn't until the following day. He'd have to spend the night here and decide whether he'd stay longer in Thailand or just get on the next plane bound for LA.

LATER that evening Trent lay in his bed in the little guesthouse and tried to think. It was sticky-hot but he was afraid to open the window and invite the local insects to feast on him, so he lay on top of the sheets under the fan as it weakly attempted to stir the thick air in the room.

How many different beds had he slept in since he'd arrived here? This was really no worse than some of the others, but it wasn't the room or the bed or the heat that made it hard to sleep this time. Little more than a week ago he wouldn't have been caught dead in a run-down dump like this. Now it seemed the most natural thing in the world.

In that short span of time *Trent* had changed.

Not that he was really a different person now; it was something more. He *wanted* to be a different person now. What he wanted in his life had changed. He'd been lucky so far, done well in school and college and breezed through life. Even his career as a writer had come surprisingly easily. Too easily, it turned out.

Just as Cassandra had told him, he'd fallen into a rut where he took the simple choice, the path of least resistance. He had become satisfied with the low-hanging fruit and given up the idea of climbing for the high, out-of-reach, and much sweeter fruit that took real effort. He went to the same restaurants and shops and knew his way around his neighborhood so well he could navigate the streets blindfolded. He looked around but he saw nothing.

It took being thrown completely out of his element to realize how much of the world around him he'd not only been missing, but had given up caring to experience. He had Cassandra and Beth to thank for kicking him out of his rut. No wonder his publisher wouldn't touch his work. It was the same thing over and over, because he hadn't changed in longer than he cared to remember. There was no life to his work because Trent hadn't really been *living*.

It was easy to write off the past few days to his gullibility, letting himself be taken in by a handsome face, a gorgeous mouth, and a sweet-talking con man, but when Trent took stock of this situation, he'd lived more in the past seven days than he had in the previous seven years. And Reed Acton was a big part of that.

Reed. Could it all have been a lie after all? Why had he bothered spinning that yarn about undercover work when they could have simply dumped Trent off at the nearest bus station to bumble his way around the Thai countryside, and he'd really never have been the wiser about what they'd been up to with the statue?

Had Reed kept him around for his own personal entertainment? Night after night they'd held each other and it had certainly *felt* like it meant something. For Trent it *had* meant more than physical comfort and pleasure. But if it meant something to Reed, wouldn't he have come after Trent like they'd planned?

In times like these, he usually called Beth for advice. It brought home to him just how far away LA really was. But this was the twenty-first century and there was no reason he couldn't call LA from Bumfuck, Thailand, was there?

Energized with an actual plan, Trent leapt out of bed, pulled on his shoes, grabbed his backpack, and raced back toward the telephone office. But it was closed. As Trent reentered the lobby, Somsak, the night clerk, shouted to him. His English was slightly better than the day clerk's, and once he figured out Trent needed to call the U.S., he had a solution.

"Skype on my computer!" Somsak said, nodding his head and grinning like the proverbial fool.

Of course! Not the most tech-savvy person, Trent had to travel halfway around the world to a tiny town in the middle of nowhere for someone to remind him he could use the Internet to make a phone call. Within a minute, Trent was set up with headphones and heard the familiar ringing tone.

"'llo?" The greeting was barely audible.

"Beth?"

"Trent?" Beth's sleepy voice sounded as if she were right in the same room and it gave Trent a feeling of hope. "Are you okay? What happened?" Concern replaced drowsiness.

Fuck. He'd calculated the time difference backward. It was early morning, not evening, there. Tomorrow, or yesterday, he still wasn't clear on that—but now he wished he hadn't called.

"Uh, hey, Beth. I'm fine...."

"Then why did you wake me up at five a.m.?" Her tone had changed to a combination of confusion and annoyance. "Don't tell me you want a ride from the airport. Take a taxi. You can afford it."

"Well, I'm still in Thailand, actually. I messed up the time. Sorry." Suddenly it seemed ridiculous to ask for advice, especially after waking her up.

"You must be having fun if you're still there. Mali got e-mail from Phaibun that he'd sent you off to the countryside, but we've heard nothing since. Do tell me all about it, or *him*, or whatever's keeping you there."

"Really? You want to hear about it?"

"Sure. I'm already up."

He could hear various sounds in the background: water running and dishes rattling. Probably making coffee. Beth pretty much needed the stuff as much as she needed air. If she was awake, she was drinking coffee. He was convinced she could even brew coffee in her sleep.

"It's complicated, and I really could use your advice."

"It's your dime. My coffee will be ready soon, so I'm all ears."

"I did meet this guy…"

"I knew it! What's he like? Is he good in bed?"

"What?" Why did Beth bring up sex right away? She must be spending too much time with Mick while he was away. "Yes, but…. He's an undercover federal agent, and we met in the airport…." Trent proceeded to summarize what had happened since he'd arrived: the map, the bus, the hut, the kidnapping, the escape. He ended with his doubts about whether Reed was in danger or if Trent was making a mistake thinking Reed cared.

"Whoa, honey. That's fantastic. I love the idea. Very vivid, and a wonderful mix of adventure and romance. How far along are you?"

"Huh?"

"With the book? If you're that inspired, you probably want to stay there until it's finished, right? I'll let Cass know what you're working on so she can talk to your publisher and whet their appetite—"

"No, no. Beth, this isn't a plotline. This really happened."

"Trent, I know I told you to have new experiences, but I was hoping opium wouldn't be one of them."

"Opium? No! I didn't try opium."

Beth laughed. "You're not joking?" Her voice got serious. "Then why don't you start from the beginning and go slowly?"

Trent did.

"So you just escaped from some Thai mobsters and your biggest dilemma is whether or not this guy likes you?"

"Yes."

"Trent! Are you sure you're okay?" Beth sounded really worried now. "Last week you were afraid to leave town without your hair dryer and now you're talking about guns and mobsters as if this happens all the time."

"I'm fine. Really, I am." He paused and laughed at himself. Beth was right, though from what he'd seen on TV, mobsters could very well be an everyday part of Thai life. "Beth, please just help me figure out what to do about Reed." Trent did his best to assuage her concerns. Of course she couldn't understand how much had changed in his life since they'd argued over how many shampoos he could pack. How being with Reed had changed Trent's life.

"Okay, back to Reed. Do you want to see him again? Even if what the embassy told you is true and he's a criminal?"

Trent considered for a moment. Whoever and whatever Reed really was, Trent cared for the man he'd spent the past few days with. Even if Reed had lied about everything, he'd treated Trent well. Actions were supposed to speak louder than words, right? Reed's actions, not anything he'd said, had made Trent fall for him.

"Yes, I want to see him again. But what if he doesn't want to see me?"

"How do you know until you try?"

"I think he does, but if everything was lies and subterfuge, then I'm scared everything he said he felt about me was fake too."

"Ah." Beth paused for a very loud slurp of coffee. "What have you got to lose?"

"I'd *know* he didn't want me." Trent bit the inside of his bottom lip.

"Is that better or worse than not knowing, and definitely losing out if everything is true?"

"You're right." Trent let out a huge sigh. He hadn't realized he'd been holding his breath, but now his head was spinning, either from lack of air or just general anxiety. "I have more to gain by trusting him than I have to lose. I should wait."

"There's your answer. But why do you have to wait for him to get you? Why can't *you* find *him*?"

"Find him?" Trent repeated. "Find him! I can go find him. Thanks, Beth!"

He hung up in the middle of Beth's response.

BY THE time he got back to his room, Trent wasn't quite as sure as he'd been while talking to Beth. He lay on the bed, staring up at the now very familiar fan on the ceiling.

Trent decided he wouldn't take the easy way out this time. He wouldn't sulk back to Bangkok and then Los Angeles to lick his wounds and hide like he had after Marc died. No, siree. This time he was going to enter the lion's den, or however the saying went. He had to know for sure who and what Reed was, and whether everything between them was truth or lie.

Did it matter if Reed was a crook? If he'd killed someone? Maybe more than one someone? That might have been a lie too. But the way Reed spoke about Kao Lung and the young boys and girls whose lives he bought and sold, that had to be more than a story. Reed made Trent feel the disgust and Reed's determination to stop it. There was no way Reed could willingly do business with a man like that without a higher objective. It had to be about much more than money.

What if Reed was part of a group of conmen who hid a fake Ruby Buddha in order to scam Kao Lung? Pay him back for all those ill-gotten gains? Did it make the scheme okay if a despicable triad leader was the victim? Trent could come up with dozens of scenarios to explain what Reed had told him, but it would be pointless. He didn't need any more.

The last proof Trent needed: those scars on Reed's back were real and the pain in his eyes when the topic came up was absolutely genuine. Reed had endured something terrible in the past, and Trent was willing to cut him some slack.

Forget Mr. Green and Mr. White from the embassy. Trent would go to the golf resort, find Reed, and get the truth. It might not be what he'd want but he wouldn't spend the rest of his life wondering.

Once he'd made this decision, sleep came easily.

The sun was high in the sky by the time he woke the next morning. It had been the first restful night's sleep he'd had since he'd escaped from Boontung's camp.

He packed and checked out, asking Jaran about the golf resort. The most expensive and luxurious hotel in the area—the kind of place a rich Chinese gangster would stay.

With a last wave to the card-playing ladies in the lobby, Trent headed out to discover the truth.

16

WITH his newfound confidence, Trent hired a tuk-tuk to take him to the resort where he expected Kao Lung to be staying. It was the only likely place in about a hundred-mile radius. He knew he was in the right place when he saw Boontung's truck with its bashed-in door in the parking lot.

The front desk clerk eyed him warily when he tried to check in without a reservation. Trent realized he didn't look much like a wealthy tourist anymore and laughed at the transformation in his appearance and attitude during the past week. He was wearing the inexpensive Thai-made clothes he'd bought in the little town he'd been staying in, and he only had his backpack, no luggage. Hell, *he* would have given himself a wide berth if they'd passed on the street.

Money talks, so he tossed his Amex Platinum card at the clerk and told him to check the limit if there were any doubts about Trent's ability to pay.

Apologizing, the clerk checked Trent in and had a bellboy show him to his room.

Once there, Trent barely noticed the luxurious furnishings or plush carpet. The AC was on too high, and he adjusted the temperature. A week ago, he'd have gone straight to the room service menu and ordered a meal to be served at one of the three pools at the resort, but now he had more important matters at hand. How on earth was he going to find Reed in this enormous resort?

Trent decided to walk around the grounds to see if he might run into Reed or even Boontung. Down in the lobby gift shop, he bought a cap sporting the resort's logo, hoping no one would recognize him. The guests here were predominantly Asian, so Trent stood out for being both

Caucasian and particularly tall. With the cap on he was only slightly less obvious, but it made him feel better.

A quick turn through the lobby, restaurants, and shops didn't produce results, so Trent went outside, wandering the spacious grounds. The resort boasted two golf courses and he hoped he wouldn't have to check there. He could just plant himself at the bar and assume sooner or later Kung Pao would come by. Too bad Trent didn't have a clue what he looked like. He was likely to have a group of bodyguards or some sort of entourage befitting a crime kingpin, or at least Trent's expectation of a crime kingpin.

The bar wasn't such a bad place to start after all, and Trent took a seat where he could chat with the bartender, Kwan, if his name tag could be trusted. Thankfully, it was just before the pre-dinner rush; the place was quiet, with only a handful of tables occupied. Trent sipped ice-cold beer from an impeccably clean glass as he watched Kwan restock supplies of lemons, limes, cherries, olives, and cocktail onions. He called on his knowledge of famous fictional detectives to adopt a persona and a plan of action.

"There's a group from Hong Kong that came in a day or two ago," the bartender responded to what Trent hoped were subtle questions. "Guy ordered my last bottle of Louis XIII last night, and I had to send someone down to Bangkok this morning to get more." Kwan's English was excellent, with a slight British accent, which surprised Trent. Then again, a world-class resort like this would be staffed with well-educated people—even the bartenders.

Kwan shook his head and tsked as if he couldn't figure out why anyone would spend that much for a drink. Trent agreed, but he knew Mick would be drooling over the chance for a glass of the super-premium aged cognac. Trent never would have even heard of it if not for Mick's expensive taste, particularly when Trent was paying.

"Good thing I didn't order it, huh?" Trent laughed and wracked his brain for a way to find out what room the big spender was in. "I sure wouldn't mind a taste of that. I'll bet just a glass costs more than a room here."

"Most of the rooms, yeah." Kwan looked disapproving again. "This guy's in one of the royal suites up in the tower." He craned his head in the general direction before turning his back to Trent so he could restock the bottles on the shelves behind the bar.

"Royal suite? You mean the king stays here?" Trent recalled how much the Thais revered their king, though the idea of a king golfing made him want to laugh.

"Not the king, but other members of his family have been here. Maybe some royals from Europe too." Kwan answered courteously but it was clear Trent was wearing out his welcome here. "I don't know. They all look the same to me, and they're usually crap tippers."

"Thanks, Kwan. See you." Trent left about three times what he thought his beer cost on the bar and headed for the tower. *Let's check out this royal suite.*

KWAN might have had loose lips about the resort's guests, but the security staff weren't quite as lax. Trent couldn't get past the elevator on the top floor without a room key unless his name was on a special guest list or he had an engraved invitation. He tried using the stairs from a lower floor but the stair doors required an electronic room key, and Trent's didn't work. He'd have to rethink his plan.

He went outside and wandered around the grounds, eyeing the tower. The resort was beautiful: gorgeous landscaping with copious flowering plants that perfumed the air. The grass was lushly green and Trent wondered how much water it required to keep it beautiful. Despite the strange sudden storms he'd seen, it was not yet rainy season, and most of the country was hot and parched. The resort was a lovely oasis and it was clear why it was so crowded—and so expensive. At any other time he would have loved to stay in a place like this, but his focus wasn't on amenities now, it was on finding Reed.

As Trent eyed the windows on the upper floors, a flash of color caught his attention in the periphery of his vision: a tattered scrap of purple fabric fluttered, caught between the window and sill of a room on the third floor. Not purple. *Lilac.*

Reed? Trent knew exactly what the little rag was: the strip of his boxers Reed had sliced off that day in the rain. Trent had taken that pair of boxers in his backpack when he'd escaped Boontung's camp, so the only explanation was Reed was in that room. Was the scrap a signal? It seemed a long shot since Reed expected him to be waiting in the Sawatdee Hotel in the little town whose name Trent couldn't even pronounce.

It couldn't be a coincidence.

Mimicking something he'd seen in countless films, Trent bent to find a pebble and tossed it at the window. Nothing. He tried again, and this time Reed appeared at the window, looking down, but Trent hid behind a giant elephant-shaped topiary. At least he knew for a fact Reed was here. His face looked battered, but he could walk. That was good news! Trent's heart gave a little flutter. Other parts, farther south, may also have reacted, but he forced himself to focus on the task at hand.

He counted windows so he could figure out which room Reed was in and headed back inside the hotel to the front desk. The room was not registered to Reed, and the clerk refused to reveal who had booked it. Did that mean Reed was still a prisoner and not here completely of his own accord? It probably wasn't a great idea to just knock on the door. He'd case out the third floor first.

He located the room and wandered around the hall as if he belonged on the third floor. There was some activity in the room and Trent thought he recognized one of Boontung's men leaving with a much larger guy who didn't look familiar. He had a different physical build from most Thais, so Trent assumed he must be one of the Hong Kong group.

Reed was nowhere in sight, but it appeared that there were two other men in the room, and one or the other would go in or out, never both at once—odd behavior if nothing suspicious was going on. They must be taking turns guarding Reed. The weather was hot and no one wore jackets but Trent didn't notice any telltale gun bulges under their shirts. Hopefully they were unarmed. In a fight Trent could probably take one of them, but not both. Not that he did much fighting, but he was in pretty good shape, despite his lack of aerobic training.

While he staked out the room, Trent worked out the bare bones of a plan. He knew how he'd get in the room and how he'd subdue the guard, but he didn't have a clue what came next. Hopefully he and Reed could just run out at that point.

It was time to put the plan—such as it was—into action.

First, he had to get into disguise.

Well, not quite a disguise. It was a hotel staff uniform: a white polo shirt with the hotel's name embroidered over the left breast and khaki shorts. Thankfully they didn't wear trousers because Trent never would have found any in his size. As it was, the shorts were a bit tight around the thighs. He'd discovered where the hotel laundry was located and had pilfered these from the racks of clean uniforms neatly hanging at one end of the room. He even grabbed a name tag from a shelf over the desk. He had grabbed one that proclaimed his new name "PORN." Mick would absolutely approve the choice. Trent chuckled softly as he pinned the tag to his shirt, and it helped him relax.

It was well past dinnertime and Trent roamed the halls on the third floor until he found a dinner cart outside of a room. He glanced around a few times, hoping he didn't look like he was stealing it, until he realized that alone made him look suspicious. He had to act like he belonged there. His breath came in shallow bursts and he tried to control his breathing and calm down. He headed for the room where Reed was being held and waited nearby in a spot affording him a good view of the door without being completely obvious to anyone going in or out.

Within ten minutes one of the Chinese guards left the room. He pulled a pack of cigarettes out of a breast pocket and hastily put one to his lips as he headed for the elevator. Apparently the other guard didn't like him smoking in there, and it only helped Trent with his plan. He hoped the guy would smoke two before he went back inside.

Trent rushed to the door and knocked. The other guard opened the door with a look of surprise at the dinner cart.

"Already order dinner." The guard shook his head and waved Trent away.

"Special from manager." Trent tried to mimic Phaibun's accent and pronunciation. Hell, how would a Chinese guy know what a Thai speaking English would sound like?

"Manager sent more dinner?"

"Yes. Free. No charge." Trent grinned. "Lobster."

The guard nodded furiously and smiled. Evidently his per diem didn't cover his expensive taste in seafood. Trent rolled the cart into the room: it appeared to be a large suite, with no beds in sight.

Before the guy could grab the silver cover, Trent put his hand on it, and waited a moment. The guard looked like he was already salivating at the idea of a free lobster dinner. Trent took advantage of surprise and his greater height to quickly raise the lid and bring it down on the top of the man's head. The motion sent an unexpected jolt though Trent's body, but to his delight, the man crumpled to the floor with a satisfying thud and an *ooomph*.

"Yeah!" Trent couldn't suppress his gleeful shout.

That was when he noticed the man rising from the couch—apparently a third guard. He was already halfway to Trent and tackled him. Trent made his own *ooomph* when he hit the floor.

The guy, who was even larger now that he was sitting on Trent's chest, got up and hauled Trent to his feet, nearly dislocating his shoulder. The hungry guard picked himself up off the floor and rubbed his head. He glared at Trent, then glanced at the dinner cart.

"Fuck!" That's how Trent translated whatever the guy really said—in Chinese—when he discovered there was no lobster on the platter. In fact, it was the remains of someone else's dinner, which seemed to make him ever angrier. Fuck was right.

Hulky and Hungry exchanged heated words while the larger one kept a painful grip on Trent's arm. When they apparently came to a decision, Hulky yanked Trent in the direction of a closed door on the far side of the room. He pulled a gun from the small of his back and waved it menacingly in Trent's direction.

Trent nodded his understanding that resistance was futile. Then Hulky opened the door and pushed Trent inside roughly.

He stumbled and would have landed on his face but for the pair of hands that steadied him and helped him to his feet.

Reed. And he didn't look particularly pleased to see Trent. For the first time, Trent was really scared about what would happen next.

"WHAT are you doing here?" Reed kept his voice quiet but he was shouting inside.

"I came here to… uh… save you." Trent shrugged and avoided eye contact with Reed. Clearly, he hadn't exactly succeeded.

"Of all the idiotic, lame-brained, stupid—" Reed stopped himself before he said something he couldn't take back. Trent already looked like a wounded deer, and Reed barely kept his temper in check. "Well, great job." Reed tried to keep the sarcasm out of his voice as he gave Trent a once-over, his gaze pausing over the too-tight shorts. He wanted to laugh but Trent was in danger. Again. After all Reed had done to keep him safe. "You shouldn't have come."

"Yeah, I pretty much suck at this adventure stuff. Now you know why I write romance novels." He sat down heavily on the edge of the bed with a forlorn sigh.

"What the hell were you thinking? I don't need your help. I can take care of myself just fine. Now I have to worry about you too. Again."

Trent cringed at that last word and Reed bit his lip so hard he tasted blood. Why the hell couldn't Trent have followed the plan and stayed safe until Reed came to get him?

"Yeah, you're fine. You're locked up in a room with three enormous Chinese guys guarding you."

"That's temporary. I could get out if I really wanted or needed to."

Trent's expression showed he didn't buy it for a minute.

"Why do you have to do everything on your own, Reed? Why can't you let someone help *you* for once?" Trent raised his voice, practically shouting. "You go around shutting out everyone else, never letting anyone in on your plan, or your thoughts. That's stupid." He calmed down and softened his tone. "Just let someone in. Let me in." Trent glared at Reed with a mixture of defiance and anger.

But Trent was right; about all of it. Reed justified shutting others out as keeping them safe, but it got to be a habit, and now Reed didn't even know how to let someone else into his life. He told himself he didn't want anyone, but over the past few days he knew he'd been lying to himself. He'd shut Trent out because it was safer for *Reed*—physically and emotionally.

But look at Trent. Just coming to Thailand had been difficult, breaking out of a self-imposed cocoon and overcoming his fear of new experiences. Yet, he'd found the courage to come after Reed, despite knowing the risks. No one had ever done anything like that for him before, risked so much for *him*. How could Reed answer with any less? Trent had risked his life, and proven himself more than worthy of Reed risking his heart.

"When you come out of your shell, you don't go for half measures, do you?"

"Maybe I believe you're worth taking a chance on." As soon as Trent spoke, he looked away and let out another sigh.

"So are you, Trent. Thank you." Reed reached out for Trent's hand and pulled him in. "You just need to do some more research…" Reed chuckled and he stepped forward and gently stroked the back of Trent's neck.

TRENT'S head shot up at the caress, though it wasn't particularly sensual. God, he'd missed Reed's touch, missed Reed so much. Now even though Trent had pretty much fucked up the rescue, Reed was actually joking with him. At least now he had his answer to whether or not Reed shared his feelings. The sense of relief was incredible, but it battled with his growing excitement from being in Reed's arms again.

"What kind of research?" Trent smiled, recalling their first night together and how much he'd disliked Reed at the time. Now, he'd enjoy any sort of research Reed suggested.

"Rescue tactics, evasion, escape. But we could save that for later."

"Later." Trent tugged Reed's arm until he sat on the bed. He glanced into Reed's eyes, saw how battered one side of his face still was. Guilt gnawed at him. Boontung must have beaten Reed because he helped Trent escape. He held back at first until he saw Reed seemed to have missed him just as much. With butterflies swarming in his stomach, Trent leaned toward Reed ever so slightly, hoping he hadn't made a mistake coming here or misinterpreted Reed's responses.

"Later."

Reed leaned in toward Trent and their lips brushed together for a fraction of a second before he wrapped his arms around Trent and pulled him in close for a deep, hungry kiss. Trent returned the kiss eagerly, almost instantly hard at the feel of Reed's body pressed against his. He didn't even care if it turned out to be just about sex this time. There was no way Trent would give up the chance to be with Reed again.

Trent lay back on the bed and pulled Reed on top of him, enjoying the way Reed's hands slid under his shirt and traced lines of fire across his back. They'd spent three nights apart, but it seemed like years. Trent forced himself to take it slowly and concentrate on the way Reed's tongue snaked around his own and the familiar scent and taste. Reed tangled one hand in Trent's hair, the slight tug as arousing as the way Reed's hard-on pressed against Trent's own. Of their own accord,

Trent's hips bucked up, allowing him harder contact against Reed, while he skimmed his hands down the curve of Reed's ass, tracing the contours he'd missed so much.

Somehow they got each other's clothes off, barely breaking contact, and they were naked, hot and hard.

THE sun was coming up when Trent got dressed again. The guards hadn't even bothered to look in on them at all since they tossed Trent in with Reed. Looking around the room for the first time since he'd arrived, Trent was surprised to see his suitcase on a rack near the door to the bathroom.

"You've got a pretty nice cell here, haven't you?" he joked as Reed dressed. He was wearing one of Trent's shirts, and it made Trent smile. "Private bathroom?"

"Yeah. It's a suite in a nice hotel. I really can't complain, except for the being locked in here part."

"What've you been doing while you were locked up?"

"Catching up on my reading." Reed pulled Trent's e-book reader out of the night table drawer. "I managed to read all of yours, though I can't say I'm a real fan of the genre."

Trent laughed and took the reader from Reed. When he dropped it back in the drawer, he spotted his little blue spiral notebook—the X-rated personal one—at the bottom. Had Reed read that too? Trent's face flamed and he looked at Reed. Then he quickly turned away again, mortified.

"Kept your things safe for you." If Reed noticed Trent's reaction he didn't let on.

If they'd been anywhere else, Reed's words would have elated Trent. It proved Reed fully intended to find him again! He hadn't misinterpreted Reed's feelings after all. Trent blinked back tears stinging his eyes, hoping Reed hadn't seen the spectrum of emotion he'd just displayed.

When the wave had passed, Trent looked Reed in the face, and reached out to touch the bruises. "These seem to be clearing up. Kung Pao's guys didn't do any more damage, did they?"

"No, they pretty much leave me alone while their boss negotiates with Boontung. They even feed me twice a day." Reed glanced at the clock on the bedside table. "It's just about breakfast time."

"I guess they haven't exactly been serving lobster, have they?"

"Lobster? No, why?"

Trent explained about his lobster ruse to gain entry to the room, earning hearty laughter and an impressed nod from Reed.

"That's pretty original. I'll have to remember that one." Reed grinned.

"SO, WHAT was your big escape plan?"

"It wasn't my plan so much as *the* plan. The Thais were supposed to arrest Kao Lung when he came to inspect the Buddha. Then they'd come and find me if I wasn't with the group when they made the arrests."

"How would they know where and when to arrest him?"

"GPS tracker in the statue."

"Of course. Clever." Trent smiled weakly. "But not clever enough, or they should have gotten him by now, and come looking for you. Shouldn't they?"

"Maybe they have. I haven't been in touch with my team for over a week. I did expect they'd come get me by now." Reed motioned toward the window. "You found my marker—the strip of fabric in the window—so they certainly should have."

"Gee, thanks. You're a pro with the backhanded compliments, did anyone ever tell you?"

"I didn't mean it like that. Sorry." Until he'd met Trent, Reed rarely found himself apologizing for anything. But now he seemed to put his foot in his mouth every time he opened it. Why was it so difficult to stop pushing Trent away with half insults? Reed had to work on that much harder in the future.

Future: not a concept Reed contemplated much. He usually focused on the here and now and strategized his next few steps, but never more than that.

Now there were so many things to look forward to. When they got out of here. *If* they got out of here. The Thais or Reed's team should have shown up by now—unless they thought he was dead and didn't bother looking for him.

"Why aren't they here yet, Reed?" Trent still used that trusting tone that cut through Reed's heart.

"Probably because they don't think I need any help. Unfortunately, I can't exactly break out. I need these guys to believe I'm sticking around waiting for my cut."

"Maybe they're going to kill you instead of paying you."

Trust Trent to come up with the worst-case scenario, but it wasn't particularly unreasonable. Reed knew he was perfectly safe until the deal went down, then it was likely Kao Lung or Boontung would want to eliminate him instead of paying his fee. It was the one risk in the original plan. Reed couldn't take the typical upfront payment as a go-between because he needed to be involved until the final deal.

"You do know they might kill you now too."

"I suspected as much." Trent's jawline was tight and Reed could see he was trying to play down the fear that must be controlling him at this moment. As much as he hated Trent getting himself captured, Reed couldn't help but love the man even more for even attempting to help him. Love? When had what he felt for Trent turned into love? Reed had no idea, but he suspected it had happened long before Trent ended up in this room. He hadn't recognized how much Trent meant to him until he was once again in danger.

"Hopefully they'll do it fast." Trent had been talking and paused, clearly waiting for Reed to respond. "They'll do it fast, right?"

"Probably not." Reed immediately wished he had lied. Trent looked genuinely frightened now and again it was Reed's fault. Hell, it was all Reed's fault. That Trent had ever left Bangkok. That he'd been at the caves. That he'd shown up here trying to help Reed escape. Reed reached out to stroke Trent's cheek, knowing how little such a gesture would help now. But Trent leaned into the touch and, with a slight smile, took hold of Reed's hand. "What on earth were you thinking coming here in the first place? I told you how dangerous Kao Lung and his men are."

"No matter what you did before we met, I don't think you deserve to get killed. That's why I came. I couldn't get anyone at the embassy to listen to me. I suppose if they had you'd end up in prison and not dead. Which do you think is worse?" Trent babbled for a few moments, in his inimitable way, and it was only when he'd finished his words began to sink in.

"Embassy? Trent, you called the American embassy?"

"Yeah. I believed that story about being an undercover agent." Trent paused and frowned slightly. He shook it off and went on. "I thought the embassy would want to know what had happened to you, even if your cover was blown. Only when I called, they said you weren't working for them. You were just an American who got in trouble for drugs and smuggling." Trent had a slight look of distaste on his lips as he finished, and Reed's heart fell at the disappointment he saw there.

"That's what they told you?"

Trent nodded, then he found his voice again.

"But I realized even if you were all those things, even if you'd lied, I'd still ended up falling in love with you—whoever or whatever you really are. You looked out for me, and made me feel safe, and maybe some of what I hoped you felt about me was real. Regardless of the lies, I didn't want that man to end up dead. You didn't deserve it."

"Fuck." Reed blinked a few times as tears stung his eyes, but he kept control. His own boss had left him out to dry but a pampered, soft writer from LA had risked his life to help him, because he'd fallen in love. Right now, Reed would do anything in the world to turn back time and get Trent as far the hell away from this hotel room as he could. Even if it meant they'd never met. He hated knowing he'd be the cause of Trent's death, when all Trent had wanted to do was to help Reed.

"Maybe later." Trent choked out a weak laugh as the seriousness of his situation finally sunk in completely. Reed put his arms around Trent and pulled him close.

"Trent, I've never met anyone as brave as you are, but right now I wish we'd never met. I wish you hadn't tried to help me, because it's going to be so much harder for me knowing I've hurt you so badly."

"I'm disappointed you lied to me about being a federal agent. And I'm sorry that if we do end up getting out of here you will probably go to prison. But I'm not sorry we met. Even if I end up getting killed, at least

I found you. Maybe we're only going to be together a short time, but you know I'll never forget you." Tears spilled out of Trent's eyes and he laughed away the fear and the pain.

It took every ounce of Reed's Buddhist training to keep from crying too.

"Did I tell you how adorable you look in those shorts?"

"Shut up." Trent pulled away from Reed.

Reed leaned over for a kiss and to tug at Trent's shoulder, but Trent pushed him away. At least Reed had lightened the mood, for however long it would last. He tried again to kiss Trent, and when Trent put out a hand to stop him, Reed grabbed the wrist and quickly—but carefully— pinned it behind Trent's back.

"Are you going to overpower me too?" Trent's voice held a teasing note and he broke into a huge grin.

"Only if you say 'please.'"

"Please."

Reed didn't have a chance to act on the request because the door opened.

SOMEONE rolled a dining cart into the room and quickly shut the door again. Trent heard the lock click home. Reed brought the cart over to the table near the window and served the dishes. It wasn't lobster, but the bowls of rice with vegetables looked delicious and they ate in silence for a few moments. The only utensils on the tray had been plastic spoons, not particularly useful weapons.

"Did you know Porn is a girl's name?"

Trent's eyebrows furrowed briefly, then his eyes went to the name tag pinned to his shirt. He fumbled with it briefly then let out a loud sigh.

"I can't do one fucking thing right, can I?"

"Sorry, it just popped out. It wasn't an admonition. It's almost as cute as the shorts."

"Fine. Now I won't tell you my plan."

"Your plan?"

"Yes. I didn't just bumble my way in here." Despite Reed's laughter, Trent continued. "I devised a plan. See? I even brought a screwdriver." Trent got up and picked the tool off the floor, where it had fallen earlier when Reed had pulled his shorts off.

"Why?" Reed sounded aloof, but Trent could tell he'd piqued Reed's interest.

"The windows don't open far enough to climb out; I checked. But if we take the window off its hinges we can escape that way."

"We're on the third floor and there's no balcony." Reed's smirk and tone reminded Trent of the night in the hut when he'd mocked Trent and his writing.

"Do you have to find fault with everything?" Trent's plastic spoon rattled against the plate, startling Reed. He took a breath before replying. "We throw the mattress out first."

"You've thought this through pretty carefully, haven't you?"

"Yes."

"That's actually not a bad plan. I'm really impressed." Reed reached for Trent's hand, stroking his fingers. "Really."

"Really?"

"Yes. But it's still pretty dangerous. Even with the mattress."

"I know. I'm scared, but I couldn't think of anything else." Trent tried to shake off his fear and grinned. "You can go first; that'll break *my* fall."

"Thanks." Reed gave a wry smile. "But now we've got a weapon. I've got an idea…." His voice trailed off and he shoved a forkful of food into his mouth. "With two of us, I think it should work."

Trent stirred a spoon through the chili sauce on the ubiquitous condiments tray. One of the constants in Thailand: at least two different kinds of chili served with every single meal. Since he'd arrived he'd experimented and gotten more adventurous with the condiments.

"No jumping out the window?" Trent had just about resigned himself to the inevitability.

"No. I'd never make you jump out of a window. Not after…." Reed stopped, but Trent suspected he worried that the plan brought up Trent's memories—and fears—associated with Marc.

"I'd do it to help you." Trent meant it, too. Reed was worth taking the risk.

"Finish your dinner while I explain what I'm thinking."

"HELP! Hey, come in here. My friend needs help!" Trent pounded on the door, hoping one of the guards would check on the commotion, even if they couldn't understand him. Reed was doubled up on the floor, clutching his stomach.

The door opened and one of the Chinese guards came in and his expression turned from annoyance to concern as he spotted Reed. He knelt down and was taken by surprise as Reed swung the screwdriver and stabbed him in the gut, dropping him quickly and efficiently. Unfortunately, he managed to shout something before he passed out—or died. Trent wasn't quite sure.

A second thug came in and Trent splashed chili sauce into his eyes, disorienting him enough to overpower him by hitting him over the head with a lamp. Then Reed bound his wrists to the dinner cart using strips of torn bedsheets. The worst he could do now would be to roll after them with the cart, which would greatly slow him down.

The third guard never showed, probably on another smoke break. Reed entered the suite's main room first, brandishing the screwdriver, making sure it was safe before he beckoned to Trent. They ran out into the hallway and down the stairs to Trent's room, and safety.

"Oh.... My.... God!" Trent huffed out the syllables, heart still pounding a mile a minute as he slammed the door and leaned up against it, trying to catch his breath.

"You okay?"

"Yeah, I'm fine. It was actually kind of fun."

"Fun?" Reed laughed. "Loved the thing with the chili sauce, MacGyver. That's another one I'll have to remember."

Trent's heart lifted when Reed called him MacGyver. So much better than "Lilac."

"I know it shouldn't be fun to hit someone over the head, but he hit me first, when I went to rescue you." Trent stopped when he noticed Reed didn't look happy. "Is that guy you stabbed dead?"

"Not yet. He might bleed out if he doesn't get medical help fairly soon. I'll call for an ambulance. Then I need to call my team for a status update." He picked up the bedside phone and spoke in Thai to the hotel operator.

Trent felt pretty bad about hitting the guy, but he now knew without a doubt that Reed had been worth everything Trent had gone through—and more. Who else would call an ambulance for the bad guy?

Reed hung up the phone. "Ambulance on the way. The Thai authorities can arrest him at the hospital. He won't be going anywhere on his own for a while."

The next few hours were a blur for Trent.

When two Thai police officers arrived wearing their usual elaborate military-style uniforms, Trent almost didn't let them into his room, worried they might be there to arrest Reed. He still wasn't certain Reed was on the up-and-up until a third man, an American wearing an off-the-rack suit that shouted bureaucrat pushed his way through, displaying FBI credentials. He then tossed a similar wallet to Reed.

"I guess you need your real ID again, Acton."

Trent let out a breath. Reed hadn't lied to him after all. The man turned out to be Reed's boss—introduced to Trent only as "Tom." The Thais didn't even bother to speak to him, so Trent settled onto the bed, scribbling in his green notebook—the one he used for story ideas—while Reed got a status update from Tom and the Thai officers.

They'd arrested Kao Lung, Boontung, and everyone involved in the physical transfer of the Buddha that morning out on one of the golf courses. Their Chinese guards had been arrested too, including the chain-smoker, who'd been picked up when he went back to the room where they'd been holding Reed.

"The takedown didn't go precisely as planned." Tom turned to Reed. "Supachai wasn't there, but a body fitting his description was found not far from Khorat. We're adding murder charges to Boontung's list, though we're willing to negotiate on that if he turns in others from their organization."

Trent noticed Reed didn't even react to mention of Supachai's name. It was a little frightening how well Reed could lie even to his own boss. No wonder Trent had so much trouble trusting him before. Now, he knew he could rely on Reed, but they'd been through some rough patches together for him to get there.

"We fully expected to find you with the statue at the transfer, Acton. It didn't occur to us you'd need rescuing." Tom chuckled and Trent held back his own smile, but stayed silent.

"I'm afraid I owe you an apology, Mr. Copeland." Reed's boss turned to Trent once he'd finished his business with Reed and the Thai police had left.

Trent sat up and stared at Tom. How had he known Trent's surname? Reed hadn't used it when he'd introduced them.

"I don't understand." Trent shut the little notebook and gave Tom his full attention.

"I wouldn't expect you to." Tom chuckled softly.

Trent couldn't place it, but there was something familiar about his voice, and his slightly condescending tone. "Mr. White?" Trent guessed when everything finally clicked.

"Yes. You recognize my voice?" He smiled in surprise. "I had to lie to you when you called the embassy, for your safety. Apparently my warnings fell on deaf ears, though I never expected you'd be the one to locate and retrieve Acton." Tom turned to Reed. "You've got your work cut out with him. Good luck to both of you."

As he headed out the door Tom paused and looked back at Trent. "Let me know if you're looking for a job. We could use more agents who can think on their feet the way you can. Though generally we prefer them to actually follow directions." He stared pointedly at Reed and Trent in turn and opened the door.

Tom left before Trent could formulate an answer, but he couldn't suppress a self-satisfied grin.

"Looks like you just got a job offer." Reed chuckled and moved toward Trent and the bed.

Another knock sounded at the door.

"It's like Grand Central freaking Station here!" Trent had hoped the parade of U.S. and Thai authorities had stopped. He let Reed get the door. The visitor was probably for him, anyway.

"Your suitcase," a high-pitched Thai voice said from the hallway.

"*Khob khun*," Reed thanked the bellboy. He pulled some money out of his pocket and shut the door. "*Your* suitcase," he told Trent.

"My suitcase?" Trent couldn't help the first thought that crossed his mind: a shower with the body wash. It would mean the ordeal was really over and life might return to normal. He pulled the bottle out of the toiletries bag. It was almost empty.

"Oh, yeah, I used it to clean up when I got to the hotel." Reed didn't even sound like he was sorry!

"The whole bottle?" The words slipped out before Trent could stop them. "Do you know how much this costs? You only need to use a little bit—"

Reed planted his lips on Trent's, shutting him up quickly and efficiently.

"I know. But it reminded me of you, so… maybe I used more than I needed." Reed shrugged.

"Of me?" Trent's heart rate accelerated again. "Well, if you aren't a closet romantic after all."

"Don't push your luck, buddy."

"Why not? Gonna punish me?"

"Definitely. After your shower."

"After?"

"Or during." Reed smacked Trent's ass and followed him into the bathroom. "Hey, how 'bout we try that thing on page twelve of your little notebook?"

Trent stopped in his tracks. Fucking Reed had read everything Trent had written and fantasized about him? He'd never been more humiliated in his life.

"Or page twenty-one."

On the other hand, as long as Reed wanted everything in there as much as Trent did, what did it matter?

"Page twenty-one it is." And Trent turned on the shower.

17

THEY started out hot and heavy under the spray, Reed pressing Trent against the clean tiled shower wall, but after a few moments of kissing, it was clear Reed's injuries were worse than he'd let on while they'd been with the Chinese guards. The stress and exertion of their escape had exhausted him and while his cock signaled Trent to "go," the occasional wince when their bodies came into contact told Trent to slow things down.

Instead, he suggested a bath and filled the tub in the spacious bathroom, splashing in a healthy dose of the last of his precious body wash. Reed was worth it. While Reed soaked in the scented water, Trent bathed him, seeing Reed relax and unwind.

For the first time, Trent saw Reed completely vulnerable, and putting himself in Trent's hands, and not in the same way at all as when he'd bottomed for Trent in the little hut after he'd killed Supachai. This was different and they both knew it.

The body wash perfumed the air, hot and thick with steam, condensing on the mirrors and tiled walls.

Trent washed and soothed every inch of Reed, easing over the bruised and battered flesh, purple bruises covering his side and arm. Boontung had beaten him with something like a stick or pipe leaving long stripes on Reed's smooth skin. Reed let out occasional sighs or grunts of pleasure, stiffening when Trent attempted to wash his back. But he soon relaxed again as Trent spread suds.

Trent wondered whether Reed still felt pain or if it was just psychological. Perhaps just the memory of the injury. He vowed never to ask Reed about it, and hoped someday Reed would feel able to tell him how he'd gotten them.

"How about a foot rub?" Trent asked, sliding one hand down Reed's well-muscled leg, gliding along the curve of the calf, the bony ankle and cupping the heel in his palm.

"Oh, God, yes." Reed sighed rather than spoke and that made Trent happy. He massaged along the arch of the foot, giving ample attention to each toe, then moving back up the calf, and repeating the process on the other foot.

As Reed reacted with obvious enjoyment, Trent felt as needed and desired as when Reed wanted him in a more carnal way. This satisfied both of them in ways sex or other physical contact didn't. For Trent it meant their relationship could move beyond the physical and still work.

"This might be better than sex," Reed said as he watched Trent work, eyes heavy lidded. He looked so damn delicious Trent wanted him more than ever, but he could wait. It wasn't like him to be so insistent but seeing firsthand what Reed went through and the results pay off, impressed Trent more than ever. How could he have doubted Reed?

"If this is better than sex, then I'm doing one of those two things wrong." Trent pouted.

"Sex with anyone else," Reed added. He reached up and traced a line from Trent's jaw down his throat, wet fingers igniting Trent's skin. Reed circled a nipple and Trent's cock hardened. When he glanced back at Reed, Trent saw his eyes were closed and his breathing had grown shallow. He'd fallen asleep.

Still aroused and disappointed Trent gathered towels and laid them out on the bed, then went back and carefully picked Reed up, carried him into the bedroom and laid him down. He mumbled a few incoherent endearments then fell into a deep slumber.

Trent watched Reed for a while before returning to the bathroom and cleaning up and crawling into bed beside Reed. His pulse quickened when Reed rolled over and spooned behind him, kissing his shoulder and murmuring Trent's name in his sleep.

IN THE morning, bright sunlight woke Trent. Reed still snuggled up behind him, the scent of sandalwood and ginger emanating from his skin. Trent inhaled the familiar smells and sighed as Reed's arm tightened around his waist. Reed's cock, morning-hard, pressed against his ass and

Trent's cock thickened in response. But Reed rolled away when his fingers brushed against Trent's hardness.

"What—?" Trent craned his neck to look back at Reed.

"Shhh." Reed put two fingers on Trent's lips to silence him, then followed through with a caress, tracing a line down his throat, just as he had the night before in the bath, before Reed had fallen asleep. "Shhh," he repeated. "Lie back, arms at your side."

Trent rolled onto his back as directed. Reed, still favoring one arm, settled between Trent's knees. One fingertip continued sketching random shapes along Trent's shoulder and collarbone, sending electrical messages down through every nerve in his body. The energy flowed and concentrated near the base of his cock and it throbbed as Reed's fingers found a nipple and pinched it to attention.

"Mmmm," Trent groaned, trying to keep his eyes open as his body short-circuited reactions that didn't bother to pass through his brain.

"Mmmm," Reed replied and leaned down for a kiss, just brushing his lips against Trent's. His cock brushed against Trent as Reed hovered. The rough stubble of Reed's chin scratching against Trent's left him craving more contact. Harder, rougher. Now.

But Reed only kissed, tongue at first licking at the corner of Trent's mouth, following the line of his lower lip, lapping at it before Reed pulled Trent's lip into his mouth, sucking at it, scraping it lightly with his teeth. His arms would stay still no longer and of their own accord came up to embrace Reed, pull him tight against Trent's chest, at which point Reed broke the kiss. Only when Trent let go did Reed continue. This time his tongue explored Trent's lips again, then his mouth, dueling with his tongue. Trent's body was on fire, his cock achingly hard, reminding him that kissing wasn't going to get either of them off. He moaned and Reed laughed through the kiss before his mouth traveled farther south.

He kissed and licked and nibbled a meandering path, hitting every highlight and erogenous zone Trent had and a few he hadn't realized existed. The lightning shot through him as Reed's mouth fastened onto a nipple, sucking, teeth scraping then sucking again. Tongue-tip swirled and lapped and teased and Trent cried out as the teeth sent more electricity throughout his aching and increasingly impatient body. His hips bucked and his hands tightened into fists. His toes curled and his knees trembled.

When Reed's lips finally neared Trent's navel he thought he might shoot his load any second, whether Reed touched his cock or not. And he didn't fucking care. Reed sat up then scooted back on his heels, catching Trent's gaze for a moment.

That one look said everything Trent needed to know. Reed's desire was as obvious in the thundercloud-dark eyes, as in his hard, jutting cock, but this wasn't about Reed's pleasure: he was doing this for Trent. More than arousal, Trent sensed genuine emotion in every glance, every caress.

Finally, Reed bent to Trent's cock, tongue peeking into the slit, tracing the contours of the head, once, twice, three times before licking wet heat down the length of his shaft. A flick against the sensitive bundle of nerves and Trent groaned. He fought to keep his eyes open, knowing if he closed them he'd give in to the overwhelming arousal. He watched Reed's muscles glide under the dark bruises, understanding how much strength and power Reed kept in check as he lovingly and languorously licked and sucked at Trent.

Reed took Trent's full length into his mouth, combining heat and suction, while his hand played at first with Trent's nipples, then moved to tickle his balls and probe farther back, one fingertip tracing the sensitive nerves of his perineum and anus. Trent could feel Reed's throat against the head of his cock and thrust up, craving friction against the firm wetness. When the combination of incredible sensations overwhelmed Trent's ability to fight back his release he tangled his fingers through Reed's short dark hair and shouted Reed's name as the dull heat in his balls exploded and sharpened and he shot down Reed's throat.

He felt like he was coming for hours, and Reed prolonged the sensations with hands and mouth until Trent could take no more.

"Oh, fucking God, you killed me." Trent let go of Reed's hair and lay completely drained of energy and come. His limbs were leaden and his heart raced. He fought to catch his breath.

Reed lifted his mouth from Trent, still swallowing, and licked a stray dribble from his chin. His smile changed to a frown. "That means I may have to consider necrophilia at some point."

Trent bit back his snappy rejoinder, not wanting to ruin the moment. "Come here." He pulled Reed down next to him and wondered if he should thank Reed. The few times Marc had given him such magnificent orgasms he seemed to expect special recognition, but—

Reed is not Marc. He refused to allow himself to compare them ever again, especially not in bed.

A hard heat pressed into Trent's side reminded him of Reed's need. Trent rolled over to face Reed, folding his body into Reed's, his softening cock brushing against Reed's solid desire.

"How would you like to fuck this very grateful corpse?" He kissed Reed, felt Reed's erection respond. Damn, Trent was jelly but he wanted Reed in every single way. Wanted to open himself up and let Reed take and take and take. His hole throbbed at the thought of Reed's cock pounding into him. Without waiting for a reply, Trent rolled away from Reed, pulled a pillow under his hips and spread his legs apart.

"Quite an appetizing display, but not what I had in mind." Reed rolled Trent back onto his side and spooned up behind him, kissing his neck, one hand caressing Trent's back and shoulder and arm. He broke away for a moment to reach toward the night table—lube—and Trent could hear the soft squish as the fluid oozed from the tube and the air was filled with the scent of fake strawberry. Deftly, with the good hand, Reed prepped Trent, again teasing the sensitive nerves in and around Trent's hole for far longer than was necessary. Reed put on a condom and still he didn't enter Trent. He played his cock around Trent's ass, between the cheeks, along the perineum and balls until finally he pressed the tip against Trent and slid inside: one smooth welcome push.

One arm circled Trent, holding him tight to Reed's chest as Reed waited.

Reed's breath rustled in Trent's ear and he thought he could feel the blood pulsing in Reed's cock as they lay together, connected in this most intimate way. Instead of thrusting and pumping, Reed kissed Trent's shoulder, nibbling at the skin, his fingers drawing aimlessly on Trent's abs or teasing at a nipple. After several moments of intense intimacy, Reed started to move, soft gentle pushes, mere stutters of his hips rather than quick, deep strokes before elongating the movements. Trent felt every inch of Reed slide in and out of him, and back in, the ache and pressure of orgasm again swelling inside, even though his cock lay limp and exhausted. Trent had never in his life felt so connected to anyone, aware of every single breath, Reed's soft moans echoing in his ears, and when Reed's orgasm took over, Trent felt it coming, as if were his own, the subtle shift in Reed's breathing, the more intense heat of his skin pressed against Trent, his muscles tensing before the eruption. Reed pumped into Trent who sensed each splash of come inside the condom. After it was all over, Reed didn't pull out, his cock still sending aftershocks and jolts into Trent for a long time.

Finally, Reed slipped out and into the bathroom.

Despite what Reed said about fucking, this lovemaking was incredible. Trent had never known such intimacy was even possible. Then as he listened to Reed washing up it dawned on Trent that he had known.

He'd written a scene like this in one of his books.

"HEY, Reed?"

"Hmmm?"

They were draped across each other later that afternoon in the enormous, clean, and incredibly comfortable hotel bed with ultra-high-thread-count sheets. It was the first time they could relax together in a real bed, and not as someone's prisoners. He'd worried their lovemaking would have lost that edge of danger and turned into something ordinary.

He'd been wrong. Being with Reed in clean, safe, *privacy* was even better, because it meant everything they felt, everything they did or said, was completely one-hundred-percent real. Not a product of forced circumstances or chance encounter. They were together now by choice. And even though Reed had wrapped up his mission, he didn't leave Trent. He hadn't just fucked him a few more times and hit the road. He'd stayed. They'd shared meals and watched awful Thai television and slept in each other's arms.

They couldn't yet go back to Bangkok. Not until it was safe.

"I don't get how they can protect you."

"Both sides think I turned them in to the authorities. But White and the Thai authorities put out the rumor to Supachai's gang and their affiliates that I'd been killed by the Chinese, and the Chinese think my Thai co-conspirators killed me."

"That way neither side realizes you were undercover?"

"Right. It means no one will be looking for me. I'd be a dead man if they knew I was alive. Worse if they knew I was an agent. But they've captured all of the ringleaders of both groups and none of the lower-level soldiers know who I am or how I'm involved."

Trent wondered how Reed could be so nonchalant about imminent death from two incredibly dangerous underworld criminal enterprises.

"What if they don't end up in jail?"

"This is Asia. They don't have quite as many instances where cases get thrown out. It's one of the advantages of poor civil rights here."

But now, butterflies raced inside Trent's gut as he brought up the subject he'd waited so long to discuss.

"Reed, what if there was a real Ruby Buddha?"

"There's not. It's just a myth or a legend, like I told you." Reed rolled onto his side and pressed against Trent, reaching up one hand to trail his fingertips down the most sensitive spot on Trent's throat. Trent's skin tingled at the caress.

But Trent didn't want to be distracted and caught Reed's wrist. Reed's brows shot up and he started to pull his hand back, but Trent didn't let go. He didn't want to worry Reed, but he did want his full attention.

"Damn, I forget how strong you are." Reed's tone was casual as he rubbed his wrist. "What's up?"

"Nothing. I just want to talk about this."

Reed let out a soft laugh. "Okay, whatever. But I still can't understand why it matters. If a Ruby Buddha of legend exists it would have been found by now." Reed chuckled again. "Oh, is this for a book idea? More research?"

"Yeah." Trent relaxed, glad Reed had given him a good way to approach the subject. "I had an idea for a story."

"Ask away."

"So, who would own it, you know, if someone found it?" Trent sucked in a quick breath, now that he'd gotten this far.

"Thai government. Most countries have a legal right to any items of cultural significance discovered within their borders. But you can try to sell it to someone without the government finding out. Best to find someone local. You'd have a much more difficult time trying to get it out of the country, unless you had connections and a lot of money, like Kao

Lung. A lot of the machinery for smuggling in Thailand has been shut down."

"How much would it be worth?"

"Depends on how much someone wants to pay. Kao Lung would have paid several million U.S. dollars—but you also risk ending up in a Thai prison. To the Thais, the Ruby Buddha would be priceless, an amazing discovery for the country and for Buddhists."

Trent stared at the ceiling as he considered what Reed had told him. Millions of dollars. Thai prison. Priceless cultural and religious artifact.

"What's a Thai prison like?"

Reed just stared at him for a second, until Trent grinned. "You really do ask some remarkable questions."

"Joking aside."

"You gonna have your hero end up in a Thai prison?"

"It's an interesting possibility, but no, not why I was asking."

"You wouldn't want to be in a Thai prison, even just for research. Trust me."

"You've been in prison here?"

"Part of building my cover. Let's just say I hope never to repeat anything even remotely like the experience."

Trent didn't want to go to a Thai prison either, that was for damn sure. He'd had enough of being a prisoner. But then again he wasn't seriously considering selling it, was he?

"If someone *did* find an artifact, like your hypothetical Ruby Buddha…," Reed began, and Trent was all ears. "And they turned it over to the government, there would probably be a reward."

"Reward? They would just, what, dig it up and carry the thing into a government office?"

"You mean if you found the real thing in the cave?"

Trent nodded.

"You wouldn't want to remove it from the cave. It would destroy the archaeological context of the find. There's an incredibly active archaeological community in Thailand, and the experts would want to excavate it themselves so as to study it."

"What would there be to study?"

"The Ruby Buddha legend—I still can't understand your continued fascination with this subject—was an old Khmer-Thai story, so it could shed light on a facet of Thai history which has obviously been lost."

Trent hadn't considered this aspect. The amount of research Reed had done in preparation for this mission impressed him. If Trent didn't have a legitimate reason for asking, this really would make a great story line for a novel.

"What if I told you...." Trent paused, heart pounding in his chest so loudly he feared it might explode. "I know where the real Buddha may be buried. A Buddha. Maybe not a Ruby Buddha." He didn't know if what he'd found was *the* Buddha of the legend. Maybe it wasn't even a Buddha.

Reed's burst of laughter answered Trent's question.

"Don't laugh." Trent unconsciously stuck out his lower lip. He hadn't even realized he'd done it until Reed leaned over and kissed it.

"You know I can't resist you when you pout."

"I'm not pouting." Trent consciously pulled the lip back in. "But I did find *something* in the cave where I was hiding."

"Something? What did you find?" Reed seemed to take Trent more seriously, or at least was humoring him more politely. "A pile of bat guano?"

Okay, maybe Reed wasn't taking this seriously enough. Trent let out a slightly exasperated sigh and began.

"The night I escaped from Boontung's camp, I hid in the cave with the big boulder blocking the entrance, like you told me."

Reed nodded.

"I got bored waiting so I wandered around. I found a lot of little rooms—chambers off the main cave—and each had a Buddha statue."

"What?" Reed sat up, his attention now fully focused on Trent. "You found a bunch of Buddhas in a cave in Thailand?" There was still a hint of sarcasm in his tone. "Look, Trent, caves all over the country have Buddha statues. They're a dime—or ten baht—a dozen. Now if they were all gold Buddhas, that would be a real find."

"No. Each room contained a stone statue, each one in a different mudra—hand position. I remembered reading each pose had a specific meaning and I decided to—"

"Get to the point, already, Encyclopedia Brown! What did you find?"

"Oh, now you believe me?" Trent aimed for a light tone, but he was still disappointed Reed doubted him at first.

"Yes, I believe you."

"One of the statues had a corner missing, chipped off." He glossed over the fact *he'd* broken the corner off. "And there was something gold and shiny underneath. I didn't break it open, but it could be something important and—"

"So those hypothetical questions about finding Buddhas were leading up to this?" Reed nodded in apparent comprehension. "You want to dig it up and sell it?"

"No, of course not. We should let the archaeology agency, or whatever they call themselves, know about it. I don't need a few million dollars."

"You don't? You mean you've *got* a few million dollars?" Reed's eyes widened and his eyebrows shot up again. "You sell that much of your…?" His voice faded away.

"Crap?"

An embarrassed look clouded Reed's features, but Trent smiled, brushing off the memory of Reed's insults about his writing.

"I do pretty well, but not quite *that* well. I don't need or want money enough to risk Thai prison. I won't go that far even for research. Though, I will admit that research *we* did together is going to more than pay off in my future writing."

"Not just your writing, I hope."

"Me, too." Trent snuggled closer to Reed. "But about that Buddha statue?"

"It's likely whatever you found has only historical or cultural significance."

"Which is fine. I didn't come here for a treasure hunt. I'd be happy to tell the Thais where to look. But wouldn't it be great if they find something really valuable?" Trent tried not to sound like an excited kid but knew he'd failed. So what.

"Okay. How about if tomorrow I call the archaeologist who designed the fake Buddha? He's a university professor in Bangkok."

"Really?"

"Sure. He'll want to talk to you, and you may have to show him what you found. But don't get your hopes up, okay?"

"Okay." Trent's mood deflated. He'd thought Reed would be much more excited about what he'd found in the cave. Trent knew next to nothing about archaeology and Reed had built a strong base of knowledge from planning this operation.

"Even if they don't find anything, it would make a good story," Reed added. "For one of your books."

"Considering all the flack you've given me about writing, did you notice you're the one coming up with the plot ideas? Pretty decent ideas, I have to admit."

"Really?"

"Not bad."

"Well, if my boss hires you, someone's got to write that fluffy smut. I could give it a shot. I'd have to do a lot more research though."

"You know what *would* make a great story?"

"What?"

Trent leaned over and whispered into Reed's ear. From the way Reed got almost instantly hard, it seemed he liked the idea as well, so Trent let him finish the story.

AS PROMISED, the following morning, Reed called his university contact and Trent explained what he'd found and where. Dr. Hoonchamlong of Silpakorn University in Bangkok went by the unfortunate nickname of Dr. Hoo, and Trent struggled to keep a straight face as Reed introduced him as such. Dr. Hoo asked a number of questions and Reed gave him specifics of the cave's location. A team would be dispatched to investigate and Dr. Hoo would contact Reed as soon as he had any information about what Trent had discovered.

"That was kind of anticlimactic." Trent had been flipping through the room service menu while Reed wrapped up the conversation in Thai. He put the menu back on the night table.

"Did you think he'd immediately run out there to check?"

"Yeah. I mean, I would."

"That's not how they work. Even once they find the cave and locate the statue, it could be weeks or months before they determine its archaeological or religious value. And even longer to pay out any reward. Sorry."

"I guess it's a good thing I'm not in a hurry. I'll contain my enthusiasm and not expect any news for a while."

"I've got some news for you. Not about the Buddha, though."

"What kind of news?"

"I'm going to quit. As soon as we get back to Bangkok, I'm resigning from the Bureau."

"Why?"

"How can you even ask? Of all people, you should understand it."

"You just wrapped up this big transnational"—possibly Trent's new favorite word—"operation and helped catch at least a dozen people involved in antiquities smuggling, not to mention bringing down Kung Pao's Hong Kong triad. You're a hero in half of Asia."

"Kao Lung." Reed shook his head and let out an exasperated laugh.

"Whatever. That reminds me. I'm hungry." Trent glanced longingly at the menu, weighing his desire for food against his interest in staying in bed with Reed for a few more hours before they were scheduled to leave for Bangkok.

"You're always hungry." Reed smirked. "Half of Asia loves me. The other half wants to kill me. It's time to get out."

"What are you going to do now? Go back to the States?"

"I was hoping a guy I know would invite me to LA."

"Really?" Trent's tone was incredulous. "Who? Should I be jealous?" He feigned concern.

"You, you giant moron."

"Oh, I'm not going back to LA." Trent grinned at the look of surprise on Reed's face. "Not yet, anyway. I have a few things I want to wrap up myself."

"I'd like to wrap you up."

"I certainly wouldn't argue with you if you tried."

"You're constantly arguing with me." Reed rolled his eyes, then leaned over to plant an affectionate kiss on Trent's mouth.

Trent pulled him back in with a hand on the back of his neck when Reed tried to lean away. The kiss deepened. Trent's cock took over and he forgot the signals his stomach had been sending. Time enough for food. Later.

REED'S boss had arranged for an official car to take them back to Bangkok, and despite Trent's initial trepidation about Thai drivers, the excitement of the past week caught up with him and he fell asleep in the backseat, at first on Reed's shoulder then draped across his lap. He woke up as they navigated the congestion of the city and eventually the car deposited them in front of Reed's apartment building as dusk settled over the city.

"If I remember correctly, you still owe me a fancy dinner." Trent's stomach growled as they rode the elevator of the surprisingly upscale and modern high-rise. Reed lived on the top floor of the sleek, glass-and-chrome building.

"I'd be happy to show you the best places in Bangkok, the ones the locals like to keep secret from the tourists."

"This time you're guaranteed to get lucky if you buy me dinner."

"I would have gotten lucky the first time around, had I been able to keep our date."

"You're awfully sure of yourself, aren't you?"

"No. I'm just sure of you." Reed flashed the sexy smirk Trent found more irresistible than ever. "I know just what you like, and you'd be a fool to turn me down… ever again."

Not that Reed hadn't ended up getting lucky even when Trent did turn him down, the first night in the little hut. Trent liked that Reed joked about it, and that he'd understood just what had happened: Trent had changed his mind.

Reed unlocked his apartment and opened the door, motioning for Trent to go in first. He switched on the lights as he followed inside, pulling the now-battered suitcase behind him.

Trent glanced around and an involuntary sigh escaped. He took in the full effect of the floor-to-ceiling windows along one side of the room, affording a spectacular view of the sun setting over the river, and the understated, elegant décor. The apartment was beautiful, with high ceilings, and the living room had an elegant airiness to it. The furniture was evidently expensive, and display cases along one of the walls held what appeared to be museum-quality artifacts. Trent threw a glance at Reed and nodded in approval.

"You look surprised."

"Marc would have given his left... arm to own pieces like these." *Marc.* Trent started to turn away from Reed, but this time mentioning Marc brought no tears, no emotion, just a comfortable memory. But Trent immediately regretted mentioning Marc, here with Reed.

Reed didn't acknowledge the comment about Marc, but a flash of something that might have been hurt crossed his features for a split second.

"It's not at all what I expected—"

"From someone like me?" Reed shook his head and any last trace of uncertainty was gone when he turned his gaze back on Trent. "Remember, I was posing as an illegal art dealer. No one would believe that cover if I lived in a pit, would they?"

Reed walked over to one of the cases and ran his fingertips along the case, which held a small Buddha image, almost a miniature of the fake Buddha that had been used to lure Kao Lung. "This is my favorite piece. It's from the university museum, from the period the Ruby Buddha would have been made." He motioned around the room. "Most of these are real artifacts loaned to the task force for this project from the university and a few legit art dealers."

For the first time, Trent understood how much the operation had meant to Reed, not just for shutting down the illegal trade, but because he had a real love for what the objects represented. There were plenty of layers to Reed Acton, and the chance to explore them thrilled Trent.

"You know, Reed, if the statue you found turns out to be the real Ruby Buddha, you'll be able to afford to buy pieces like these for yourself."

Reed laughed. "If there's any reward, it belongs to you."

"You don't think I'd share it with you?"

"I didn't do anything to earn it. I wouldn't take the money."

Reed really was too good to be true. The description "Boy Scout" came to mind. He needed to learn to treat himself better than he had; another thing Trent was eager to help with.

"Then I'd buy you a piece like that. It would be a gift."

"A gift?"

Reed's tone gave the impression he hadn't received many gifts in his life. If Trent had anything to do with it, that was going to change.

"Fine. I'll give you a chance to earn it." Trent copied Reed's sassy smirk and planted a kiss on his mouth—a long, lingering kiss that left no doubt about Trent's expectations or Reed's willingness to comply.

"Would you like to see the bedroom?"

"Yes, I would."

Reed started to unbutton Trent's shirt but Trent pushed his hands away.

"After dinner. At the best place in town." Mick might have asked for the "most expensive," but Trent had quickly learned that in Thailand—as in most places—expensive didn't necessarily mean top quality.

"That can certainly be arranged."

18

ON THEIR third night back Reed prepared a special dinner for Trent. They had spent several relatively uneventful but pleasurable days in Bangkok. Reed spent mornings in his office writing endless reports, while Trent occupied himself outlining his next novel. They filled afternoons with visits to Reed's favorite spots followed by unhurried romantic dinners and nights on the town, where he introduced Trent to the gay Bangkok tourists never discovered and most Thais didn't even know existed.

"This makes the second meal you've cooked for me. It looks a lot better than those old noodles we had in the hut." Trent closed his eyes and inhaled deeply before digging in. They'd mainly been eating Thai food, so this was a treat.

"I don't remember the last time I cooked a real meal. I never had time or anyone I wanted to cook for before." Reed sipped wine and watched Trent eat. "Oh, before I forget, I've got a present for you." Reed got up from the table and headed for the bedroom.

"Present? Besides this fantastic meal?" Trent wondered what Reed could have gotten him. Butterflies zoomed in his stomach. Jewelry? A ring? No, that was stupid. It was probably handcuffs or rambutan-flavored lube. Or a huge new box of condoms, since they *were* running low. Mick would be so happy to hear Trent had used most of the ones he'd put in Trent's backpack.

Reed came back with a package the size of a shoe box. He handed it to Trent, kissed his cheek then sat back down.

Definitely not a ring.

Trent took the box and shook it. Heavier than he'd expected. He hesitated for a moment before opening it up. Inside was a familiar blue and gold bottle. His favorite body wash in the extra-large size.

"Wow. Not what I expected at all. Thank you! How'd you get this? Is there a place in Bangkok that sells it?" A guy could hope, couldn't he?

"Diplomatic pouch."

"What?" It sounded so cloak-and-dagger.

"Basically, the embassy has a weekly run from the States for those things you just can't find here. Whoever's coming back brings the package."

"That's so sweet."

"You better enjoy it; you have no idea how much ridicule I had to endure just asking for that. Tom White made sure it happened. He likes you."

Trent's cheeks heated and he was glad for the candlelight. He focused his attention on the meal again.

"I can't remember the last time I had a romantic candlelight dinner. This steak with balsamic sauce is delicious. And those twice-baked potatoes? Sinful. My personal trainer is gonna kill me."

Reed just laughed as Trent patted his abs with one hand and shoveled in another forkful with the other.

"You're in perfect shape. And I don't want you getting sick of Thai food just yet." Reed gave a cryptic grin and took another bite.

"Yet? What have you got in mind?"

"I've given my notice, but they won't let me leave Thailand until all the paperwork clears the upper channels, in case there are questions from any of the other organizations involved. But I'm now officially on vacation. All I have to do is check in once a week by phone. So we should get out of Bangkok."

"I remember the last time someone suggested that; I ended up in a bus crash and prisoner of some Thai gangsters before being captured by a Chinese triad."

Reed laughed. "Promise. I'll make sure no one but me captures you for at least two weeks. How do you feel about heading to one of the islands?"

"Sounds great. Which one?"

"You won't read about this one in a guidebook. Need your own boat to get there."

"I think I saw that movie. The one with Leonardo DiCaprio?" Trent frowned. "Pass."

"It's nothing like the film. I promise."

"I hope not. I've had my share of excitement for the foreseeable future."

Trent hoped Reed didn't hear the catch in his throat when he said "excitement."

Too late. Reed reached out and covered Trent's hand with his own, giving a reassuring squeeze. Trent glanced up seeing nothing but understanding and love in his gaze.

"Don't worry, Reed. I trust you." Trent backed his words up with a smile. "So, have you got a boat?" he added with a hopeful tone.

"I know a guy who runs a sailboat rental company…"

EARLY the following afternoon they arrived in Phuket after a short flight from Bangkok. Trent had a few initial reservations: given what he knew about Thai drivers, he wasn't in any hurry to experience Thai airplane pilots, but the alternative was a twelve-hour bus ride, which Trent immediately rejected. After a meal of fresh-caught fish, Reed's friend Randy set them up with a fully equipped boat, and they made their escape from the crowded tourist destination by way of the sea.

The scenery of the area had been incredible as they'd flown past towering limestone crags covered with emerald-green trees, but once on the water it was even more spectacular. Sheer cliffs jutted out of the jewel-like sea hundreds of feet in the air, as they sailed out toward the open water. Reed watched Trent's reactions to the natural beauty of the place and smiled, as if seeing everything for the first time, through Trent. The fresh tang of the sea air and the cool breezes were as welcome as the stunning visuals, and Trent felt rejuvenated almost immediately.

He was impressed with Reed's ability to handle the boat, but then again, pretty much everything Reed did impressed Trent. Nothing wrong with that. The boat wasn't large, enough space for the two of them, but clearly easy enough to handle for just one experienced sailor. Reed skippered and instructed Trent how to handle the ropes—*sheets*, Reed kept reminding him—but Trent couldn't help getting distracted by the sheer natural beauty surrounding them.

They'd been out about an hour and the shoreline was nearly invisible when it seemed as if the wind just disappeared. The sails fluttered uselessly as the boat lost speed and started to drift.

"Now what? Do we use the engine?"

"Why would we do that?" Reed grinned, but Trent couldn't tell what was so damn funny about being stranded miles away from shore. He could swim, but he didn't really want to leave his belongings behind yet again.

"To get back to shore?" Trent stood up and stared back toward the beach, slightly rocking the boat.

"Are you in a big hurry?"

"No." Trent glanced at Reed's face and noticed the smile. He'd seen that smile before and he knew exactly what it meant. "No hurry at all." This time Trent smiled back.

Reed reached out for Trent's hand and pulled him down beside him on the bench near the back of the boat, then leaned in for a kiss. A long, deep kiss to let Trent know Reed didn't intend to rush right now, probably for the first time since they'd met.

When Reed finally let go of Trent, he reached under the bench and retrieved a small cooler. He pulled out two beers and handed one to Trent.

"As usual, you're prepared for everything." Trent laughed.

"Yes, I am." Reed picked up the cooler and nodded toward the cabin. "After you."

Trent went down the three steps and continued until he got to a small cabin in the back, large enough for little more than a bed. It didn't take either of them long to pull the other's clothes off and settle onto the surprisingly comfortable bed.

"I guess I don't mind getting stranded this far from shore after all."

"I figured you'd come around to my way of thinking, eventually. You usually do."

"You're awfully persuasive."

"You're easily persuaded." Reed rained kisses along Trent's throat.

"But why do I have this feeling we're in the final scene of a James Bond film?"

"Because you have an overactive imagination?"

"You have no idea just how imaginative I can be."

"What are you waiting for? Show me."

They began to make love slowly and silently, using the rocking motion of the boat to enjoyable advantage.

"Reed?"

"Yeah?" Reed slowed his movements and looked into Trent's eyes.

"This is nice and all. But...."

"But what?" Reed stopped completely. "Are you okay?" His tone turned concerned.

"Well... sometimes a guy just really wants to get fucked. You know?"

Reed let out a soft laugh. "Fucked?"

"You remember how to fuck, don't you, Reed?" Trent teased, paraphrasing Bacall's famous line from *To Have and Have Not* and bringing back memories of their first time together.

Reed's only reply was a low whistle. Then he grabbed hold of Trent's hips and gave him a good fucking. A very good fucking, which left them exhausted and breathless in each other's arms.

Reed was the first to break the silence with words, his voice still low and rough. "I'd say that research really paid off."

"You're a good teacher. Even if you do say so yourself." Trent grinned and kissed Reed.

"What if the Buddha you found isn't the Ruby Buddha after all?"

"It doesn't really matter. It's not like I need the reward money. I'm perfectly comfortable with what I earn. Besides, from what you told me of the legend, and what we've been through, maybe the Buddha should stay lost."

"But it would be pretty exciting if it was the real thing. The Ruby Buddha, lost for centuries...." Reed's tone was wistful as he rolled onto his back and stared at the ceiling.

Trent nearly laughed at Reed's change of heart about the Buddha. Just another way they'd reversed roles in the space of little more than a week. He'd never have dreamed up a plot like this for one of his books. Or written so much amazing sex—making love as well as fucking—into his own life.

He snuggled back up to Reed and traced circles on his chest with a fingertip. "Besides, what I've already got is far more valuable. Something rarer than rubies."

EM LYNLEY works in the wine industry, though she'd rather be writing hot, sexy man-on-man action. She spent ten years as an economist and financial analyst, including a year as a White House staff economist, but only because all the intern positions were filled. Tired of boring herself and others with dry business reports and articles, her creative muse is back and naughtier than ever. She has lived and worked in London, Tokyo, and Washington, DC, but the San Francisco Bay Area is home for now.

Visit her web site at http://www.emlynley.com, her blog at http://emlynley.livejournal.com, her Twitter page at http://twitter.com/emlynley, and her Facebook at http://www.facebook.com/emlynley.

Also by EM LYNLEY

http://www.dreamspinnerpress.com